THE BOOK OF IRA

The Book of Ira

Nachash Keeper

STONE PULP PRESS PRESENTS

A MYSTIC ISLAND STORY

The Book of Ira
Copyright © 2024 by Nachash Keeper

Printed in the United States of America

Stone Pulp Press
Imprint Mailing Address: PO Box 23
Zip: 02339 US States: MA
Country: US

Paperback ISBN: 979-8-9898749-4-1
E-book ISBN: 979-8-9898749-5-8
LCCN: 2024946175

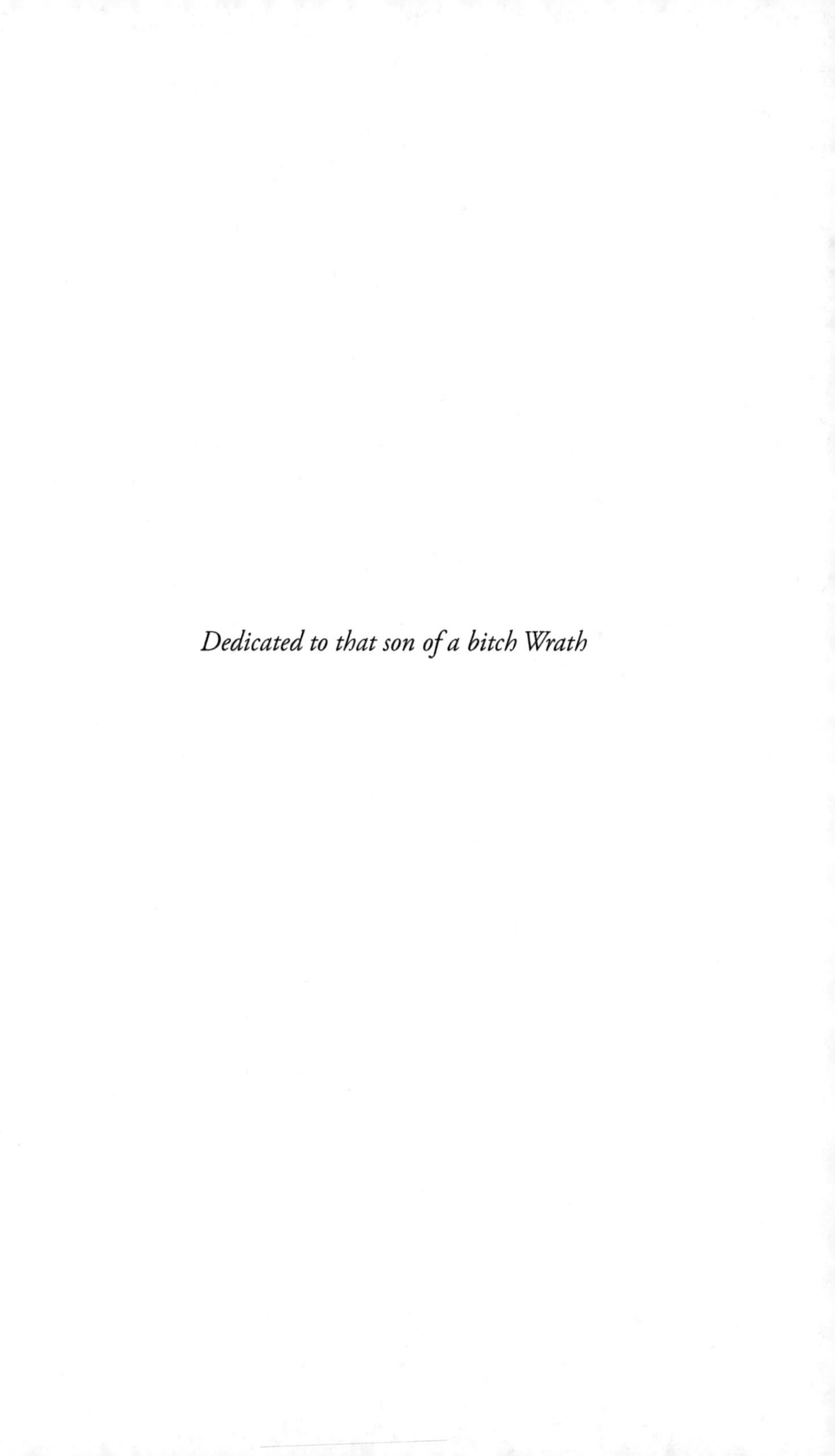

Dedicated to that son of a bitch Wrath

GENESIS

1. In the beginning there was The Fall. And The Fallen lived among the Sons and Daughters of Cain. And The Fallen did demand offerings.

2. Unto Beelzebub the Sons and Daughters of Cain did bequeath their livestock, for did he enjoy the flesh. And unto Mammon they did commit their gold. And unto Belial they did cede their secrets. And to Moloch they giveth their children in sacrifice.

3. Until that day that Moloch did forcibly take the virginity of Cain's youngest daughter Maac, and she and Moloch did begat the Nephilim Iratus. The Nephilim survived the birth, but Maac did not.

4. The Sons and Daughters of Cain did beseech The Lord to cast away The Fallen, and so He did, saying that they not be worthy of the Earth He did create for man, and the Sons and Daughters of Cain did say that it was good.

5. The Fallen, cast from the land of Man, did create a kingdom in the bowels of Earth.

6. In the New Kingdom, Lucifer did appoint the Nephilim Iratus, Son of Moloch, Punisher in the rings of Tartarus. And it was good.

7. And the Son of Moloch did punish those takers of innocence for the many generations, unto the day of his awakening and terrestrial ascent, seeking the names of The Book on Earth, and lo enact his punishment upon the wicked, and it was good.

8. Until the silver-eyed one would demand the seraphim Urial smite the Son of Moloch, upon which the One True Son did....

9. You know what? Fuck this.

Genesis Redux

The wind was picking up, sending white caps scurrying along the dark sea and drenching the air with a reek of salt. The stars vanished behind a newly drawn blanket of clouds, heralding a coming storm. A figure, blacker than the night, stood on Damon's Point, which the residents called Demon's Point, although no one was quite sure why. The beach was deserted—no one knew the figure was there. As it approached the sea, the rising tide seemed to scurry away from its giant plodding feet. The clouds above hid the moon's face, as if even it didn't want to watch what stood at the water's edge.

The figure looked down and saw something it had not seen for a very long time. There was blood on its hands. It had not expected the blood. When it had tried wiping it away, it had noticed something else it did not expect. A patch of red skin beneath the smudged black soot. The figure then stepped into the sea with an explosion of steam, and it washed the soot from its body.

The Seekers

1

FBI agent Frank Jacobs was taking a sip of coffee when a folder slid to a rest in front him.

"There you go," Emmanuel Diaz said.

Jacobs raised his eyebrows and peeked into the file as if checking hole cards. "What is it?"

"It's your new case. You can thank Thompson." Diaz turned and walked away with the self-important stride of a runway model.

Jacobs shook his head and, opening the file on his desk, called out, "What the hell is this?" There was no answer from Diaz; he'd already crossed the warehouse-sized office of non-partitioned desks, putting the sounds of agents talking on phones and fingers clacking on computer keyboards between them. "Seriously, what is this?"

Tyrone Malone, who was walking past his desk, stopped and said, "Looks like a file, Frank."

"Thanks, Ty." Jacobs began thumbing through the file.

"So what is it?" Ty said. "I saw that little shit, Diaz, running around all morning, sniffing around the SAC's office, just itching to get in there. Looked like he had a hard-on for something. Why's Thompson giving it to you?"

"I have no idea," Jacobs said, scanning the pages in the file. "What is this shit?"

Tyrone tilted his head, reading over Jacobs's shoulder. "A demon?" he said.

"You've got to be kidding me."

"Go find Diaz and ask him."

"He's not going to give me answers to something Thompson snatched from him."

"Then ask Thompson."

Jacobs gathered up the file, saying, "I'll go ask Thompson."

"Good idea. Glad I could help. Oh, and just so you know, that's all the help you're getting on this one," Ty said.

"Okay," Jacobs said.

"No, seriously. Thompson always gives you the weirdest shit, and I always get sucked into helping you with it. I'm not touching this one. You're on your own."

"Okay," Jacobs said, walking away from the desk, then called over his shoulder, "I'll let you know what you can do to help."

"Come on, man. I got a bad feeling about this one."

When Jacobs walked into the SAC's office, Thompson did not immediately look up from the papers on his desk. Instead, he focused on a memo, his brow knotted into a caricature of concentration.

Jacobs said, "Care to explain why Diaz is giving me my cases now?"

Thompson still regarded the memo on his desk, but Jacobs could tell his eyes were not following the words written upon it.

Jacobs sighed and cleared his throat. "Excuse me. Care to tell me why Diaz is giving me my assignments now, Special Agent in Charge Thompson?"

Thompson raised his head from the memo. "Ah, yes, Agent Jacobs, what can I do for you?" he said in a friendly manner.

"Knock it off, Harrison. I've known you too long to buy into this *Art of War* management shit you're doing. You may insist everyone else address you as Special Agent in Charge Thompson, but don't forget, I knew you when you were known as Pudge."

Thompson sighed. "Fine. What is it, Frank?"

"You tell me. Diaz just dropped this on my desk," Jacobs said, waving the file.

"That is a case I need you to handle."

"Diaz said it was *his* case. Why isn't *he* handling it?"

"It's not *his* case. It's *a* case. He just happened to find it. But I think it is better suited to you."

"Why?"

"It just is."

"He called you Harrison, didn't he?"

Thompson flinched and let out a breath. "No, Frank. This type of case is going to require some…let's say finesse. Diaz is overzealous. He's a busybody. He'll go running off chasing every minute detail, missing the bigger picture. You, on the other hand, have the proper investigative technique for this situation."

"Yeah? What technique is that?"

"Luck. Shit always seems to fall in your lap. That tends to be effective."

"Is that what Sun Tzu says?"

"Just do this for me, Frank?"

Jacobs looked at the file in his hand. "I don't even know what *this* is."

"Did you read it?"

"Not past the word demon."

"What is that, like the fifth word?"

"Third."

Thompson held out his hand. Jacobs handed him the file. Thompson opened it and, glancing through the pages, said, "Last week the police in the small community of Mystic Island received a call from a young girl stating there was someone in her house attacking her uncle. A"—he looked at the file to confirm the name—"Stewart Brookes. She claimed she did not know the man attacking her uncle—or even if it was a man. She described him as"—he read from the file again—"'eight feet tall, as wide as a doorway, and totally painted black.'"

Thompson glanced up at Jacobs for a reaction. He received none.

"Anyway, the girl's uncle was found upstairs by police with his head completely crushed. Like mush. Like someone put it in a vice. The girl was left unharmed." Thompson looked up, saying, "Well, obviously she was unharmed, because she reported it." Thompson laughed. Jacobs still looked unimpressed. Thompson cleared his throat and said, "It turns out that this girl, Molly Simmons, her uncle had been inappropriately touching her while her parents were away."

Jacobs said, "You want me to track down a little girl's description of a monster? Maybe we can start with her closet. I'll put out an APB: 'Be on the lookout for a Purple-People-Eater.'"

"Black People-Eater. He was painted black. The girl's description is hard to follow."

"Probably because she's a kid. Look, her uncle is molesting her, her father kills him, and she copes by describing a fantasy about a monster. Case solved. Glad you gave it to me. We done?"

"Wasn't the father. He's got a whole cruise ship's staff and passengers as his alibi. Little girl said the giant was about the same height as her bedroom's ceiling, and that he appeared to be painted black. Investigators found soot on a blanket, where it appears the perpetrator wiped his hands."

"Soot? What kind of soot?"

"Nothing of note—traces of sulfur, carbon, common elements present in a number of chemical reactions that would produce soot."

"Any tool marks on the victim's crushed head?"

"It would appear the perpetrator did this with his hands. No fingerprints."

Jacobs said, "Isn't this Mystic Island PD's problem?"

Thompson shuffled the pages, saying, "There was another attack in Hobart, Oklahoma, twenty-six hours after the call on Mystic Island. Same description, although the caller, a Louise Martin, referred to him as a demon. She said he was red. Like sunburned, or cooked."

"Why the change in color?"

"I don't know. Guy likes to paint himself or something."

"Is it, like, ritualistic or something?"

"I don't know. That's what an investigator will have to figure out. And, seeing as this could be the same man, and the murders have crossed state lines, it is now an FBI matter. Whatever it was in that house in Oklahoma tore apart four armed men."

"What do you mean tore apart?"

"Well, let's see," Thompson said, looking at the file. "The owner of the house, after apparently firing a shotgun blast at the perpetrator, had his genitals ripped off and shoved into his mouth. Another victim had one of those Desert Eagle handguns shoved so far down his throat that his stomach contents were found on its barrel."

"Desert Eagle? Why the guns?"

"It's Oklahoma. What else is there to do?" Thompson shrugged. "Let's see. Another victim was decapitated, and another watched his heart torn out before his own eyes."

Of course Thompson had no way of actually knowing that the heart was torn out before the victim's own eyes. He just thought it sounded better. However, for the record, Roscoe Van Everey's heart *was* torn out of his chest while he was still quite conscious enough to watch its final beats.

Thompson said, "It turns out that the victims in Oklahoma are also child molesters. One of them was drugging and pimping out his daughter to his friends. This giant man apparently broke up one of their parties."

"So it would appear that an eight-foot-tall, painted, cross-country, vigilante serial killer who can tear people apart with his bare hands is offing child molesters?"

"It would appear so."

"Is it even possible to drive from Mystic Island to Oklahoma in twenty-six hours? I doubt an eight-foot tall man is going to take an airplane."

"It is possible, but it requires driving with no stopping. Still, I told Diaz to check with airport security in surrounding areas."

"Why isn't Diaz doing the rest of it, too?"

"I told you, I want you on this one. Diaz is too young and too eager and he talks too much. He's always looking for some angle to make a name for himself. Whereas you are...." Thompson shrugged.

"Old and don't give a shit?"

"Reliable. And predictable."

"You see the possible media attention in this, and you know I will avoid it."

"I think it best that I manage the media involvement should any arise," Thompson said.

"Give it to Diaz," Jacobs said. "I don't want to touch this thing."

"I'm giving it to you. It's an order."

Jacobs sighed and turned to leave, huffing, "All right."

"Have the voice analyzed," Thompson said.

"What voice?"

"The 911 calls from the two incidents. The perp can be heard in the background."

"Diaz gave me no sound recordings."

"He must have held onto them," Thompson said. "He is a weaselly little shit, isn't he? Get the recordings from him and get them analyzed."

"Analyzed for what?"

"You'll see when you listen to them," Thompson said, going back to his memo.

2

Jacobs sat in his apartment. It was a one-bedroom, still furnished with the secondhand furniture he'd gathered four years ago when he'd left Beth. Or when Beth had kicked him out. Or when they'd mutually agreed that their marriage didn't work. Or maybe it was when he'd first discovered she was having the affair. The reasons were a little mixed up in his mind, the coherent thread of their relationship wiped clean by the hand of fate and the heart's and mind's childish game of King of the Hill. The biggest question had been how could he love someone so much, only to come to hate someone so much, only to realize, when she was gone, how much he'd loved her the whole time?

He leaned back in a chair with his feet up on his desk—a small card table in his living room's corner. He had been searching Google Maps for every route someone could drive from Mystic Island, Massachusetts, to Hobart, Oklahoma. Like Thompson said, it could be done in twenty-six hours, but it must have been quite a ride. Jacobs scruffed the head of his Yellow Lab, Old Yellah. Beth, being from the Midwest, had always hated his Boston way of dropping his Rs, so, at the end of their marriage, when he brought the puppy home, he dubbed him "Old Yellah"—even spelled it that exact way on the dog license.

It was after 1:00 am, and on the television was a woman with lips so full of collagen they barely moved when she spoke. She squawked about the unparalleled beauty of a porcelain plate emblazoned with the face of Jesus, who looked strikingly like Brad Pitt, for an act-now price of $39.99.

Jacobs took a sip of his coffee. He winced at its coldness, but lacked the resolve to make another pot. The case files were pushed off to the side of the table, but he was working on it in his mind, trying to find the edge pieces of an impossible puzzle.

After leaving Thompson's office earlier, Jacobs tracked Diaz down in the break room. "Hey," Jacobs had barked. Diaz jerked, spilling a small puddle of coffee on the counter. "Got something for me?" Jacobs said.

"What?" Diaz said.

"Sound recordings. Give them to me."

"It's my case, and you stole it from me," Diaz said, his shaking hand returning the coffee pot to the machine with a wind chime clattering of glass and plastic.

"For someone to steal something, they have to have an active role in the taking. I have no idea what this is." Jacobs waved the file in his hand. "I mean, look at this. A fucking demon? What is this, *The X-Files*?"

Diaz squinted his eyes and grimaced "What's *The X-Files*?"

"You were going to keep the killer's voice from me?"

"I forgot to put it in the file." Diaz pulled a digital audio recorder from his pocket and handed it to Jacobs. "You should probably take it to linguistics to make sure it's human."

"I thought it's the killer's voice."

"It is," Diaz said before he walked away.

Now, in his apartment, Jacobs took his feet off the table, muted the television, and picked up the audio recorder with the 911 calls. He hesitated to press the play button, maybe due to his weariness with the confusion of it all. Or maybe because he, once again in his life, felt fate rolling its dice. The voice on that recording sounded like something that should be left alone. At least he could confidently call it a voice now. Carol Pierce in Linguistics had determined that it was speaking Latin.

He pressed play and heard the dispatcher's voice stating, *"911, what's your emergency?"*

And then Molly Simmons's tiny voice, sounding even more lost and small when carried on the tinny, airy reverberations of the speakers. *"Is this the police?"*

The dispatcher said, *"Yes, dear, this is the 911 dispatcher, what is your emergency?*

Molly said, *"There's a…man in the house."*

Jacobs noted Molly's pause before saying the word *man.*

"There's a man in your house?" the dispatcher said.

"Not my house. It's my uncle's."

"It's your uncle?"

"No. The man is in my uncle's house."

"Do you know this man?"

"No."

"Does your uncle know this man?"

"No. But it seems to know my uncle."

"Okay, what is the address where you are, dear?"

"Um, I'm not sure…it's…I don't know, it's my uncle's house."

"It's okay, hon, I can see you are calling from a landline. I have the address. Stay on the line, honey, okay?"

"Yes."

"Okay, you're going to be all right, hold for one moment—All units, Signal 21 in progress. 14 Wild Rose Road. Caller is a female child stating an unidentified male is inside the residence—Are you still there, honey?"

"Yes."

"Good. What's your name, dear?"

"Molly Simmons."

"Molly? Okay, Molly, you're doing great. How old are you?"

"Eight."

"What is your uncle's name?"

"Stewart Brookes."

"Okay, can you describe the man in your house?"

"He's all black."

"He's black?"

"No."

"He's not black?"

"No, he is black, but not African American…he's…like painted."

"He's painted black? Like makeup?"

"No."

"I don't under—"

"He's like covered in something black…and like really tall."

"Really tall? How tall do you think?"

"His head hits the ceiling."

"He's as tall as the ceiling? How high is your—? Molly, what's that sound? Is there a…is there a dog on the premises?"

"That's the man talking."

"That's the…that's someone speaking?"

"The man. It talks in strange words, except when it told me to call the police. Now it's saying those strange words at my uncle."

"Where are they now, dear?"

"They're upstairs in my uncle's bedroom. I'm downstairs."

"Okay. Hold on, dear—All units, be advised that the caller is an eight-year-old female. The Intruder is described as… intruder is described as a black male…or…rather a male painted black, or…covered in something black? It…he…the intruder is described as very large. There is a possible battery on another adult male in the house—Molly, are you—? Molly… is that a woman screaming?"

"It's my uncle…my uncle, he's—"

"Molly? Hello? Hello? Molly, can you hear me? If you can speak, please tell me what is happening…. All units, be advised that there is screaming in the residence. Caller is no longer responding to the phone…. Molly? Molly, are you there? Molly? Oh God, what is that?"

Jacobs stopped the recorder and stared at the last route mapped out on his computer's screen. "Shit," he whispered. "She says he's painted black."

The other description, the one in Oklahoma, said the man, this demon, was painted red. He thought, wasn't there a Stones song about painting something black? A red door. The song was about painting a red door black. Could that have something to do with it? He doubted it. Did the suspect being painted black have something to do with the soot? It had to be two different people.

Jacobs rewound the recording.

Molly said, *"He's like covered in something black…and, like, really tall."*

The dispatcher said, *"Really tall? How tall do you think?"*

"His head hits the ceiling."

"Shit," Jacobs said again, thinking, *two different eight-foot-tall people?* The call in Oklahoma specifically described him as eight feet. And most ceilings are eight feet. He wouldn't know for sure until he visited Stewart Brooke's house, but… he glanced up at his own ceiling.

"Molly, what's that sound? Is there a…is there a dog on the premises?"

Jacobs squinted, listening to the sounds in the background. The distant pleading of her uncle over the phone static. And then the voice: like the low tectonic rumbling the Earth makes before an earthquake.

Molly said, *"That's the man talking."*

"That's the…that's someone speaking?"

Jacobs fast-forwarded a bit.

"Molly? Hello? Hello? Molly, can you hear me? If you can speak, please tell me what is happening….

Jacobs now knew the dispatcher was unaware that Molly had fainted.

"All units, be advised that there is screaming in the residence. Caller is no longer responding to the phone…."

Here, that rumbling, tectonic voice *became* the earthquake, or the angry sea, or a freight train passing, or a lion's roar on stadium speakers.

At his feet, Old Yellah whimpered, shifted uneasily, and got up to leave. Jacobs watched the dog go, hearing its padding footfalls travel into the bedroom. Then the sliding sound as Yellah squeezed under the bed.

"Molly? Molly, are you there? Molly? Oh God, what is that?"

Jacobs stopped the recorder and opened the file. He took out a piece of notebook paper with Carol Pierce's scribbled translation on it. The voice had been screaming: *I am wrath, the taker of takers. I sentence you to death. But death is only the beginning.*

3

In a substantial home in Brookline, Massachusetts, Dennis Callahan woke from a deep sleep. He'd heard a noise and his mind began racing. His first thought was that the "liberal faction" of the Deep State had arrived in his home. He figured atheist CIA spooks dressed in black had come on the behest of The New World Order. To cart him off to The Ministry of Truth and shut him up. To tear down his website, his beacon of knowledge to the true believers. They could stop him, he thought, but they could never stop God's truth. After all, he knew they, too, would be judged when Jesus returned with Michael's army of angels to bring order to the chaos of The Apocalypse.

But what if it's not the government? he thought. What if it were Islamic fundamentalists enacting a fatwa on a true Christian soldier? *Those dirty bastards could be sneaking up my steps with their cloven hooves right now, coming to video-tape my beheading.* He wondered if he would whimper and blubber and cry as the knife pressed against his skin? Or would he piss himself on camera? Would this bold Christian soldier's crying and pissing be on the digital airwaves of You-Tube until End Times? That seemed like a long time, even though he knew that End Times were coming soon. Coming soon to plow the followers of false prophets under the soil of Jesus's reign.

Such a gruesome death was little worry to Callahan, who knew he would be resurrected to the Kingdom just like Jesus had been. *I am ready to be the martyr*, he thought, but then reassessed his feelings. *If I am taken early, I will miss the Rapture.* He was looking forward to experiencing the moment when he and his fellow true believers were taken whole into the air, up, up, up, looking down on the sinners, who were begging, too late, for salvation. If he were already dead, he would miss such a glorious moment. *But if I go to Heaven now, I'll be there to greet the other souls flooding God's Kingdom.* He figured he'd be like a Paradise upperclassman giving tours to the newly arrived. He liked that. *So bring on the CIA spooks and the Jihadist hit squads,* he thought to himself—knowing that the sound was most likely the wind or the refrigerator kicking on. *Or teenage meth-heads here to kill me for spare change,* he thought.

His eyes widened and his grip on the blankets tightened. *What if it is desperate meth-heads?* They would kill him just because they were tweaked out, and there would be no martyrdom, no glory in the name of The Lord. He'd be forever lumped into the boring statistics associated with drugs and pointless violence. Or worse. *Will they rape me?* If they raped him, he'd be shunned from Heaven for the homosexual act. *Then I'll no longer be Raptured,* he thought. *I'll be stuck here on Earth with the other sinners and heathens, forced to watch the armies of the Antichrist storm the world.* He'd have to go to Jerusalem to wait for Michael, and he'd actually have to fight. And when it was over, he'd be a nobody in the new Paradise on Earth. Second class. Third class even. He'd be a third class citizen of Christ's new world. After all the work he'd done to be God's messenger to the masses, he'd end up an abomination tainted with homosexual rape. *But that's not fair,* he thought.

The noise came again. This time closer. Callahan slowly turned in his bed. He slid through the blankets to keep them tightly wrapped around his head, only his peeking eyes showing. When he was facing the other way, he lifted his head from the pillow to see the bedroom's door. A thin band of light lined the door's bottom edge. *Did I leave the hallway light on?* he thought. *I never leave the hallway light on.* The light flickered, as if someone had passed in front of it. Someone was outside his door. His mind gave up the last grasp of hope that the sound was the wind or the refrigerator kicking on. *The wind doesn't turn on lights. Meth-heads do.*

He whispered, "Why, God? Why have you forsaken me?"

As if in response to his question, the flickering light beneath his bedroom door steadied and intensified until it became brighter than a sunlit day.

A booming, mellifluous voice spoke, and the voice said, "Dennis Callahan, come hear the Word of God."

4

Jacobs headed to Thompson's office, not even knocking on his door before barging in and saying, "I got it. I figured it out—" He stopped.

Thompson sat at his desk. Agent Diaz stood in the corner of the office; he had a shit-eating grin on his face. A man sat across the desk from Thompson. The man turned to look at Jacobs and then stood to greet him.

Thompson said, "Agent Jacobs, I'd like you to meet Dennis Callahan."

Callahan smiled and shot out his hand, saying, "Nice to meet you, Agent Jacobs. We have much work to do."

Jacobs did not take the hand. Instead, he shot a glare at Diaz and then at Thompson. "What is this?" he said.

Thompson grinned his best politician smile and said, "Mr. Callahan may be able to help us with our case. He has information that could lead us in the right direction."

"Mr. Callahan is a religion expert," Diaz cut in. "He came in bright and early this morning asking for the agent in charge of the case involving the killer demon. Said he could offer help. I told him I'd be glad to take him to Frank Jacobs. You know, because *he's* the agent in charge of the case." A smarmy smile spread across his face. "Mr. Callahan, here, says he already knew you were the agent on the case. Do you know how he knew?"

"Because you told him?" Jacobs said.

"Nah. The Archangel Gabriel told him. Told him to find you. Says he mentioned you specifically by name. You're on a first name basis with an Archangel, Frank."

Jacobs stared at Diaz a moment, and then looked at Thompson. "What is this?"

Callahan offered his hand to Frank again, saying, "I'm eager to help vanquish Lucifer's first foot soldier."

Jacobs didn't take the hand. He said, "Seriously, what is going on here?"

Thompson cleared his throat and said, "Gentlemen, can I please have a moment alone with Agent Jacobs?"

Callahan looked dumbly at his hand. Diaz smiled as he and Callahan shuffled out of the office. The door shut behind them.

Thompson cleared his throat. "Look—"

"Did Diaz put him up to this? Diaz is pissed he didn't get the case, so he finds some crackpot to waste my time?"

"It's not like that. This guy has friends in high places."

"Yeah, angels, apparently."

"No, as far as we're concerned, higher." Thompson raised his eyebrows.

Jacobs understood. The guy had friends in the big white buildings in Washington.

Thompson said, "We are to extend him every courtesy, I am told."

"So the FBI is taking on true-crime tourists now?"

"No. This guy is no tourist. Look, your suspect has been busy."

"Busy doing what?"

"Doing what he does. This guy Callahan is a religious nut. He's the man behind *Global Watch*." Thompson paused as if Jacobs was supposed to recognize the name.

Jacobs stared at him blankly.

"It's an investigative blog into religious phenomena."

"I can't believe I'm hearing this."

"He's been following the trail of your suspect in the media. He has an eye for this type of thing, connecting news stories to bizarre conspiracy theories. He may be crazy, but he is good at recognizing patterns."

"Sir, with all due respect, this is totally fucked."

"I agree with your assessment, Agent Jacobs. But I would mind you to watch your tone with me. I give you a lot of leeway, Frank, but that leeway has limits. Something is going on here. Something bigger than we initially thought, or could have comprehended. A reaping of child abusers that borders on genocidal."

"With all due respect, sir, you're sounding like the religious nut now."

"This may be world-wide, Jacobs. I'm pumping a lot of resources into this. I'm putting tech on chat-rooms and social media. Going to assign agents to look into different cult organizations. I need you to take this angle."

"What angle is that, exactly?"

Thompson cleared his throat one more time. "The demon angle."

"All right, I'm leaving. Fire me if you want. Give the case to Diaz." Jacobs started for the door.

"Jacobs," Thompson barked, with just enough growl to sound menacing.

Jacobs stopped and turned toward his boss.

Thompson said, "Diaz is…what's the word?"

"A dick."

"Overzealous."

"You've called him that word before. I think you're meaning dick."

"Diaz and this Callahan guy will go off turning this into some kind of demon-busting-exorcism thing. I need someone rational on this. Maybe even overly rational, to balance out the crazy."

"I don't think there is a rational counterpoint to this level of crazy."

"The guy specifically asked for you. How did he know that you were the agent on this case?"

"The Archangel Gabriel told him," Jacobs said.

"Or, he's involved somehow. I don't know."

"Could just be that he's crazy."

"Crazy or not, he knows something and someone. I told you this comes from the top. I just got off the phone with the director before you came in. We are to extend Callahan every courtesy."

Jacobs stared at Thompson. He had no response to this.

Thompson tossed a yellow legal pad across his desk so that it faced Jacobs.

"What's this?" Jacobs picked up the pad and looked at location after location scribbled down the left hand margin.

"Those are possible hits."

"Of what? Acid?"

"No. Places where child abusers got killed in some drastic way. This guy, Callahan, has a large following. He put out to his followers a kind of APB, if you will, searching media stories for certain criteria. It was pretty good detective work, really, same kind of search we would have run."

Jacobs read the locations, each jumping from country to country, continent to continent. "Are these in chronological order?"

"To the best they could get them, yes."

"There're several hits between Mystic Island and Hobart."

"I know."

"But that's impossible."

Thompson shrugged and said, "Callahan has put together a kind of profile of our killer. Well, it's a demon profile." Thompson's voice dropped a little, realizing how foolish it sounded. "Callahan says this demon is a kind of reaper, who has most likely come to Earth to collect souls for the coming battle of Armageddon."

Jacobs tossed the pad onto the desk. "You almost had me convinced to do this."

"Look, I obviously know that this is not a demon doing this. I know it has to be some kind of organization of people. Very motivated and organized people. People who possibly believe they are doing some kind of religious duty."

"That's what I was coming to tell you. I figured it out. This is obviously a group of religious extremists doing this. Fanatics dressed as demons…on stilts…and steroids…." Jacobs paused a moment, as if mentally calculating a math problem. "Anyway, we don't need a religious fanatic to track down…." He paused again to check his math.

"To track down religious fanatics?" Thompson said. "See? That's why I need you to let this Callahan guy out on the leash. See where he leads us."

"Take him for a walk and clean up his shit."

"I don't think this will be a waste of time. I think this guy knows something. And I think he'll lead you right to it. After all, let's face it, you're good at finding the shit."

5

Jacobs asked Ty to join them. He didn't want to be alone with this Callahan nut. He wanted another perspective, or at least a witness. Not to mention, Ty was a good investigator, asking the right questions and providing the right feedback to keep the investigative juices flowing. He and Jacobs worked well together. And besides, Jacobs liked Ty, considered him a friend.

Ty was waiting beside the standard government-issued, black Denali when Jacobs and Callahan exited the building, Jacobs holding two Styrofoam cups of coffee.

"Our driver?" Callahan said to Jacobs.

"An agent," Jacobs said. When they were close enough, Jacobs said, with muted enthusiasm, "Ty Malone, meet Dennis Callahan."

"Nice to meet you, Mr. Callahan," Ty said, holding out his hand.

Callahan, not taking the hand, said, "Likewise, Agent Malone." He climbed into the back seat of the Denali.

Ty looked at Jacobs with his hand still held out. Jacobs put a coffee in it.

Ty grinned, saying, "Haughty little fella, huh?"

"You have no idea."

"Did I hear him ask if I'm *the driver*?"

"This is going to be a long ride," Jacobs said, walking toward the passenger seat. "But you are driving."

"Great."

Jacobs and Ty got into the vehicle, and Callahan said, "I think our first order of business is—"

Jacobs, about to sip his coffee, turned to face Callahan. "Look, we're going to Mystic Island. I'm making the decisions here. You're here as a resource. We don't need any true-crime tourist telling us what sites he'd like to see."

"I can assure you, I'm not—"

"Look, I don't care. Just sit there and be quiet until we ask you something. Okay? That's how this will work."

"Special Agent in Charge Thompson told me—"

"I don't care what he told you or who you know or whatever. I don't want to hear from you unless it is in response to a question. You got that?"

"Is that a question?"

"Yes."

"Then, yes."

"Good." Jacobs turned to Ty and gestured forward with his coffee. "Please proceed."

"Yessa, Miss Daisy."

Jacobs glanced at Ty and shook his head.

They'd yet to make the highway before Jacobs turned toward Callahan and said, "Okay, start."

"Is that a question?"

"Yes, I am asking you to start."

"Start what?"

"Helping."

"Start where?"

"How the fuck should I know?"

"There's no need for rudeness, Agent Jacobs. Nor blasphemy. I was told you are in charge of the case and that you need my help. If it continues to be met with such hostility, then perhaps I should take that help elsewhere. Maybe I should be talking with Agent Diaz. He seemed far more open and appreciative of my expertise."

"I thought I was assigned to this by an angel," Jacobs said.

"No, you were assigned by your boss. I was told of you by an angel. I am happy to pull some strings and have you replaced."

"You can pull strings with angels?"

"No, I can pull strings with your boss."

Jacobs sighed and said, "Okay. You're right. I was rude. Let's start over. Go ahead."

"Go ahead with what?"

"Tell us what you know."

"I know a lot, Agent Jacobs. Can we maybe narrow it down some?"

Jacobs glanced at Ty. Ty shrugged. Jacobs said, "Okay. Who is killing all these child abusers?"

"I believe it is a demon."

"Look, let's get this right out there. I don't think it is a demon. There are no demons. So can we pull this back into the realm of reality?"

"Do you want the real answers to your questions, or do you want only what you are willing to believe?"

Jacobs glanced at Ty again. Ty grinned as he pulled the Denali onto the highway.

Jacobs asked Callahan. "Who is killing these child abusers?"

"A demon," Callahan answered.

Jacobs nodded. "Okay. Fine. I'll play. Why's a demon killing child abusers?"

"This is no game, Agent Jacobs. It is a demon killing these sinners. That's what demons do. They kill and torture the wicked. And they try to corrupt the good."

"Come on, man. You need to meet me halfway, here," Jacobs said, leaning back in his seat. "Look, let's try this again.

Maybe start with some kind of a timeline. When do you think these killings started? And why?"

Callahan looked out the vehicle's windows. "How long a drive do we have? This could take a while."

6

It was late in the day when the Denali, encased in a cocoon of fog, made its return trip from Mystic Island. None of them in the SUV were able to see the water that surrounded the bridge leading back to the mainland. Jacobs was now especially glad Ty had agreed to accompany them to Mystic Island. Not only as a buffer against Callahan's nuttiness, but also, something seemed not quite right on that island. Something seemed… he couldn't put a word on it.

"That was weird, right?" Jacobs said.

Ty said. "Hold on, we're almost off the bridge."

Jacobs had no idea why Ty wanted to wait until they were off the bridge before talking—that statement in itself was weird. Jacobs could see the intense concentration on Ty's face, and the way he gripped the wheel with both hands. Jacobs figured the fog was making Ty uncomfortable. Or, he wondered if it was the bridge that was making him uncomfortable? Jacobs knew the fog would most likely clear as soon as they were off the bridge, solving both possibilities. A local old-timer had told them that the bridge—and only the bridge—was often encased in fog. It had something to do with the currents around the island trapping warmer water or colder water or something. Callahan contradicted this assessment by telling Jacobs, "Actually, it is from the dimension of Hell slipping into our own dimension." Jacobs figured he'd go with the ocean currents explanation. Although earlier, coming through the fog onto the island was like an old B horror movie effect—traveling to a mythical land, or ripping back in time—and the nineteenth century buildings scattered across the island only added to this effect.

With a gentle bump of the car carrying over the lip of the bridge's end, they were born into sunlight. Jacobs felt a marked relief, though he figured he'd never pinpoint quite why, unsure himself if it was the fog or the bridge itself. Whatever it was, it was—

"Weird, right?" Jacobs said—for a moment not realizing if he'd voiced the words or merely thought them.

"Is that a question?" Callahan said from the backseat.

"Not for you," Jacobs called toward him. He'd just about had enough of this guy, and that was before they'd even left the field office.

"What's weird?" Ty said.

"The whole thing. Everything that just happened on the island. It was weird, right?"

Ty chuckled. "Yeah, I'd say so. But which part stuck out as the most weird to you?"

"I think maybe the girl has me a little freaked out."

"Explain."

"She was too calm for what happened."

They'd interviewed Molly Simmons. Her parents had returned from their trip and were already packing to move off "this godforsaken island," as Molly's mother, Alice, had put it. The father, Steve, had just shrugged. Alice and Steve had grown up on the island, along with Stewart, and Alice was long done with the place. For Steve, it was home. Jacobs could see Alice's point. Ty could see Steve's. "Sometimes places, no matter how bad they are, are just home to some people," Ty had said.

Callahan had interjected *his* theory of the place, telling Alice that, "God has indeed forsaken this island."

Jacobs, Ty, and Callahan had then sat with Molly and her father—Alice didn't join them, not wanting to, "relive that insanity"—as Molly recounted the story of her uncle's grisly death without so much as a quiver in her voice. "It was a monster," she'd assured them. It was like the night came to life. But while she'd described the thing as a monster and horrifying, she'd kept referring to it as her friend.

Callahan had said, "Never a friend is a demon."

Jacobs turned toward him and said, "What does that even mean?"

"It's foolish to call a demon a friend," Callahan said.

Jacobs growled at him, "Look, not another word, got it?" He then said to Molly, "Had you ever seen this man before?"

"It wasn't a man," Molly said.

"Okay, then had you ever seen this thing before?"

"No."

"Have you seen him since?"

Molly shot him a scolding look.

"Have you seen *it* since?"

"No."

"Then why do you call it your friend?"

"It saved me from having to play Uncle Stewie's games. And it was nice."

"Nice?" Callahan said. "It crushed your uncle's head until his eyeballs shot across the room."

Ty winced. Jacobs gave Callahan a look as if he were about to backhand him.

Molly shrugged. "It was nice to me. It told me to go and call the police, and it said I would never have to worry about Uncle Stewie again."

"You could understand it?" Callahan said.

"Sure," Molly said. "It spoke strange words at times, but it spoke English to me."

Now, in the car, out of the fog, Jacobs told Ty, "She was describing the guy like it was an imaginary friend or something."

"Are you sure it was a guy?"

"Jesus, not you, too. You really think the night came to life?"

"It was a demon," Callahan called in a singsong voice from the backseat.

"Didn't ask," Jacobs sang back.

Ty said, "I'm just saying she seemed pretty convinced it wasn't a man. And you said it yourself. What man can crush a human skull with that kind of force?"

"No man," Callahan said.

Ty said to Jacobs, "And you saw the ceiling in Uncle Stewie's room."

Ty was referring to what they'd found when they'd visited the crime scene. Molly had stated that the guy—the thing—had to stoop in Uncle Stewie's room. "That looks a standard height to me," Ty had said, pointing up at the ceiling. "Which makes it about eight feet." He'd even held up his arm, gauging the distance. "Yeah, I'd say it's eight feet. And what's that black shit right there? Those streaks?"

"Soot," Jacobs had said reluctantly.

"What, was he a burner, this Uncle Stewie? He hit the pipe?"

"No." Jacobs had swallowed, glancing at Callahan, not wanting to answer. "The lab found traces of soot on the ceiling, the floor, the comforter, and on Stewart's head."

"What kind of soot?"

Jacobs shrugged. "I don't know. Soot. Are there different kinds?"

Callahan said, "Of course there are different kinds of soot.

Each ring of Hell has—"

"Not a word, remember?" Jacobs said to him.

Ty said, "Well, looks like this sooty guy was bumping his head on an eight-foot ceiling."

Now in the car, Jacobs squeezed his eyes with his thumb and forefinger, a habit he had when thinking too hard, or when he didn't want to think at all.

Callahan said, as if to himself, "Nephilim are known to be at least eight-foot-tall. It's not that hard to imag—"

"I said—" Jacobs began, but then said, "All right, fine, let us recap a little here for clarification of our conversation earlier. You think this demon, this Nephilim"—Jacobs turned and looked at Callahan, making sure he had the correct terminology; Callahan nodded—"this Nephilim has come to orchestrate the End Times. And the Archangel Michael told you all of this."

"Not Michael. Gabriel. Gabriel is the Word of God. Only he can have direct influence over the matters of man. Michael is the guardian of sacred sites. And the leader of Jesus's army."

Jacobs sighed and said, "So Gabriel told you a Nephilim has come to orchestrate End Times?"

"Well, not the Nephilim part," Callahan said. "I figured that part out myself." He puffed up his chest a little with pride.

"And how did you figure that out?"

"The physical descriptions from the survivors. I've shown you the composite drawings of your so-called suspect. You yourself said they looked familiar."

"I said they look like those Easter Island head thingies."

"Exactly. And those Moai are depictions of the Nephilim. Giants with six fingers."

"And you think this demon came through to our world on Mystic Island? Did Gabriel tell you this, too?"

"No, I deduced that as well from my research. Look, I told you, Gabriel told me I needed to contact Agent Frank Jacobs to help track down a demon that has breached our world with the intent of driving forward Satan's army to Armageddon."

"And Armageddon is a place, not a thing?" Jacobs said, his voice showing his exhaustion. He looked at Ty.

Ty shrugged. "I thought it was a shitty Bruce Willis movie."

Callahan ignored Ty. He said, "Armageddon is the location of the battlefield where the war between good and evil will come to its climax and the Apocalypse will occur."

"The end of the world," Jacobs said.

"No," Callahan moaned. "We've been over this, too. The Apocalypse is a revealing. It literally means the lifting of a veil; a revelation."

"I really should've paid more attention in Sunday School," Jacobs said to Ty.

"Don't think it would help with any of this," Ty said.

Jacobs said to Callahan, "And you think this demon is killing these child abusers because he is amassing an army of dead people that you call the Wicked Dead?" He turned to Ty, saying, "Of course, here in the Boston area, that would mean *really* dead."

Ty said, "Yeah, I've come to realize that since being transferred here."

Jacobs said to Callahan, "So why did this Nephilim rise on Mystic Island? Why not Easter Island or this Armageddon place?"

"Mystic Island seems to be some kind of paranormal hotspot. In fact, Puritan settlers had found a tunnel—a place the indigenous people of the island had called wunn… wunnau…" He paused, looking at the car's ceiling, as if the word were up there for him to read. "Wanna-chick-o-muck," he said. "Which translates roughly as 'smoke hole.' The settlers attempted to explore its depths, but they never got more than a couple of hundred yards before they turned back nauseated and overwhelmed with fear. They believed the place to be a pathway to Hell, and so they built a church atop it, bolting the entranceway shut with a three-inch thick iron door. They supposed no demon would be able to come up through a holy place. Apparently they were wrong."

Jacobs said, "You're telling me there is a church on that island with a supposed doorway to Hell in its basement? Why didn't we go check out this church?"

"Why would we need to check out the church?"

"To see if there is evidence that a demon came through this doorway."

"It isn't enough evidence that Archangel Gabriel told me it is so? We know the demon has come up through the doorway from Hell. You just saw the evidence on Stewart Brookes's bedroom ceiling."

Jacobs turned fully to face Callahan. "You didn't take us to this church because you know if that doorway is still bolted shut, then it disproves your theory that a demon came from Hell. I'm not going to be manipulated here to try and prove your narrative. If there is something to investigate, then you tell me."

"It wasn't manipulation, Agent Jacobs. If we had gone to the basement of that church and saw that the door *was* open, what would you believe?"

"That someone had pried open the door to make it look like a demon had come up to Earth."

"Exactly. That door being open or shut would influence neither of our opinions on what happened. So, of what use would going into that basement be?"

Jacobs didn't answer. Instead, he stared out the windshield.

Ty said, "I have a question. Why child abusers?"

Jacobs said, "Yeah, why child abusers? Why not murderers or something really nasty?"

"There is nothing more wicked than a taker of innocence. One that harms a child is the worst thing there is," Callahan said. He paused a moment, looking out the window. "I almost envy him."

Jacobs said, "Him, who? Your demon?"

"Yes. In my life, I've only had my faith shaken once, and it was due to the church's commission of that very sin. It's the reason I left the Catholic faith and was born again."

Ty said, "I have another question. So, the reason your supposed demon wants the Wicked Dead army is because when the time comes for Armageddon, when the bell rings, so to speak, Satan fears that the Wicked Living will pussy out and not fight?"

"I'm not sure I said those words, but yes."

"So, he kills these wicked people so they can rise from the dead, zombie-style, and be under Satan's control?"

"Yes. Exactly."

"A zombie army sounds pretty cool," Ty said to Jacobs.

"I agree," Jacobs said.

Ty said to Callahan, "And you won't be here during all of this because all you good Christians will have been Raptured to the Holy Land."

"Not the Holy Land. The Kingdom of Heaven."

"So why won't all you good Christian soldiers be fighting?"

"Yeah," Jacobs said. "Where will you all be?"

"We have been promised the Rapture."

Ty said, "Isn't fighting against the forces of evil more important? I mean, you say that the whole reason Satan is amassing this army is because he fears the wicked won't fight. So why don't all you Christian soldiers just roll right over the army of Satan?"

"Because we were promised the Rapture."

"Sounds a little like you all are pussying out," Ty said.

"He has a point," Jacobs said.

Callahan's fists clenched. "Agent Jacobs," he said, his voice quivering, "I fight my battle for the Lord *now*. Gabriel himself has entrusted me with this responsibility." He looked out at the passing landscape, saying under his breath, "Why did they give me agents that are so insulting?"

"*Give* you agents?" Ty said.

Jacobs said. "Sorry, but we're all you got. Unless any other angels intervene. And I'm not trying to be insulting. Just getting a handle on the story."

"It's not a story. It is prophecy."

Ty said, "If it's prophecy, then we already know God wins, so then why does Gabriel need your help?"

Callahan was visibly shaking. "You don't understand," he said, his voice rising. "The Antichrist has already come. You've already destroyed this country's fabric of morality. It all started back when you put that Islamic half-breed in the White House."

Ty's face dropped as he glared at Callahan in the rearview mirror. "Excuse me?"

"That mongrel will rise to power again."

"Um," Ty said.

"And you sit here and mock me," Callahan said, sneering and glaring at Ty's eyes in the mirror. "The pieces are in place on the chessboard. The time to strike at the heart of evil is now." Breathing heavily, he tried to get hold of his emotions. "You people," he growled, glaring at Ty's eyes again.

"You people?" Ty said. "Do I need to pull this thing over?"

Jacobs ran his hand over his face. "All right, gentlemen, please stop. I don't have the patience for this shit."

Callahan and Ty shared a final contemptuous look in the mirror.

"I don't think it's a demon," Jacobs said to Callahan. "I think it's a group of costumed religious freaks. And you're gonna help me find them."

7

Thayer Hill was a spook, but not in the ghost sense. He was an agent with the Central Intelligence Agency. He was tall, but not too tall. He was muscular, but not too muscular. He looked average, which was good because his job entailed blending in. However, Thayer Hill was far from average. If he were ordered to do so, he could—and would—kill someone just as soon as look at them. He had a smile and a twinkle in his eyes that made one believe he didn't want to do so, even if he did. Thayer's assignment was to act as a smuggler of weapons and blood diamonds in and out of the Democratic Republic of Congo, but he'd received a strange message from Langley that was contrary to that assignment. It had told him that despite the potential for breaking cover or being killed by the Hutu, he was to go to a militia camp just outside the town of Bukavu, and to report back to Langley what had happened there. Thayer Hill had never received such ambiguous direction. *Report what happened there.*

Thayer stepped from the jungle undergrowth with a Sig Sauer pointing at the ground. The birds, usually squawking in the jungle, were silent. No vultures circled above in the cloudless sky, despite the overabundance of carrion. The only sound was an overwhelming buzz of flies. The air, oppressive with the humid heat, felt heavier still. The sickly sweet stench of decomposition intensified with the hot, stale air.

Thayer glanced around, making sure there were no survivors, and then he glanced over at Philippe Mamboui, who emerged from the jungle behind him. Mamboui was a local man who worked with Thayer Hill. He was not a CIA agent, but the CIA was his employer. Mamboui glanced around at the carnage and sheathed the only weapon he had: a machete he'd used to cut through the jungle vegetation. He'd realized that if whoever, or whatever, had done this to the camp were still around, the machete would do little good.

Thayer estimated there were about fifteen dead militiamen. There were actually twelve—it is difficult to count bodies when they are in pieces. At first, Thayer thought it looked like the camp had been attacked by men with machetes, and, surveying the dead, he wondered why no one had such a weapon in hand. The militiamen had all had guns, and the shredded vegetation proved that those guns had been used to excess, yet they'd not seemed to hit a single attacker. Thayer approached a decapitated body. Beside it, a pile of entrails offered refuge for scores of buzzing flies. No cut marks, no defensive wounds consistent with one being attacked with a straight-edged weapon. It looked more like the men were torn apart.

An animal, maybe? he thought. *Animals?* But there were no animal carcasses either. *The men would have hit at least one, right?* Thayer crouched beside another body. The man's finger still gripped the trigger of an AK-47, the weapon having long ago spent its last shells. His head looked like a soup bowl. Thayer tried to imagine what could make such a perfect dent in a human skull. All he could come up with was a shot-put maybe? A ball and chain? Thayer picked up a spent cartridge from a pile beside the man. The militiaman had unloaded an entire magazine. But no one lay before him riddled with bullets. Thayer glanced at Mamboui again.

Mamboui said, "Shetani," the Swahili word for *Devil*.

Thayer bobbed his head, looking around at the bodies. He dropped the cartridge and absently wiped his fingers on his pants, saying, "Maybe." Mamboui was not the first person to formulate this theory. The local priest who had reported this incident to authorities said that the Devil had come and killed all the Hutu militiamen. It was the most logical explanation so far. Because, to Thayer, none of it made sense. There was something else wrong, but Thayer couldn't quite place it. Mamboui voiced it for him.

Mamboui said, "Where are the women and children?"

Militia camps were generally full of women and children—the girls acting as sex slaves, the boys as soldiers. There were no signs of them. No bodies. No one crying. No one running to them for help.

Thayer needed to speak to the priest.

It was a two-hour hike through the rough, twisting, machete-cut paths leading to the small village to the south. By the time they arrived, the sun had nearly set.

The deeper colors of twilight made the quiet village seem abandoned. No one moving about in the streets or the yards or the houses. Occasionally, Thayer caught eyes peering from windows or doorways, but no one made himself or herself known. Thayer and Mamboui went to the open doors of the church, Thayer's hand on the butt of the Sig Sauer at his side.

The pews were filled with women and children. They looked at Thayer and Mamboui with blank stares. Thayer had seen that look before. They were in shock. They had seen something so unreal that their brains gave up making any sense of it. Thayer walked to the front of the church, the blank stares of the pews' occupants following him. In the silence, each of his and Mamboui's footfalls brought creaking protests from the floor's wooden planks. They felt as if they were onstage before a captive audience, but in reality, maybe one or two would comprehend that they'd even been there. Still, Thayer raised his voice and said, "I am looking for Father Himbata." He said this in French, the official language of The Democratic Republic of Congo. The reply he received, however, was in heavily accented English.

The voice said, "I am Father Himbata."

Thayer turned to see a man sitting in the church's corner. He was an old man dressed in a black cassock. He held his head in his only hand—his other hand had been cut off, with most of his forearm, by the Hutu two years prior. He said, "I suppose you are here to ask about the Devil."

The Wrath

1

Huang Mingde had never held a machine gun. In fact, he had never held any kind of gun. At least, not with any intent of using it. He had once carried a gun—and in carrying, he had transported it from one place to another place. That gun had been a Glock 9mm, and he had carried the thing as if it were radioactive. Huang had thought about the bullets inside of it that were just itching to go kinetic, but he figured that, with his perpetual bad luck, the gun would go off accidentally, and then Jimmy Wang would have used the next bullet on him. At that time, Huang had wondered what it would feel like to squeeze off a round, to bring that kinetic energy to life, but he'd wondered it while carrying the gun by the barrel. Today, however, Jimmy had grabbed Huang from the kitchen, where Huang had been finishing up the dishes. Jimmy told him that Pin-jui, The Rat, hadn't shown up for a few days now, and he needed another body during a delivery. Jimmy said to Huang in Mandarin, "You know how to use one of these?" He held out an MP5 machine gun.

Huang nodded even though he had absolutely no idea how to use it. He guessed he could figure it out, sure that it was as easy as pulling the trigger and pointing the thing, not realizing that these steps were backwards.

Huang now stood by the rear exit of the warehouse—an abandoned sweatshop with a full kitchen and living quarters for Jimmy's henchmen. Jimmy had told him, "Just stand beside this door and don't let anyone through." He added, "And if any mothafucka starts anything, you light the mothafucka up." He said all of this in Mandarin, except for the word "mothafucka," which he said in English. Huang held the MP5 before him, scrunching his brow to make himself look more intimidating, like someone capable of lighting a mothafucka up. Mayaw Ciro had once told Huang that the firing of a gun was like "spewing your wanky." According to him, it was even better than sex. Huang had no idea what sex felt like. Although he worked for an organization that specialized in the peddling of flesh, Huang was still a virgin. Jimmy had yet to "throw him a bone." Jimmy often threw his other men bones, but Huang wasn't really considered one of Jimmy's men. In Jimmy's organization, Huang wasn't all that different in status than the girls now standing against the warehouse wall. Huang's father had owed Jimmy Wang a debt, and he had paid that debt with his youngest son. Tonight, Huang hoped he would be accepted into the "brotherhood." He hoped that tonight he would become bone-worthy.

Jimmy, of course, was always bone-worthy. Seeing as how, in his mind, he owned all these girls, he could do with them as he wished. He meandered along the line of twenty girls—most of them Asian, all of them under the age of eighteen. He picked the one who looked the youngest and most scared, and he led her off to his office, a small room raised about twenty feet off the warehouse's floor. Steep metal stairs led up to the room and large windows were cut into its walls. Whenever Jimmy had his bone, he would draw the windows' shades, but he would leave the lights on so all his men could see the silhouette of his boning.

This time, Jimmy did not pick the prettiest girl. At least, Huang didn't think so. The one Huang would have picked was not Asian. She was standing closest to him. She was very petite, but appeared taller than she was, due to her lithe body. She had over-large, dark eyes that were both mischievous and intelligent. And she had a closed-mouthed, sensual smile that she used with a shift of her head, bringing her long black hair to fall over half her face. This caused a physiological reaction in men, and the maneuver had saved her life more than once. Huang, of course, had no way of knowing this about her, but it was true nonetheless.

The girl's name was Raven Mijares and, despite her Spanish name and the American accent with which she spoke several languages—including Mandarin Chinese—Huang was mistaken when he thought she was not Asian. She was American, but her parents were from Asia. Her mother was from Russia, her father from the Philippines. Raven was sixteen years old. When she was thirteen, her parents were killed in a plane crash and Raven was sent to a Russian village to live with her aunt—a woman so envious of her sister's life in America that death wasn't a good enough remedy. In true Cinderella fashion, her aunt treated Raven like a slave, so she ran away. While cutting through a rival village, she was kidnapped as revenge for an ancient feud. The two villages had long since forgotten why they feuded—forgotten that, 122 years ago, a member of one village had not appropriately thanked a member of the other village for a shared meal. This lack of courtesy had since yielded sixty-two murders, thirteen maimings, seventy-six fistfights, and twenty-six kidnappings. That said, even if the rival village had not wanted to take Raven as part of an ancient feud, they probably still would have taken her. A thirteen-year-old girl with such a potent combination of innocence and sexuality would fetch a high price on the black market.

And she did fetch a high price. They sold her to an Albanian organization known as the Dhelpër e Zezë. They, in turn, sold her for over two hundred thousand dollars to a wealthy Saudi sheik named Nimr al Abbandhu. The sheik soon found that he had gotten more than he'd bargained for. Raven was a sponge for information, making her smarter than most, and she was unfazed by punishment or reward. She was what men of the sheik's ilk would call *unbreakable*. After being owned by the sheik, a Russian mobster, and an American doing business in Bangkok, Raven was sold to Taiwanese sex traders for three hundred dollars. The truth is, the American would have paid them to take her off his hands.

Now she was dressed in a schoolgirl uniform—short plaid skirt, tight gray sweater, gray knee-high socks, and white sneakers. It took several costume changes for Jimmy Wang to come up with this one. No matter what he put on her, she just looked too damn mature to be sold to clientele that specified "the younger the better". So he put her in the schoolgirl outfit—knowing that her smoldering maturity would add the qualifying "bad" in front of the schoolgirl moniker. She would more than likely be sold to a Bangkok brothel as "the feisty one" that the men would try to tame.

Whenever Huang glanced Raven's way, she leveled a very direct glare at him. It was the look that had both infuriated and melted all of her subjugators. She looked as if she saw every thought in their heads and every emotion in their hearts. The American businessman had once said to her, "Jesus Christ, stop looking at me like that. You're like a fucking cat." He was referring to the fact that when he was a child, his grandmother's cat had always looked at him in a manner that made him believe the cat knew something about the deepest parts of his soul, a kind of clairvoyance. When the girl leveled her gaze at Huang, he looked away immediately and lowered his brow to appear more menacing. He raised the MP5 in his hands and adjusted the shoulder strap more securely on his shoulder.

The girl said to Huang in Mandarin, "You know, that thing works much better with the safety off." She then added in English, in a very American way, "slick."

Huang looked down at the machine gun, searching for the safety.

Sammy the Bull, who was standing nearby, said to Raven, "Bì zuǐ," which means *shut up* in Mandarin. Sammy's real name was Twan Ho Le, but he'd always wanted the nickname Bull. Twan the Bull didn't have the right ring to it, so he took the name of a famous American gangster. The other men butchered the English version with their accents, creating the nickname, "Sammy the Boo." The only person who could pronounce the name correctly was Raven, but she still insisted on calling him Sammy the Boo. Sammy the Bull said, "No talking."

"Sorry, Sammy the Boo."

"I said, no talking."

"Just trying to help."

Sammy pulled Raven from the wall and cocked his arm as if to strike her. Huang cringed. Raven did not. Raven knew Sammy's threat was only for show. The men weren't allowed to hit the girls—so as to not lower the value of the merchandise. God forbid Sammy were to knock out this girl's teeth or leave a scar. Huang didn't know this rule because he was always in the kitchen. So Huang, who had become fond of Raven and didn't want to see her struck, returned his attention to the MP5, still looking for the safety.

A sound rang out from Jimmy Wang's office. Huang looked up from the machine gun. Everyone, all the men, Sammy the Bull, the eighteen other girls, and even Raven, stared slack-jawed toward the office. At first, Huang thought the sound was Jimmy yelling at the girl he had taken up there. Maybe he got another one who'd decided to bite his dick (Huang had heard a rumor of this happening before), or maybe she refused to do what he wanted her to do, or maybe she was another crier; Jimmy hated the criers—he wanted them to do what they were supposed to do without a sound. But the girl he had taken up there seemed too meek to cause Jimmy any real problems.

Actually, Huang wondered if the sound was even yelling. Or even human. It wasn't a language he'd ever heard before.

The office door opened and the young girl came screaming down the steep stairs. The girl ran to Sammy the Bull and clung to him. She screamed in Vietnamese, "Sammy the Boo. Sammy the Boo. It's the Devil. The Devil has come for him." She would not let go of Sammy the Bull, and she kept screaming that the Devil was in Jimmy Wang's office. This time, Sammy broke protocol. He backhanded the young girl to shut her up and get her off him. Raven, who had been released from Sammy's grip, grabbed the girl and backed up against the wall. The other eighteen girls cringed and began to whimper. The men looked at one another, unsure what to do.

He Lee, the one the others called "The Butcher," looked like a lost child who was trying to not piss his pants. "The Devil has come for us," he whimpered—not realizing that he may have found more mercy if it had been the Devil. Sammy the Bull, who was the only one who had any sense of action, pulled a silver .44 Magnum from the front of his pants and strode toward Jimmy's office. He stopped when something crashed through one of the windows and, after a few bounces, came to rest at his feet. Sammy pointed his gun at the object, struggling for comprehension. He lowered his gun and tilted his head, realizing he was looking at Jimmy Wang's decapitated head.

The only thing louder and shriller than the girls' screams was The Butcher screeching, "It is the Devil. It is the Devil."

"Bì zuǐ," Sammy hollered. And as Sammy raised his Magnum toward Jimmy Wang's office, the office door exploded in a cloud of debris and splintering wood. Something sprang from the room, crashing twenty feet to the warehouse floor. The thing charged Sammy the Boo as Sammy unloaded his Magnum. At first, with the thing's size and speed, Huang thought it was some kind of charging animal, like a rhino, but then Huang saw that the thing was actually a man…well, it was man-like. It was upon Sammy in a flash, and it pulled Sammy the Boo in half. Sammy the Boo, whose Magnum had run out of bullets, had time to click off a few useless trigger pulls and to look in confusion at his lower half in the giant man's other hand.

The giant tossed the halves aside and was next upon The Butcher. This time, The Butcher did piss himself. Then he fainted. The giant brought its boot down on The Butcher's head, mashing it like a melon. Next it was on a man named Lee Moo. It jammed its hand down Moo's throat—Moo's eyes widening and crossing as they focused on the elbow emerging from his mouth—and pulled out red goop as Moo fell to the floor. Mayaw Ciro emptied his MP5 at the giant. The giant turned, chased Mayaw to the far end of the sweatshop, and ripped his spine from his back.

The giant man then turned to face Huang. Huang saw its eyes glowing in the shadows. Huang raised his weapon and pulled the trigger. But even though he'd performed these steps in the correct order, the gun didn't fire. Huang had expected that surging feeling of spewing his wanky, but there was nothing. He looked at the gun. Then he looked at Raven for guidance.

Raven looked shocked for a moment, then she mouthed the word, "Safety."

Huang lifted the MP5 and inspected the weapon as the giant strode slowly across the room toward him.

"I don't know what that is," Huang said, as if to the gun.

Raven said, "It's right there. That little switch above the trigger."

The giant man, what Huang now thought of as a demon, was standing before him. Huang flipped the switch and raised the gun, but he didn't bother to pull the trigger. Instead, he closed his eyes tight and cringed. He waited for the thing to rip off his head, or disembowel him. But it didn't. Huang slowly opened his eyes.

The demon was flipping through a small leather-bound book. Huang looked to Raven for guidance. This time, she could offer none. Instead, she raised her eyebrows as she watched the demon reading the book. The demon looked from the book to Huang, and it said in Chinese, "You don't belong here."

Huang wanted to say that he agreed, but he couldn't say anything.

The demon said to Huang, "You need to leave and never come back."

Again, Huang said nothing. He looked to Raven.

Raven had no explanation, but she did offer some advice. "Run, dummy."

2

Raven watched as Huang ran a few yards left, cut a right angle, ran a few more steps, stopped again, made a hypotenuse back to his original point—looking for answers from Raven again—and then, as if just noticing the giant man for the first time, turned and sprinted for the kitchen. He disappeared through the door, leaving a wake of crashing pots and pans.

The giant watched Huang go. To Raven, he almost looked amused. The man turned toward the girls standing against the wall. All of them but Raven screamed.

The man held up his hands in a halting manner, his eyes widening. He said in Mandarin, "I will not hurt you. I will not hurt you. You are free."

The girls screamed louder and pressed themselves against the wall.

Raven understood the reason for the girls' screaming. This thing before them, savior or not, had just slaughtered five men. Tore them apart. Raven was wondering why *she* wasn't screaming. The thing's appearance was that of nightmares. She figured it had to be at least eight feet tall with gnarled muscles barely contained within its deep red skin. It had a prominent stone chin and eyes set deep beneath a serious brow. But as terrifying as this giant man's appearance was, Raven felt no fear. There was something in the man's eyes that she found comforting. His eyes were a fortress: foreboding to enemies, sanctuary to friends.

"You are free," the man called over the screaming, but the rising volume of his voice only stirred more terror in the girls. He lowered his hands, his massive shoulders sagging, and he looked at the floor, his expression twisting in defeat.

"Ānjìng," Raven shouted the Mandarin word for "quiet."

When the girls still didn't stop screaming, she shouted, "Bì zuǐ," knowing that even the non-Chinese-speaking girls would recognize the phrase that their captors had screamed at them so often. The girls stopped screaming. They huddled together and stared at Raven. Raven said to them in Chinese, "He is here to help. He has set us free." The girls stayed silent. Raven said, "We are free." Some of the girls nodded, beginning to understand, but they all huddled closer together, still looking to Raven for guidance. Raven could have used some guidance herself.

The giant nodded at her, appreciation in his fiery eyes, and he turned and walked away. Raven regarded the girls, still huddled together. They looked blankly at her as if they were cattle, having lived a life of dumb boredom until brought to the slaughterhouse floor. She turned and followed the giant. Reverting to her native English in her confused excitement, she said, "Hey, wait, where are you going?" When the man didn't stop or answer, she tried Chinese, having heard him speak it. "Wait," she said in Mandarin. "Stop." The man continued walking. Having recognized the language he was screaming at Jimmy Wang earlier, she tried Latin. "Desino."

This stopped him. He turned and responded in Latin, "You speak the Old Language?"

"Ita," she answered. "But I'd prefer speaking a new one," she said in English. "You speak English?"

"I do."

"Where are you going?" she said. She gestured at the other girls. "What are we supposed to do?"

The giant said, "You are free. Go to the police and find help."

Raven looked again at the girls huddled against the wall. Hearing their weeping and their low, unsure whispered pleas for comfort, she turned back to the man. "Find help? The police? Are you kidding me? The police will sell us right back into slavery."

The man said, "That will be their mistake."

"Oh, gee, that's helpful. Is that what I should say to them when they rape us and sell us again?"

"I will punish them."

"I'll be sure to tell them a big scary looking motherfucker told them to watch out."

The man looked at her a moment, as if trying to decipher a puzzle, then turned and walked away.

"No, hey, wait," Raven said, walking with him. "What about all of these girls? Is that really what you expect me to tell them? C'mon, you can't just leave us here. Where are you going?"

"There are others to punish."

Raven stopped. The man walked off to the far side of the warehouse. There was no exit, only a dark corner behind Jurassic machinery. A place she associated with rats and rape. She looked down at the floor where she had stopped. She was standing over Mayaw Ciro, the last man the giant had killed. Mayaw's body, which had been liberated of its spine, was bent at an impossible angle, both his blank staring face and his ass facing the ceiling. She looked back at the cowering herd, still weeping and staring at her for answers. She had none. She had become these young girls' keeper from the moment she fell into Jimmy Wang's ownership. Some of them had even dubbed her "mom" in a desperate attempt at comfort. But she didn't want to be anyone's keeper anymore. She didn't want to be anyone's comfort either. Including her own. Everyone looked to her for answers. Where had her answers gotten her? She had become fate's bitch. Orphaned, shunned by her remaining family, abused and owned by men. It was time someone else was the protector—and who better than a giant who had dispatched five armed men? Raven turned and ran into the darkness behind the ancient machinery in the far end of the warehouse. "Wait—" she called. And she was in a gray fog.

3

The cold was immediate. The kind of cold that stops breath in the lungs. The kind that feels like icicle worms burrowing into skin. The gray was all-encompassing. But then she noticed movement. Shapes in the fog. She sensed forms shuffling around her. She heard whispers—like young children sharing secrets at bedtime. Whispers and soft, shapeless moans.

Raven turned back in the direction from which she had come. She saw a sliver image of the warehouse, as if a photograph of her former prison had been rendered on a long streamer. But even this streamer view vanished as the grayness engulfed it like a closing zipper, leaving only the gray and the cold and the shifting sense of movement. And the whispers.

"Hello?" Raven called, but, as sometimes happened in her dreams, her voice was muted and she could not shout loud enough. Her voice was as frozen as her breath. For a moment, she thought she was actually dreaming. That she would wake up back in the warehouse, huddled with the other girls, not knowing where she would be sold next. This being a dream was, of course, the only logical explanation for what had happened—a giant coming and killing the Wang Gang, setting her free and disappearing into this shifting, addling landscape. Heart falling, she came to the realization that there was no rescuer. She was still a product to be sold. And to be used.

Now that she'd come to this realization, wouldn't she wake? But she didn't wake. She moved through the thick fog and the biting cold. And she heard the whispers and the soft moans getting louder. Or closer.

"Hello?" Raven called again. "Mr. Big Scary Guy?" Again, her voice was muted in the gray.

The shifting shapes around her became more defined, consolidating into figures. They climbed from the swirling gray distortions around her. Or, more accurately, the swirling gray was becoming the human-like figures. They were naked and emaciated—their faces the screaming corpses of a Poe story. They reached for Raven, trying to grab her.

She ran. But as in her dreams, she was unable to run at full speed. The figures clutched at her. They clawed at her clothing. The whispers became teakettle screams. Raven thought she heard words in the screams. One figure grabbed her by her hair. It yanked her head back and peered into her face with blank, staring eyes. Its toothy, decayed mouth smiled. She felt the thing's other hand climb up her chin like an insect. She gripped its arm with both her hands, trying to pull it away from her face. But the figure's strength was shocking, and it reached for her mouth with renewed determination. Raven pursed her lips, but those fingers—burning cold—pried open her mouth. Its long nails clicking against her teeth and brushing against her tongue. Raven gagged as the fingers continued past her tongue, the hand filling her mouth. She tried to bite down, but it didn't seem to matter. It was like biting leather. The figure looked more intently into her face, its smile widening. Then it let out a piercing scream as its mien contorted into a countenance of pain, and the creature was gone.

Something was pulling the figures away from her and tossing them aside. The giant that rescued her from Jimmy

Wang's gang was now holding one of the figures by the nape of the neck. The giant had fury in his eyes, and he said in Latin, "Do you know who I am?"

Raven felt an insane urge to burst out laughing, recognizing a phrase that every one of her owners had uttered to numerous subordinates and maître d's.

The giant scooped Raven into his arms. She felt as if she were being lifted, weightless, by steel girders. More figures rushed at the giant, trying to get at her. The giant tossed them aside, others he clobbered with his massive fist. Raven clung to his neck as more and more of the figures converged on them. The giant continued to beat his way through the crowd, smashing the figures aside.

One figure did not rush them. It was more emaciated than the others. It had a long white beard and stringy white hair. It stood and spread its arms and let out a screech. The other figures stopped and turned and looked at the old one. It spoke in the whispering, whistling language they used—an eerie mash-up of many languages combined with the cries of the wind. Raven recognized words for "punisher" and "Satan," and then "wrath" and "eternity" and "suffering." The crowd of figures regarded one another. Then they regarded the giant with the girl in his arms. Despite the warnings of the old figure—a specter that had once warned the likes of Odysseus himself—the others charged the giant and the girl.

The giant stood somehow taller, squaring his shoulders and thrusting his face forward to let out a roar that Raven felt more than heard. Her insides vibrated, as if she were standing before a powerful subwoofer. The crowd of figures stopped and cowered. The man holding Raven in his arms pulled his leather-bound book from his pocket and, with a small crescent iron blade attached to its spine by a cord, slashed through the fog. He and Raven stepped out of the grayness as the figures charged again. The sound of their screeching was snuffed as the slashed doorway sealed, and Raven found she was in the warm, fragrant night.

4

Raven said the first words that came to mind. "What the fuck?"

The giant man had placed her on the ground. They were in a parking lot behind a warehouse. It was not Jimmy Wang's warehouse. Big rigs surrounded them; their headlights—reflecting the glare of the parking lot lights—stared in silent judgment. Raven climbed to her feet, holding her stiff jaw. She could still feel the icy remnants of the figure's hand in her mouth. "What the hell was that?" she said in a choked gag.

The giant man said, "No human has ever been in the Gray Zone. That was unwise of you."

"The Gray Zone?"

"I guess you would call it Purgatory. Those are the shadow people, the Shades of Sheol. They are the most desperate of souls. You're lucky they didn't rip you apart trying to get at your life force."

"Then I guess I owe you my life. Twice. Thanks, Mr. Scary Guy."

The giant man stared down at her. He said, "Mr. Scary Guy is not my name."

"Well, it seemed apt. Do you have a name?"

"I am Iratus."

"Your name is Wrath? Did your parents not like you?"

"No. They did not," the man said.

"Your mother disliked you enough to name you Wrath?"

"My mother did not name me. She never knew me."

Raven detected a touch of sadness in the giant's deep, growling voice.

Iratus said, "She was a human and died giving birth to me, unable to suffer bearing a Nephilim."

"You're a Nephilim?" Raven said.

"You recognize the term?"

"Yeah, of course. Angels and humans getting it on to create a race of giants. All that fun Old Testament stuff. So who named you Wrath?"

Iratus paused a moment, his brow lowering. "I don't know."

"I can't very well call you Wrath, so I think I'll call you Ira," Raven said. She turned and regarded the bright parking lot and the herd of big rigs surrounding them. "Well, Ira, we need to get out of here and find someplace a little less conspicuous to hide out."

"We?" Ira said.

"Yeah. You stick out like a big red thumb. We need to find someplace to chill out. You just killed five guys."

"I am not worried about retributions for my killing. It was sanctioned. And you need to find the police. They will take care of you."

"Nope, sorry, Ira. I already told you, I'm not going to the police. They'll just sell me back."

"We are no longer in Taiwan. We covered a great distance in the Gray Zone."

Raven looked around at the parking lot and up at the sky. "I guess that explains why it's night all of a sudden. Where are we?"

"I am not sure exactly," Ira said. "I've never had to cut out suddenly like that."

The signs on the side of the big rigs were in English: Victoria Shipping. She said, "My guess is we are either in England or America." Regarding the Mack logo on the front of the trucks, she added, "But probably America."

"The police here will not harm you."

Raven chuckled. "If you say so. Actually, they'll most likely hand me over to Children Services, who will at first foul everything up with all kinds of bullshit, ship me around from one shithole home to another, eventually sending me back to my aunt in Russia, where I'll get grabbed and sent into trafficking again. If she doesn't sell me into it herself. Nope. Sorry. I've done it before. I'm better off with you and offing bad guys. Or whatever it is you do. What is it you do, exactly?"

"I am a Punisher."

"And whom do you punish?"

"Takers of innocence."

"So, like thieves?"

"Those who harm children."

"You punish those who harm children? Where the hell have you been for the last three years of my life?"

"Hell *is* where I've been."

"So why are you on Earth now?"

"I got tired of waiting for the innocence takers to come to me."

"A Nephilim from Hell that kills child abusers...boy, the priests will be running scared."

"I don't understand."

"You know? Priests? Child abuse? Never mind. Like I said, we need to find someplace to lie low, and I can come with you to punish assholes."

"You can't stay with me. You need to find the authorities," Ira said, but he felt something he had never felt before: enjoyment in the company of another. He liked the fast way she talked, the way she called him Ira, her determination and will, her survival. He didn't want her to go away. But she couldn't come with him. "I'm sorry."

"I owe you a life debt," Raven said. "Technically, two life debts. Until I save your life, you're stuck with me."

"You cannot come with me. You must find safety. I have work to do."

"Seriously? You drop me off somewhere, I don't know where, and you're gonna just bounce like that? Can't you at least help me find some money or food or something? I'm hungry. Can we Gray Zone our way into a restaurant?"

"You can never go into the Gray Zone again."

"Why not? Seems to get you around pretty well."

His voice hovered below a growl as he said, "You can never go in there again."

"All right, got ya. No Purgatory for me. Can you at least Gray Zone your way into this warehouse here?" She nodded at the trucking company's building. "I bet there's a couple of vending machines somewhere in there. How about grabbing some food and water or something?"

Ira looked at the building. He looked back at Raven. "Vending machine?"

"Yeah, you know, big machines full of food. Most places have one filled with snacks and one with water or soda. Just head in and grab me something to eat and drink."

"But that would be stealing," he said.

"Yeah?"

"It is a sin."

"Ira, you just butchered five men. Isn't killing a sin?"

"Not when they were sentenced to die. It was warranted."

"Well, if you let me starve, wouldn't that be harming an innocent?"

Ira opened his mouth, as if to mount an argument, but

instead he shut his mouth and turned to look at the building again. He took the book from his pocket and disappeared into the Gray Zone.

Raven felt a brief moment of stomach twisting anxiety. She was tired of being alone, not trusting anyone, missing her parents so badly that she'd often contemplated opening a wrist or flying from a high window to go and see them. But if she killed herself—her aunt, the sex traders, her owners— they'd all win. She'd already invested too much into this fight to cash out now. Cash out with nothing to show for it. And, besides, she hadn't necessarily believed that there was an afterlife in which to find her parents. She'd lost her notion of a Heaven or a Hell long ago. But that notion was certainly changing.

The air split open and Ira appeared again. He stepped out of the Gray Zone carrying a vending machine. He placed the machine down in front of her. She stared at the thing. It was as tall as her and as wide as him, filled with a rainbow of junk food.

"Holy shit," Raven said.

Ira turned back to the slit of the Gray Zone. "I'll go get the water machine," he said.

5

Raven sat at a high-top table, staring out the window of Morning Joe's Coffee Shop. Sammy the Boo's wide-eyed expression flashed into her mind. The expression he had as he was torn in half—the strange comprehension as his staring eyes watched his body's lower half travel in the opposite direction. Raven shut her eyes, willing the image away, but it continued as if it were a movie projected on the backs of her eyelids. Flashes of movement as Ira ripped through five armed men. She shook the images away and opened her eyes.

She took a sip of her Coke and watched the people in line at the counter. Did any of them realize that this girl sitting among them had met an honest to God demon? Behind the counter, a girl with pink hair watched a squat woman struggle to choose an item from the giant menu hanging on the wall. Behind the woman, a twenty-something man wearing a striped suit looked on with an expression of rushed annoyance. Raven needed to get out of this town. She was, in fact, in America, and she wanted to somehow get to one of the coasts. She needed a place where she could get lost in a crowd and maybe obtain a job. And a new identity. She thought of California or New York as her best bets. On that front, there was good news and there was bad news. The good news was that she'd been able to pull from the vending machine not only five bottles of water and several bags of food, but also $232.75, which, while sitting in the Victoria Shipping parking lot, she'd counted down to the last quarter. Ira, the giant, killer demon, hadn't been morally okay with taking the money either, but she'd insisted that if he was going to abandon her in the middle of a foreign land, then he would have to get morally okay with it. And, yes, although she was American, this was a foreign land. She and her parents, due to her parents' careers, had moved around so much that she had never settled long enough to feel like a resident anywhere. Ira had suggested again that she go to the authorities. She suggested that she was better off making her way to a major city. The way she calculated it, her odds of getting raped and killed were the same whether she went off on her own or got involved in foster care. So they had parted ways. Ira had disappeared into what he called The Gray Zone. Raven had wandered off down the street to the center of town.

In town, she'd found a Store 24 and spent $22.99 ($10 of which was paid in quarters) on a small faux-leather knapsack to carry her loot: the waters, several snacks from the machine, and the money, including the portion still in coins (now $3.76 after buying the bag). The other good news was that she'd been able to lift a cell phone off of a guy waiting for the bus, gambling on the phone not having a tracking app.

It was a trick she'd learned from the Dhelpër e Zezë. The first thing they taught the girls. Most of the girls would be sold to brothels, and that was a prime skill: lifting wallets from Johns who were high and drunk and euphoric. Raven was so good at it that Admir Kuteli, the boss of the Dhelpër e Zezë, thought it a shame when she was sold off to the sheik. She would have made a fortune picking pockets.

Once she'd had the smartphone, Raven discovered the bad news. When she'd checked the device's map, she discovered she was in Iowa. *Of all the places to suddenly end up*, she thought, *that walking wrath guy dropped me off in fucking Iowa*. Hunter, Iowa, to be exact. She imagined that somewhere in this shithole town there was a store selling T-shirts reading: *Where the hell is Hunter, Iowa?*

Raven scanned the people in the coffee shop for someone who might give her a ride. She thought the guy in the suit was a possibility, but, being most likely dressed for work, she doubted she could convince him to take her too far. Behind the suit was a delivery guy with a canine-look of faithful devotion. She could appeal to his sense of charity, but a salt-of-the-Earth-type would end up taking her to the police. Behind him, a nurse. Another trip to the proper authorities.

A sound of overconfident manifolds ripped through the air. Raven nearly spilled her soda as she looked out the window. A man on a Harley was backing the bike into a spot in front of the window.

Ahmad, Sheik Nimr's bodyguard, had once told Raven that men back their bikes into parking spots because they think it's more important to look cool leaving than arriving. "Now watch," Ahmad had said, nodding toward the Sheik's son and his three friends parking their bikes at the Saudi complex, "they will rev the engines three more times—twice in quick succession, and then one fading one—just to make sure that if no one has noticed them yet, they will now." Raven smiled as, outside the Iowa coffee shop, the Harley's rider gave two quick bursts of the engine, and then one fading one before cutting the engine. She missed Ahmad.

Her eyes flashed to the license plate on the bike. New Hampshire. A trip to New Hampshire may be from one boondocks to another, but it was at least closer to one of her coastal destinations. Raven took the napkin roll on the table and peeled it open, revealing the silverware packed inside. She took the butter knife and slipped it into her knee-high sock. This biker dude walking into Morning Joe right now didn't know it yet, but he was about to give Raven a ride.

6

It was a total sensory experience. Lights flying past her eyes. The roar of the engine in her ears. The smell of leather and high-octane exhaust. The weightless flying controlled-out-of-control feeling of hanging on the back of the bike, the vibration running up between her legs and rear. Ahmad had taken her for a few rides, even let her drive the bike. But those were very short rides. No more than fifteen minutes around the compound. This ride now was…how long? Had to be over ten hours. She released one of the arms she had wrapped around Benjamin and reached into her bag for her phone (*her* phone? *The* phone) to check the time. The battery was almost dead. It said it was 9:32. She also saw that there was no service. The guy she'd lifted it from had probably canceled it. It was little more than a clock now. And one almost out of juice. She let the thing fall from her hand and skip off down the highway.

"Everything all right?" Benjamin called over his shoulder.

"Yup," Raven shouted over the engine's roar.

That morning, she'd waited for him in the parking lot. He had walked out of the coffee shop with an egg sandwich (already halfway devoured) and two Snapples, then stopped when he sensed someone too close to his bike. He looked up at her with deep blue eyes that looked a lot younger than the rest of him. Not that he was old. But he was old to Raven. Fifty-six, with handsome features weathered by constant riding. Those blue eyes locked onto her. She'd been standing beside his bike, sipping her Coke, her other hand on tilted hip. "Nice," she'd said, admiring the chrome. It was an old bike. Seventies-era, when Harleys weren't worth a shit, but she still acted like it was.

He'd looked her up and down, his eyes lingering on the short skirt of her schoolgirl costume. "Shouldn't you be in school?" he said, regaining his cool composure and walking over to the bike.

"What are you, a cop?" she asked in a teasing voice.

"I was," he said.

Raven thought he'd perhaps picked up on the flicker of doubt in her eyes, but it was *only* a flicker; she never lost her composure for long.

"School's out, mister. It's summer."

"It's June. School ain't out yet."

She was going to bail. This former cop was already asking too many questions, but he was also the only person in the coffee shop who might be heading East. "College is," Raven said. "I need to get back. Got a summer internship. Paid. I lose it if I'm not there Monday."

"What school?"

"NYU."

"What internship?"

"Photography. I'll be working with Karl Farbman."

"Who?"

"Farbman. He's a famous photographer. Look him up."

"Name sounds familiar. How did you end up here needing a ride?"

"Long story. I'll tell it on the road. C'mon, your plate says New Hampshire. Can't you get me East?"

"You're telling me you're eighteen?"

"No. I'm telling you I'm nineteen. I'll be twenty on the Fourth of July." She leveled her self-assured eyes at him, raising her eyebrows and offering her crooked, pressed smile, her black hair falling over one eye. "C'mon. Can't you just get me to New Hampshire? I can catch a ride from there. I have money. I can chip in for gas."

"What's your name?"

"Raven. You?"

"Benjamin."

"Well, what do you say, Benny? You could really help a girl out. It's a big opportunity for me; I could really use the ride."

Benjamin looked off into the sky, as if he saw something no one else could see. Then he looked at her and said, "Hop on."

When they'd stopped for lunch in Naperville, Illinois, Benjamin seemed to lighten up on the age issue, or at least he didn't seem so inclined to catch her in a lie. He mostly talked about himself. Even when he'd ask her questions, the subject would shift back to being about him. She'd been trained to manipulate conversations, and she'd had years to hone her skills.

Over lunch, she'd learned that Benjamin was a retired cop in New Hampshire. He'd been part of the vice squad, busting biker gangs that tried to secure the area's drug trade for Bike Week. He'd retired after the leader of the gang Devil's Rising stabbed him in a drug-fueled rage. Benjamin knew then that if they stabbed him while thinking he was a member, what would they do to him if they discovered he was a cop? He'd just become a grandfather, and, "This gives you a new sense of what worth is," he told Raven. Now he had the time to ride to Wyoming every year to see his granddaughter, Millie.

During the conversation, Raven stuck to her story about being a photography major at NYU, offering very little more. The only suspicion he showed was when he asked her why she hadn't asked to stop anywhere to take photographs; traveling cross-country like this might be a good time to expand her portfolio to show Karl Farbman. She told him she'd left her camera at her friend's place in Denver. She doubted the bitch was going to mail it to her, was all she added. "I don't really want to talk about it," she said.

Now, riding along in the night, just west of Cleveland, she felt the bike drift over to the right lane. She saw an off ramp approaching, and the reflected amber glow of the bike's directional on the blacktop below. She'd been waiting for this. She thought Benny was a machine for an old guy, driving straight through like this for so many hours, but he was going to need a rest at some point. And now they were heading for just such a rest.

Raven reached down and felt the outline of the butter knife she'd stashed in her knee-high sock. She refused to pay for this ride with the currency she'd had to pay for everything else the last few years.

7

Seamus O'Neil was a stutterer, so his final words were taking awhile. The F of his statement, "It's not my fault," was stretching on for almost a full minute. Seamus was the janitor at the St. Jude's School for Wayward Boys. He also, at times, buggered the seven- and eight-year-olds in the shower room. Seamus was scrawny and weak, and the children, especially the older children, would laugh at his speech impediment. But Seamus had what the boys did not: unfettered access to the outside world. So he was able to "make friends" with the younger children by offering them child-enticing contraband.

It turns out that not so long ago, Seamus was a student at the school, and the priests bought his "friendship" with contraband of their own. Not that it would have swayed his judgment, but Iratus knew nothing about the priests. And as soon as Seamus finished his final word, Iratus would enact his wrath.

"fff-fau-ff-f-" Seamus said.

Iratus took the top of Seamus's head in his hand, as if he were blessing the lad, and waited.

"f-f-fff-"

Seamus tended to stutter more when he was nervous.

"ff-fault," he said. With Iratus's hand on his head, Seamus felt the need to reiterate his plea, beginning the statement again, "It's n-nn—"

Iratus cut him off, saying, "It is your fault, Seamus O'Neil, and now a reckoning for your sins."

"P-p-please," Seamus sobbed, his head raised, his eyes closed. The action made him look like a baby bird begging for its feeding. But it was too late. Iratus had caught him with the boy, interrupting Seamus's awkward foreplay. Iratus had sent the boy to find help. Help for cleaning up the mess when Iratus was through.

"I may have stopped you from harming that boy, but you must pay for the others."

Seamus opened his eyes and looked in the direction the boy had run. Seamus's eyes widened and filled with a concoction of confusion and realization. "Wh-who—"

"The boys you harmed," Iratus said.

"N-nnn-no. Wh-who's th-th—"

"The other children," Iratus said, his fingers tightening on Seamus's crown. He was growing impatient. He had allowed him a final word, and Seamus took six and a half.

Seamus raised his hand and pointed in the direction the young boy had run, still trying to say, "th-th-th—" Iratus ended the word with a twist of his hand. Seamus fell limply to the floor.

Only then did Iratus turn and look in the direction Seamus had been pointing.

The boy had not run off. In fact, the boy wasn't far away at all. He was in the arms of another young man dressed in a janitor's uniform. The man held one hand over the boy's mouth; his other hand held a knife to the boy's throat. Iratus didn't need to check his book to know that the man's name was not in it. He did not recognize the man, but he did recognize the eyes. They were bright silver. They were the eyes of someone he'd seen recently. They were the eyes of someone he'd known long ago, but he couldn't remember who.

"Let the boy go," Iratus said.

"He's right, you know," the nameless man said.

"Who?"

"Sh-sh-Seamus O'Neil," the man said, mocking Seamus's voice.

"Right about what?"

"It wasn't his fault." A wry smile slipped across his face and his silver eyes gleamed. "You hate that, don't you? But I can't figure out what you hate more, that people say it, or that it's true."

"Let the boy go."

"Where are the priests in that book of yours?" the nameless man said.

"What priests? There are no priests."

"Exactly. Not all names are in that book, demon." The man then pushed the boy away and put the blade to his own throat. When he drew it across his flesh, instead of blood, dust poured from the gaping wound. The man laughed as he sank into a pile of dirt on the floor.

The young boy stared wide-eyed at the pile of dirt. Then he looked up at Iratus.

"Go find help," the demon told him.

The boy ran off.

Iratus crouched and lifted a handful of the dirt, allowing it to run through his fingers and onto the floor.

8

The truth is, Hell exists in much the way it is depicted in movies and books and the like. It is burning and cavernous, with lakes of fire and tortured souls and demons. And Hell does have rings, as Dante made so widely known. And the rings have rings. And those rings have rings. And so on. It is in the very center of this fiery, ringed domain that the worst part of Hell exists. You might think it is here that the

Devil resides. You would be mistaken. It is here that the souls "serving damnation for the worst affronts to God and nature" do their time.

It is here in the heart of Hell that the demon Iratus resides. Or, at least, resided.

Iratus was the worst of the Punishers, and by worst, he was the best. The most effective, if you will. Six days ago, Iratus had been here in Hell's center, in an amphitheater moated by the converging rivers Styx, Acheron, Phlegethon, and Lethe, well past where these rivers had turned to fire. The glow of the flames flickered in his deep-set eyes. He was dealing with a handful of souls who had been sent down the rivers of fire like barrels from a mill. The Malebranche had fished them out of the rivers with gaffes and pikes and dragged them to Iratus's amphitheater and bound them to X-shaped crosses. Iratus poured the fiery water of Styx down a man named Onwar Hippolick's throat. He was with Iratus because during his life on Earth, he'd peddled young boys as sexual companions to rich Middle Eastern oil executives. Bound to the cross beside Onwar was Hans von Daam, who had made pornographic movies with preteen performers. Beside him, Tamgar Onowat was doing time for buying and selling babies on the black market—he'd been personally responsible for 78 child deaths. Next was Ann Parker, who'd run a daycare—she ran a popular betting pool with local gamblers wagering on which children could endure mental and physical abuse the longest. On the cross beside Ann was Mary Beth Myles, who had, one by one, drowned her three children in a bathtub because her boyfriend didn't want them around. Iratus was almost done with Onwar—Onwar had stopped gurgling against the fiery water—and it was then that a high, screechy voice called out, "It's not my fault."

Iratus raised his head and turned from his work. Behind him was a small man bound to a cross among the five others. The man looked about middle aged, his face lined with the map of a trying life. He was scrawny, his ribs protruding from his torso—the physique of a man who had never filled out. His eyes were silver, and familiar in a way that Iratus couldn't quite place. Iratus dropped his chalice of fiery river water, his eyes flickering with Hell's flames.

The man cringed against the cross.

"Where did you come from?" Iratus said.

"I was brought here by your monsters," the man squeaked, nodding toward the Malebranche.

Iratus turned and saw the Malebranche dragging souls from the fire and piling them on the shores for distribution to the Rings. "Down here," Iratus said to the silver-eyed man, "*you* are the monster."

"It's not my fault. I shouldn't be here," the man said.

This was a phenomenon the Punishers were coming across more and more lately. In the past, the damned seemed capable of accepting damnation. But now they came down *convinced* they'd done nothing wrong. "If you are here, then you are guilty," Iratus growled.

"I didn't say I wasn't guilty," the man said, his voice not as squeaky anymore, "I said it wasn't my fault."

"You have free will. You chose to do what you did."

"My brain was wired to make me do what I did. So it was God's doing. He let it happen."

Iratus took his book from his pocket and regarded the sweeping singed calligraphy. This small man with the silver eyes was not in it, and thus was unrecognizable to the demon. He was nameless.

The man said, "Sinners are no longer afraid of Hell. The

Earthbound have forgotten your name. You hide here in the flames and let them do these horrible things."

"Who are you?" Iratus demanded, his voice explosive as a lightning strike.

"I am just one of the damned. One of the blameless damned. I couldn't help what I did. None of us could." The man nodded toward the others bound to the crosses. "It's not any of our faults. God made us this way. It's His mistake."

Ann Parker said, "He's right. It's not my fault. I thought I was doing the right thing by those kids. I was going to pay them their cuts eventually, maybe even set up college funds for them. It was the bettors' fault. If I hadn't been spurred on by them to lock children in a dark closet with rats, or to beat them with wooden spoons and burn them with cigarettes, I would never have done it."

"Quiet," Iratus said.

Hans Van Daam chimed in, too. "Yeah. I didn't do any-thing, either. I didn't have sex with any of those kids. I was just a producer slash director slash writer slash cameraman. I'm an artist. It's not my fault what some people want for their art."

"Stop talking," Iratus said.

"He's right, though," Tamgar Onowat said. "I was just trying to help people who wanted children. How am I different from an adoption agency? Or one of those IVF doctors? I was just cutting through the bureaucracy. How is it my fault if some of the babies did not make it? Isn't that God's fault? Where is He during all of this?" Tamgar nodded in the direction he assumed Heaven to be. "Easy for Him to do something about it now. Where was He then to tell me those babies would die?"

"Stop talking," Iratus said.

Onwar Hippolick, who literally had a fire in his belly at that moment, spoke up, too, but his words were a garbled mess. He said, "Arp flus bovine awd verdan voo. Ip kwat ba ba haumk." What he actually meant was: "I was providing a service too. It was not my fault."

Mary Beth said, "I never would have done what I did if it wasn't for me being the way I am. I had postpartum depression. So it wasn't my fault I killed my babies, right?"

Iratus growled, "You had a choice."

"No, you didn't, Mary Beth," the nameless man said. "It wasn't your fault."

"How did you know her name?" Iratus said.

The nameless man ignored the demon's question. He said, "I had a penchant for little boys. And God just kept delivering them to me. *You* let that happen, too, demon. Why did you *let* me hurt those little boys? Where was Wrath when those boys needed it?"

Iratus looked down in his book again. He still could not find the man's name, and thus could not recognize the sinner for his sins.

All six of the cross-bound damned began whining and complaining at once, all of them screaming over one another.

Iratus was feeling his human emotions bubbling up within him. He used to feel righteous vengeance while punishing. But lately he'd felt frustration. And inadequacy. And doubt. Had the Earthbound really forgotten his name? Did the warnings and the fear of him no longer carry any weight in their decision-making?

"It's not my fault," the nameless man screamed in a falsetto voice. "Why didn't you stop me?"

Iratus had had enough of the man's voice—the whiny, screechy excuse making—so he grabbed the man's head and popped it from his body.

Still the severed head cried in Iratus's hand, "Why, demon, why?"

Iratus threw the head across the amphitheater so that it could float away on the rivers of fire—he'd let some other demon deal with him. But before it reached the fiery waters of the rivers, a gargoyle snatched it up. It flew above the amphitheater, taking up the same screeching as the man. Another gargoyle intercepted the first, and the two fought for the screaming head like seagulls fighting over a sandwich at a beach. The gargoyles' screeching and the man's screeching and the other five cross-bound damned's screeching combined into a jumbled, garbled, high-pitched symphony of excuses that was like a plucked cord in Iratus's gut. It was then that the demon Iratus burst through an iron door, shearing the rivets that had bolted it shut for centuries, and emerged Topside.

He'd crossed the church's basement to the opposite side of the empty, cavernous room and climbed stairs to Saint Sebastian's main hall—an echoing space of wooden pews and plaster statues accented by the musty stench of boredom. He'd glanced up at a giant cross with its usual resident nailed to its façade, the light of the moon accenting figures in stained glass behind it. He'd spotted the figure of a woman in the glass, her nakedness covered by golden locks, a snake at her ear. The demon's face had twisted into a scowl and then he'd trudged down the aisle to the church's front doors. Out the door and onto the island, he'd paused a moment, breathing the unscorched air, feeling a breeze wash over him. He'd then pulled his book from his pocket and read the sweeping singed calligraphy of the latest name burned into the page. The name had belonged to Stewart Brookes, who'd just happened to be a resident of the island.

That was six days ago—one for each of the fingers on his hand. He'd been busy since.

Now, he wondered about that silver-eyed stranger and his words.

Why would there be priests in his book?

There had never been any priests in his book. Ever.

The girl, Raven, had said something about priests. Did she know something about this? He needed to find her.

The Raven

1

It was dark. Raven heard the slow creak of the door opening and shutting again. Then the slow creep of bare feet across the carpeted floor. She reached slowly down her leg to the top of her knee-high sock and felt the hilt of the butter knife.

When she and Benjamin had pulled off at this dive motel, Raven blurted, "We're spending the night?"

"Yeah, I'm beat. I can't even feel my ass."

"Oh. Okay. Cool."

Benjamin, recognizing the hesitation in her voice, had said, "So here's the deal: we can split a double room, or you can get your own. I've stayed here before. It's clean. At least, clean for being so cheap. Eighty bucks on your own. Forty if you want to split. If you got the cash, you may want to invest in your own room for a little privacy, because I snore like an asthmatic bullfrog."

Raven burst out laughing. She wasn't sure why. Maybe because the awkwardness had been defused so easily. "Duly noted," she said. "My own room it is."

But her own room and his own room shared a connector door. A door, she'd noted, which had a nonfunctioning lock. A door that had just creaked open and shut, leading to the foot-falls across the floor. She had no read on what time it was. She had been deeply asleep. But she was quick to wake—familiar to the sound of men creeping in the night. The standard motel clock-radio was behind her. She didn't want to turn to check the time. She didn't want to move at all. To alert him that she was awake. If it came down to it, she wanted the butter knife against his throat to be a surprise. She inched the metal from her sock. About halfway there.

Thick, paisley curtains deprived the room of the parking lot's lights. Raven thought the curtains in these types of motels must be made of lead, to block sunlight from the perpetually hungover. She didn't need the light, however; she could always track the sweaty smell of an older man closing in.

The knife slipped free of her sock, her thumb and middle finger grasping the thing like tweezers, and she manipulated it into her hand, her palm closing around the flat steel handle. She knew that next the side of the bed would dip as he sat beside her. Then he would either climb under the covers, or he would begin stroking her hair and start calling her honey and sweetheart. Men were all alike. She tightened her grip on the knife. He seemed more like the stroke-the-hair type of guy. And when he reached over to stroke, she'd have a nice opening for the throat. If he was the climb-in-bed type, the knife goes to the balls.

She sensed him beside the bed. She could feel his eyes watching the lump that was her form. "Hey," he whispered. "Hey, Raven."

She was completely still, only her right arm, like a minute hand, slipping up into position.

"Hey, Raven." He laid his hand on her shoulder and gently rocked her. "Raven, time to wake up."

Her hand stopped. She cooed a faux waking and shifted in her bed. Stretching only her left arm. "Huh," she said.

"Raven, it's time to get up. I tried knocking. You didn't

answer. I want to get an early start. We have a lot of distance to cover."

Raven turned her head to see the digital alarm clock now. It was just after five a.m. She let the knife slide out of her hand to rest, hidden, beside her under the covers. She stretched with both arms.

"I'd like to be out of here by six or so. Think you can be ready by then?"

"Okay," she whispered.

"See you at six, then," Benjamin said. "Oh, and good morning."

"Morning," Raven said, watching him walk back toward his room. She slipped the knife back into her sock.

2

Iratus had last seen Raven in the Victoria Shipping parking lot. He stood there again the next morning, with the sun about to streak the sky red. He needed to find her, but he had no idea where the girl could have gone. The trucks still slept silently around him, but the vending machines were gone.

He went into the thin woods through which she'd departed the morning before. He saw the glints of streetlights dancing like sprites between the leaves and branches, and he heard the very early morning commuters in the far distance—mostly the heavy diesel engines of trucks groaning through low gears. He followed a path up and over a ridge, then down and up an embankment to a quiet, dark road. He stopped where the trees edged the blacktop. He could see, through another strip of trees, the lights of businesses and parking lots about a half-mile away.

Iratus heard a car engine. The leaves across the street began to glow, and then the street before him was washed in light. A car came around the corner. It slowed and edged past him. He saw two ghostly faces—a woman in the passenger seat and a man leaning forward from the driver's seat—staring at him through the passenger window. Eyes bulged, mouths dropped in O shapes.

He felt something well in his stomach and chest, a tickling sensation rising through him and spilling from his mouth in a rush of air. The feeling faded, and a warm sensation filled his body. He didn't realize it, but he had just laughed, the feel of it as foreign to him as he was to the people in the car.

The screech of tires split the air. The car fishtailed like a pendulum before the screeching gave way to the crumpled roar of metal bending metal as the car struck a guardrail a few hundred feet down the road.

That warm feeling in his stomach froze and compressed into a new feeling. This was another emotion he was not familiar with, although he'd experienced it when Raven had walked away from him the morning before. Guilt.

He tentatively approached the accident scene. The doors popped open, and the man and the woman burst from the car. They stared at Iratus, their eyes bulging somehow wider, then turned and ran screaming down the road, the man flailing his arms above his head.

Iratus watched them go, not sure which emotion he should be having.

3

Benjamin and Raven pulled into a sprawling New Hampshire suburb, passing streets ending in cul-de-sacs with kids playing ball and riding bikes. The exhaust of the Harley seemed louder now that it bounced off the sides of split-level ranches and heavily leafed shrubs. The scent of lilacs fought through the octane smell of the bike's emissions. They came to a small bungalow-style house, and Benjamin leaned the bike into a sharp, sweeping turn onto the driveway. Although he didn't back the bike into the spot, he did give two quick bursts of the engine, and then one fading one before cutting it. He ran his hand through his thick gray hair (he'd shed his helmet as soon as they'd crossed into New Hampshire, but still insisted Raven wear hers). "Well, here we are," he said.

"Okay," she said. When she realized Benjamin was waiting for her to dismount, she climbed off the bike, stripping the helmet from her head. "And where exactly is it that we are?"

"Well, this would be Standish, New Hampshire," he said. "Come on in and we'll find you a ride to NYC. But, as a man in his fifties, I get first dibs on the bathroom." He unlocked the front door and burst into the house, calling over his shoulder, "Excuse the mess, I wasn't expecting company."

Raven paused on the porch. It was furnished with two old but clean wicker chairs and a wicker table. A few houses down, a man was washing his car. The sounds of distant dog barks and children laughing settled among the houses with the hum of lawn mowers. It was like a few of the college-town neighborhoods she'd grown up in before her parents died. For the first time in a long time, she felt as if she were at a real home.

She stepped into the carpeted living room. At one end was a giant 70-inch television—one of those behemoth boxes on wheels, state-of-the art twenty years ago, before plasma screens and HD. In the corner was a small bookcase. Raven walked over to it, spotting photographs of Benjamin with a little sandy-haired, blue-eyed girl. There was also a photograph of a much younger Benjamin in a police dress uniform.

She heard the flush of a toilet and a door open and close. Raven followed the sound into the kitchen.

Benjamin grinned and said, "Wow, that was like an epic piss. You probably didn't need to know that, but I imagine, unless you're a camel, you need to take one, too."

Raven glanced around the kitchen, quickly sizing up the surroundings—inventorying the cookware, the appliances, the decorations—getting a read on the man and the situation. The appliances were older, but clean. The stove and cookware looked well used. There was a sign above the refrigerator that read: "Beer *IS* a Food Group." The refrigerator was buried beneath a child's artwork—rainbows and lemon suns and smiling stick figures.

"Where is the bathroom?"

"Right there." He motioned through the back of the kitchen to a small hallway. "While you freshen up, I'll get on finding you a lift to NYC." He held up a flip phone.

She stared at the phone and burst out laughing. "That thing is older than I am."

"You might be right." Benjamin grinned. "Sad thing is, among my friends, I'm the most technologically advanced. Anyway, there's the bathroom. It is a bathroom, not an out-house. And the toilet is from the twenty-first Century. Or at least late twentieth."

Raven chuckled and stepped into a small, clean bathroom. She regarded herself in the mirror. She looked different. Older. But only to herself, she supposed. She was, for the first time in a long time, viewing herself as herself, not viewing herself through the eyes of men that saw her as nothing more than a teenage, sex fantasy. Or, maybe she looked older due to a new wisdom of the world. The knowledge that not all men were monsters. Not even the monsters. Ira seemed more like a dream at this point than anything possible in reality. But she, former cynic and skeptic, now knew that there was a Heaven and a Hell. Or at least a Hell.

Or *had* that been a dream? A hallucination? If Ira were a hallucination, then how the hell did she get to America? Hell, indeed. The eyes staring back from the mirror looked even older than they did a moment ago.

Hearing Benjamin's deep voice rumbling as he spoke on the phone, she realized that he sounded a little like his bike when he talked excitedly. Her smile was reflected in the mirror. He was having an animated, one-sided conversation in the kitchen. She couldn't make out what he was saying. His voice faded as he walked into another room. The last thing she heard was his four-stroke sounding response of, "Yes, yeah, yeah, yeah…."

Benjamin didn't realize just how camel-like she was. In captivity, one learns how to control many aspects of one's body. And mind. On the back of the toilet was a small ceramic planter. A troll had its arms around the pot. He peeked coyly from its edge with his beady eyes and bulbous nose and mischievous grin. She peed, flushed, and washed her hands, catching her adult eyes in the mirror. When she stepped from the bathroom, Benjamin was back in the kitchen with a broad smile on his face. "Guess who found you a ride to New York?"

4

Branches reached into a canopy above as the road became dirt, the Harley's exhaust louder as it echoed off the trees. Benjamin leaned the bike into a turn and they entered a clearing. A small ranch-style house squatted at the clearing's center, tall pines like gathered sentinels around it. Benjamin pulled the bike beside two other Harleys and cut the engine with his usual three-rev flare. They sat silent for a moment. Raven regarded the two other bikes. One was much fatter than Benjamin's dinosaur. The other had ape hanger handlebars that were almost taller than she was. She looked past the bikes and saw a rusted 1980s pickup truck nestled beside the house.

Benjamin said, "Well, here we are."

Raven got off the bike and removed her helmet. She eyed the house's peeling paint and rotting porch.

"C'mon," Benjamin said. "These guys may look rough, but they're teddy bears. You'll love them. Believe me, Zippy is a much better road companion than I am."

"Zippy?" Raven said, shifting her hair over one eye and raising her brow.

"Obviously that's not his real name. We call him that—"

"Because I'm so quick with a comeback," a man called from the porch. He was bigger than Benjamin. Shorter, but wider. He had long salt-and-pepper hair and a thick, more-salt-than-pepper beard.

"Hey, there he is," Benjamin said. "What's the good word, Zipster?"

"Onomatopoeia."

"Huh?"

"That's a good word," Zippy said.

Benjamin let out a belly laugh—too heavy for the quality of the joke. He was greasing his friend up a little, maybe because of the favor Zippy was doing for him. "That is a good word, Zipster." His smile too wide for his face, he held out his hands like a model presenting a game show prize. "I'd like to introduce my new friend, Raven."

"Hey now, Raven," Zippy called down from the porch.

"Hey now," Raven said, raising her hand.

"Mi casa es su casa. I'm just finishing my preparations." Zippy turned and walked into the house.

Benjamin mounted the house's steps, but Raven hesitated. "You coming?" he asked her.

Raven inspected the dilapidated porch. "These safe enough to walk on?"

Benjamin chuckled. "What are you, the building inspector? Yeah, they're safe enough, wise ass."

Raven climbed the steps and followed him into the house.

The inside was not much different than the outside. The whole place seemed crooked. The furniture was a mishmash of old granny furniture covered with blankets and grungy afghans. She couldn't separate the smell of ancient cats from the smell of recent pot smoke. Heavy shades and tapestries covered the windows. Marvin Gaye was singing "Got to Give it Up," and there was a hunting show on the television. A lanky man with dyed auburn hair and a heavily creased face sat in the corner, drinking a beer and nodding his head to the music. He stared at Raven.

"Hi," Raven said to him.

"That's Ronald," Benjamin said. "Say hi, Ronald."

"Hi, Ronald," the man said and then drank his beer, still staring at Raven. "I like the schoolgirl outfit," he said.

Raven giggled nervously, inspecting her outfit. "Yeah? Thanks."

In a voice more aggressive than Raven had heard from him before, Benjamin said, "Shut up, Ronald, you're being rude."

Zippy emerged from the kitchen with three shot glasses filled with clear liquid.

Raven smiled and bobbed to the Marvin Gay song. "I like this music," she said.

"Yeah, well if you're going to listen to coon-screeching,

then this is the darky to listen to," Zippy said. He handed Raven and Benjamin a shot glass. "A toast to our new friendship."

"Well, that's not really—what is this?" Raven asked, looking at the shot glass.

"Mezcal," Zippy said.

"Don't I get one?" Ronald called from his seat.

"Shut up, Ronald, you ain't any part of this new friendship," Zippy shouted.

Raven said, "I probably shouldn't."

"It's bad luck to ride across state lines without a toast. Bikers' creed."

Raven chuckled and said, "Well, I don't think I can drink it."

"Why not?"

"I'm not twenty-one," she said with her hand on tilted hip.

Zippy and Benjamin looked at one another and burst into laughter.

"I think you can handle it," Zippy said. "Besides, if you refuse a shot of mezcal, you have to eat the worm."

Raven looked at Benjamin.

Benjamin flared his nose and scrunched his face in a semi-wink, looking a little like Popeye. He nodded as if saying, *Yeah, you should do this, it's the creed.*

Raven took the shot glass from Zippy. "Well, I guess, when in New Hampshire...." She looked at Benjamin.

Benjamin made his Popeye nod again.

"You are the cop," Raven said to him. "So if I get busted, it's on you."

The three of them drank.

Raven grimaced and handed the glass back to Zippy.

"You take it like a pro," Zippy said. "Okay, I'll get my stuff so we can get started." He walked back toward the kitchen.

Raven looked at Benjamin.

"You did all right with that," he said, sounding impressed.

"I guess I can keep up with the best of them," she said. But she was feeling a little lightheaded. She had never really drunk alcohol (besides a few glasses of Champagne with her captors when they wanted her to join them). Certainly no mezcal. She had heard that it could go straight to the head. And it certainly was going there now. "Wow," she said, "that went straight to the head." Did she say that? She wasn't sure. She wasn't feeling so great. The room was doing a drastic breathing thing. And she saw Ronny staring at her. His eyes burning into her. She couldn't feel her hands. And the room was now doing slow spins. "I think I need the bathroom," she said. She placed her hand on Benjamin's chest to steady herself.

"Raven?" Benjamin said. "Raven, are you okay?"

"I don't feel so great. Where's the bathroom?"

"Maybe you should lie down," Benjamin said. "Jesus, you don't look so good. Come on. We'll find you a place to lie down."

She felt her feet walking and she was moving in some direction, she wasn't sure which. The world was streaking and spinning. She sensed Zippy coming back from the kitchen and she heard him say, "She looks like she's ready to go."

5

In thick Appalachian woods, Iratus kicked Saul Ramsey's entrails aside. Beneath the mess was a large blanket. It had been Saul's intention to use the blanket to wrap the nine-year-old boy's body when he was done torturing him. But that didn't happen. Instead, Iratus used Saul's comically large hunting knife to pin Saul to a maple tree, then he set the young boy free, telling him to find help. The boy ran off into the woods. They always ran. All except for Raven.

When the boy was gone, Iratus pulled Saul's guts out of his stomach and dropped them in a steaming pile at his feet. He looked at his hand drenched in blood and viscera. He recalled the man with the silver eyes, and the dust pouring from his gaping wound.

Not all names are in that book, demon.

Iratus picked up the blanket and cleaned his hands. Could it be true that some sinners were missing from the book? Opening it now, he saw no shortage of names. He read the next one on the list.

6

Raven felt underwater. She wasn't. She was on a bed. Or a coffin. No, it was definitely a bed. But the notion of a coffin seemed eerily possible. The way the three men were looking down at her was as if she were the guest of honor at a wake. They had a well-that's-done look on their faces.

Dearly beloved, we are gathered here today to get through this thing called life—

Wait, was she thinking that or was it coming from the stereo? She tried to banish the underwater feeling and the fragmented, floating thoughts. She needed to stay sharp.

"I'm first," Benjamin said. "Been waiting long enough for this."

"I'm next. I call next," Ronny said.

"Shut up, Ronald," Zippy said. "I'm next. Go fuck the other one."

Ronny twisted his face. "I think the other one's dead."

"Go fuck her anyway," Zippy said.

Raven attempted to curl her body into a fetal position. This was much harder than she thought it would be. It was as if she were in a vacuum, unable to find any purchase on which to pivot her body. She was the Star Child in her space womb, feeling only the cold cocoon of nothingness…. *Stop it. Pull it together. Think clearly*, she thought.

The guitar riffs of "Let's Go Crazy" looped in her head. She tried to separate the notes, but it all spun endlessly in the air. Her knees were in her hands. They felt like sandpaper in her palms, like she could feel the microscopic mountain range of each skin cell and hair stubble. Her hand moved down to the forest of threads on her sock. She worked her fingers into her knee-high.

"What's she doing?" Ronny asked.

Raven felt the hilt of the butter knife in her fingers, but she stopped. She knew she had to be inconspicuous. Stealthy.

"I think she has something in her sock," Ronny said.

So much for inconspicuousness. Some deep down part of her wanted to laugh at the word—and she tried again, her fingers feeling like an inflated surgical glove. After gripping the knife's hilt and pulling it from her sock, she rolled onto her back and lifted the blade toward her captors.

Zippy said, "She's gonna fight us with a butter knife? Oh I like this one. Where'd you find her, Benji?"

"Of all places, Iowa."

Raven attempted to sit up and jam the knife into Benji's nutsack, but instead, she just lay there. The knife fell from her grip.

"I'm gonna want some privacy here, boys," Benjamin said.

"I'm next. I'm next," Ronny called.

"Shut up, Ronald, you're not next," Zippy shouted. He turned to Benjamin and said, "Sure we can't stay and watch?"

"Nah," Benjamin said. "We need some alone time."

"Aw," Ronny whined as he and Zippy left the room.

The bed dipped as Benjamin sat beside her and stroked her hair. "Alone at last, honey," he said.

Raven closed her eyes, but when she felt the teeter-totter lurching of the room and heard the same guitar riffs spinning over and over, she forced her eyes open again. She willed her hand along the bed, searching for the knife.

"I think we really had something," Benjamin said. "Like Butch and Sundance crossing the country, no?"

Raven found the knife on the endless bedspread. She gripped it. She only needed to will it into Benjamin's throat.

Benjamin smoothed her hair. "You really are just so beautiful," he said. "And fun. Man, you got some spunk."

I got spunk all right, motherfucker. Now was the time to jam the knife into his neck. But she hadn't actually said the words, and the knife, still held loosely in her grip, was lying on the bedspread.

Benjamin stood. His fingers crawled spider-like up her thighs. "And I loved that Karl Farbman thing. Ha, I'm a big Seinfeld fan." His fingers continued to her panties. "Thought I wouldn't notice—" His fingers stopped. "Assholes," he said.

Raven's head flopped to the left, following his gaze, where she saw Zippy's and Ronny's eager faces peeking in through the window. Benjamin went to the window, closing a makeshift shade—a black flag with a dark figure astride a flaming motorcycle, the words "Devil's Rising" emblazoned above the figure's head. The room darkened.

Benjamin returned to the bed. "Sorry," he said. "That was rude. Now where were we? Oh yeah." He placed a knee on the bed and bent forward. The spider hands began running up her thighs again, creeping below her skirt, fingers hooking onto her panties and sliding them down.

"We don't need those," Benjamin said, tossing the panties aside.

Raven's fingers closed around the hilt of the butter knife. Benjamin leaned forward again.

Some other guitar riff was spinning in the air now.

She couldn't separate it. *Concentrate.* Her eyelids were drooping. She fought them open. Sending everything she could to her hand. The knife rose from the bed sheet.

Benjamin stopped. He stared a moment at the knife and smiled. "Aw, c'mon, sweetie, I thought we were friends." He plucked the knife from her hand and tossed it in the direction of her panties. Raven heard it clang on the floor, sounding both loud and extremely far away. Benjamin undid his belt buckle and unbuttoned his jeans, reaching in to retrieve his still-floppy dick.

Raven closed her eyes, knowing that floppy thing would stiffen if he saw any fear, and she braced herself for the initial push of the thing, not wanting to make any sound, or wince, willing herself to keep perfectly still. She'd found her rapists actually thought she'd like it, actually come to want it, and any wince or coo of pain somehow emboldened their feeble minds onward. She would not give that to this one. Instead, she would run off on the drug. Go to that place where the guitar riffs spun in endless, twisting confusion. If he was going to take her, she wasn't going to be here.

A crackle of pain exploded against her cheek as Benjamin slapped her. His smirking face hovered above her. "Wake up. I want you here for this, sweetie. You're gonna take what I got for you. And you're gonna like it."

The slap had done what Benjamin intended, momentarily bringing her back. A thought broke through the tangled beats and spinning room. A memory materializing clearly in her mind: Ira charging at Sammy the Boo like a rhino.

Benjamin had his hands planted on the bed as he rubbed

his flaccidity up and down her thigh. He whispered into Raven's ear, "I'm gonna fuck you so nice."

For some reason she suddenly remembered Sammy being torn in half, his confused eyes regarding his separated torso. Raven whispered into Benjamin's ear, "Oh, sweetie, no you won't." She bit down on his earlobe as she brought her knee up into his groin. He made a breathy grunt, and, despite the situation, the peril she was in, her drug-addled mind wanted to giggle at the expression on his face, the way his eyes had crossed. But she struggled for awareness, and absently realized there was a fleshy, grape-sized object in her mouth. With his eyes still crossed, Benjamin began to slide off the bed, but before he disappeared over the edge, Raven had time to spit his earlobe into his face.

Following the sound of his body's hard thud on the floor and his gasping for breath, she lurched off the bed and flopped onto him.

Her mind fought through the music, through the spinning room, searching for the strength to get up and run, but there wasn't much strength left. Benjamin was gulping for air, recovering from his testicular trauma. She straddled him and almost toppled, but then righted herself. With a shake of her head, she fought her eyes open and saw the butter knife lying beside her discarded panties. The objects were in reach, but they were multiplying and dancing in her vision. She reached for the knife and ended up with her panties.

"You bi—" he wheezed, but she shoved her panties into his gaping mouth.

Focus, she thought.

She heard the music's thumping baseline, but the rest of the instruments were gone. She noted a pungent smell she took for Benjamin's cologne. A musky, charred, leathery smell, tickling some part of her memory. The knife glinted. It looked huge, seeming to float up to her. Like she was an ant viewing its giant edge. She gripped it. Raised it. With a satisfied awareness seeping through her body, she noted a new expression of fear creep into Benjamin's eyes. As if she were something unworldly which had come to enact vengeance. And she imagined it was the look Ira saw in the eyes of those whose names appeared in his book. Benjamin's cry of horror choked off as he sucked her panties down his throat. Raven held the knife in both hands above her head like an ancient priestess about to make her sacrifice, but she no longer straddled him.

She was in the air. Then on the bed. The room was filled with red and then Benjamin was off the floor and Ira was smashing him through the bedroom door with an explosion of splintering wood. Light spilled in through the doorway, and Raven heard more screams erupt from the living room. Zippy and Ronny shouting, "What the fuck? What the fuck?" Three gunshots. Then there was only the sound of the sopping, fleshy ripping of bodies. And Raven ran off on the drug to sleep.

7

Raven woke to a dull, pulsing headache and a flat stone of nausea sitting in her stomach. She rarely knew where she was when she woke. So many nightmarish beds; she always woke fearful she was in any of them. But this was a more complete unknown. The room was dimly lit by what felt like early-morning light. It streamed in around the edges of a flag with a demonic figure astride a flaming motorcycle. She stared at the figure, faceless and cloaked in black. The flag reminded her of twisting guitar riffs and limp dicks. And then of liberation. The memories crept into her mind like fingers running up her thigh. Betrayal. Rape. Destruction. And finally, Wrath. Her eyes widened. Ira.

She shuffled off the bed with a swinging roundhouse of a headache and the corkscrew of nausea. The bedroom's door was in pieces, neatly piled against the wall. She stepped into the living room. The couch had been pulled about three feet from the wall. A blanket traversed the space between wall and couch like a child's fort. Raven inspected the blanket's lumpy contours. She lifted its edge to see Zippy's staring eyes and twisted face peeking up at her. He and the other two men had been piled there like junk shoved into a closet in anticipation of company. There was no sign of their killer.

"Ira?" she called. Then, under her breath, she said, "Did that asshole leave me again?" She looked out the front window and saw him outside, his back to her. He was perfectly still, his head tilted downward, as if he were studying the ground. Relief swept through her and she ran out the front door, bounding up to him, wanting to hug him. But he looked too stoic for hugs at the moment—or any moment, really. He was looking down at another lumpy blanket.

"You woke up?" he said to her.

"You sound surprised."

"Relieved."

"Do you always do housekeeping after slaughtering bad guys?"

Ira glanced back at the house.

"That's pretty good," Raven said. "Vigilante Maid Service. We take out the trash in more ways than one."

"I didn't want you to see the carnage I wrought."

"The carnage you wrought, huh? You couldn't mop up the blood splatters on the walls and floor? Looks like a Jackson Pollock work in there."

Ira glanced back at the house again. "Sorry."

"I'm kidding. To be honest, I wish I got to see it. I hope they suffered."

"They did," Ira said, his gaze lingering on the house a moment before returning to the lumpy blanket at his feet.

"Who's this?" Raven smiled, nodding at the lumpy blanket.

"Girl."

Her smile fell. "A girl?"

"Young, like you. She was tied to the bed in the other bedroom."

The reality of the situation hit her with another spinning wave of nausea. Raven was almost another lump under the blanket at Ira's feet. Even if she had overpowered Benjamin, Zippy and Ronald would have killed her.

"I couldn't save her," Ira said.

"You can't save all of them." It was the first thing that came to mind.

"There's not enough time here to keep up with all the book's names."

"You saved me."

He looked down at her, his face still stoic. "I need your help," he said.

"Help with what?"

"You know something about the priests being abusers?"

Raven chuckled. "Ira, everyone knows about priests being abusers. It's the biggest scandal to hit the church since—I don't know, new rules were hammered to their door. How do you not know about this? You'd think when priests were faced with a demon in Hell, they'd try and use their religious panache for clemency."

"I don't think their names are appearing in my book. And they certainly aren't appearing in Hell."

"Well they've appeared in plenty of newspapers. The story was huge."

"Can you get me the names of these priests?"

Raven shrugged. "I'm sure I could. But it would take a huge amount of research to track down individual priests." She looked back at the house. "I'll need internet access, which, judging from that dickhead's wall phone, I doubt there is in this shithole."

"Then we will find you this interstate access."

"Internet. It's internet."

He stared at her.

"Never mind. Is that all you need? Info about priests? Ira, any asshole with a five minute memory span can tell you about diddler priests."

Ira was quiet a moment. He looked down at the lumpy blanket at his feet. "I should find a shovel to bury this girl."

Raven shook her head. "We'll put her back inside on the bed and anonymously call the cops. Her family will want to give her a burial." She paused a moment. "Or at least someone will give her one. She deserves better than to be buried here. I'm sure someone will want to know what happened to her." She looked back at the house again. "If anything, we should bury those assholes in an unmarked hole here." She paused and said, "What's happening to them in Hell right now?"

Ira turned and stared at the house, but his eyes seemed to be focused far beyond it. "I don't know," he said.

Iratus really didn't know. However, the three assholes, as Raven referred to them, were bobbing their way down the River Styx. They would be pulled from the fiery water and piled onto Iratus's amphitheater, where a very large backlog was developing.

8

Raven adjusted the girl into what she thought of as the "dead person's pose." The girl on her back, head on a pillow, chin nestled to breastbone, hands, one over the other, gently resting on the chest. Raven stepped back. She couldn't tear her gaze from the girl. Raven had been her. But when the men loomed over this girl, no savior materialized to take her from the horror. The girl suffered that moment of realization, same as Raven had, that it was really about to happen, but for this girl, it did happen. And then it most likely happened again and again, until the next this-is-really-happening moment: her death. Raven placed her hand on the girl's hands. They were cold. They were still. They felt like plastic or rubber. She was now just an object. There was no girl.

"Is there a heaven?" Raven said.

Ira, standing behind her, said, "I would assume so."

"How do you not know for sure?"

"I've never been there."

"Then why do you assume so?"

"Because there is a God."

"You know that for sure?"

"Yes."

"Well, I guess that's a good thing."

"That depends," Ira said.

Raven turned and looked at him. He was in what she had already come to think of as "one of his moods." Lost in his own past, the fire in his eyes flickering more intensely and more distantly. She also already knew not to push him too much in these moments. "Would you like to say anything?" she said.

"Say anything?"

"Yeah, for her." Raven nodded down at the girl.

"She's dead."

"I know, but it's customary to say something when people have died."

"Like what?"

"Sometimes you share a memory, comfort those who have lost her, make a witty observation about mortality." Raven glanced over her shoulder at him. "Sometimes you say something to the person, hoping that maybe her soul can hear you."

"It can't," Ira said.

"Saying something is not for her, Ira. It's for you."

He looked down at the body on the bed. "I'm sorry I couldn't save you," he said and turned and left the room.

Raven caressed the girl's hair from her face. For a moment, she questioned if she should be touching a murder victim. Her days locked away in the Bangkok apartment as the American's property had been an endless loop of *CSI* and *SVU* marathons. But she figured there was already too much evidence of her throughout the house to do anything about it now. To them, she was evidence that there had been another victim. One they'd assume was probably buried somewhere in the woods, lost forever. Let them think that.

She went to find Ira.

He was in the living room taking Zippy's body from behind the couch.

"What are you doing?" Raven asked.

"You said to bury them."

"Fuck it. Leave them. Let the cops know who did this. Just drop the fucker there."

Ira did what he was told. Zippy's body dropped to the floor. His arm flopped up over his head with a hard clack of metal on wood. Raven looked down to see a Beretta held, white-knuckled, in his hand. Raven's eyes widened, and she darted forward to take it. Rigor-mortis had set in, and Zippy, an asshole even in death, refused to give up the gun. Raven grunted, playing tug-of-war with a corpse, and said to Ira, "C'mon, help me."

"No."

"No? Why? I need this thing."

"No you don't."

"Ira, I was just almost raped and killed. I need protection."

"You'll end up in the Pit if you kill someone. You don't want to end up in the Pit. I don't want you to end up in the Pit."

"I'll be fine," Raven grunted, pulling on the gun again with both hands, as if she and Zippy were children fighting over a toy.

"It is merely a talisman. And talismans are dangerous."

"Not a talisman. A tool. A tool to shoot people trying to stick their dicks in me."

"It is a foolish trinket."

Raven turned her body and tried to rip the gun from the hand. "Well, when have I ever been foolish?" she said, tugging harder.

The gun went off with a deafening report.

Raven fell back on her ass, feeling the air vibrate from the passing bullet. She let go of the gun, which was still held tightly in Zippy's hand. It hit the floor with another clack. Raven stared at the thing, its barrel puking whiffs of smoke. She looked at Ira. "Holy shit," she said, "that was…." She didn't know how to finish her sentence.

"Foolish," Ira completed for her. "Leave the gun."

"And take the cannoli," Raven said under her breath, knowing full well Ira would not get the reference, but she didn't care. Her heart was pounding in her chest. She'd already surpassed a cat's allotment of lives, and she wondered how many she had left. Climbing from the floor and backing away from Zippy, she glanced around the living room, searching for the hole in the wall made by the bullet that almost got her. She found, in spatters of blood on the far wall, four bullet holes. Three of them were most likely from earlier.

Raven said, "Is that why you stopped me from killing Benjamin? You're keeping me out of the Pit?"

"He was my responsibility."

She turned and looked at him. Then she looked at the bodies and said,

"We should get out of here. Let's Gray-Zone somewhere."

"I told you. No Gray Zone."

"C'mon. I'll be fine."

"You lose a piece of your life-light every time you go in there."

"What does that even mean?"

"It means your soul wears thin."

"What about you? You go in there all the time."

"My soul can't get any thinner," Ira said.

"Okay, so we need another way out of here. I suppose we could walk, but we're pretty far in the woods...." She stopped as her eyes fell on the three motorcycles outside.

9

The decapitated body was Benjamin's; his fly still open with his limp dick hanging out. She reached into the pocket and fished out a keychain. She darted outside to find Ira standing beside the motorcycles, looking like something from an eighties metal band's album cover. She thought if Devil's Rising wanted a new emblem, this was it.

"You sure you don't want to take one of these things?" Raven said, nodding toward the bikes. "These are definitely more you. Forget that Gray Zone shit."

"The Gray Zone is more efficient."

"But you'd look way cooler showing up to diddlers' houses on a motorcycle," she said, tightening her small, faux-leather backpack to her shoulders and putting the helmet Benjamin had given her on her head. She climbed onto Benjamin's bike, barely able to reach the gears and the handlebars at the same time.

"You can drive one of these?" Ira asked.

"Yeah," she said, popping the key into the ignition and suppressing the clutch. "Well, maybe not one of those monsters," she nodded to the other two Harleys. "But I should be able to drive Benny's bike here. My friend Ahmad taught me to ride." She sprang up and down on the kick-starter. The engine turned but didn't start. "I didn't get a lot of practice, but I know the basics." She jumped on the kick-starter again. The engine turned but didn't start. "I've never driven one this big." She kicked and the bike didn't start. "But I'm not going far. Just back to town where we can find someplace to hole up."

"Hold up?"

"Hole up. You know, hide out." She kicked again. It didn't start. "Of course this could be a problem if this doesn't start."

"How will I find you wherever you end up?"

Raven, about to try the kick-starter again, stopped and looked up at him. "You mean you aren't getting on this thing with me?"

Ira regarded her on the bike and shook his head.

Raven smiled. "I'll just find the creepiest looking guy in town and wait for him to show up in your book."

"But—"

She kicked the starter again. This time it roared to life. She revved the engine in three increasing lengths of ear-splitting roars.

Ira flinched, surprised by the noise. When the engine settled to a manageable decibel, he shouted, "That is a terrible plan."

Raven gave him a wry smile and said, "Ira, you need to learn to recognize sarcasm. I'm messing with you. I'll head back to town. It looked pretty suburbanized, and I assume they have libraries in New Hampshire. Meet me at the library in Standish tonight at midnight."

"How will I find the library?" Ira shouted over the engine.

"Just Gray Zone in there," Raven shouted back.

"I need to know where to come out of the Gray Zone."

"How do you usually do it?"

"The book leads me."

Raven's shoulders slumped. "Shit, back to the creepy guy plan."

Ira paused a moment before saying, "Sarcasm?"

"You're getting it," she called.

Ira tore a blank page from his book and handed it to Raven. "Here, have this with you in the library," he said. "The book should find its missing page."

"Should?"

"It's been a long time since I've used the book Topside, and my memories of that are fragmented, at best. But I have a strong feeling it will work."

"Why haven't we just done this before?"

"Because another possibility is that with the book now missing a page, the next time I enter the Gray Zone, I could become lost and not be able to get back out."

Raven let the motorcycle engine die.

"What? You could become trapped in the Gray Zone?"

"I think it will find its missing page," he said with mounting confidence. "I will command it to do so."

"Are you sure that will work?"

"I think—"

"You *think*?"

"It *will* work."

"All right, then I will see you at midnight," Raven said, folding the paper and putting it in her backpack.

"Are libraries open at midnight?"

"No. But I'll be in there." She kick-started the bike again.

"What if you get caught?" Ira shouted over the engine.

"Then you'll have to bust me out of jail. You've already found me twice, and now I have your book's page that may or may not lead you to me. Now go do that voodoo that you do so well, and…don't go getting caught in the Gray Zone on me."

"It will work."

"I'll have a list of diddler priests for you by midnight," Raven said. She revved the engine and disengaged the clutch. The engine jerkily slipped into gear and Raven started forward, wobbly at first, then straightening as she picked up speed. Ira watched her go about twenty yards before the wobbling returned and she had to jump off the thing. The bike crashed to the ground.

"Are you okay?" Ira called.

Raven threw her hands over her head and called, "And she sticks the landing."

"What are you going to do now?" Ira said.

She pointed at the rusted truck nestled beside the house. "Let's hope that piece of shit still runs."

The Damned

1

Jacobs had just gotten into the office. He was sitting at his desk, staring at unopened files and sipping coffee when Ty walked up. "Where's Mr. Onward Christian Soldier?"

"You mean Backwards Christian Soldier? Remember? He doesn't intend to fight in Armageddon."

"Oh yeah, how could I forget?" Ty grinned. "So where is he?"

"I put him in the conference room yesterday afternoon. Told him to put together a chart tracking all of his demon's movements…in order, chronologically. Figured that should keep him busy for a while."

"How far did he get?"

"I don't know. I never went back to check on him."

"Are you sure he did it?"

Jacobs shrugged.

Ty said, "Knowing him, he probably never left yesterday. He might still be in there working on it."

"Yeah, right," Jacobs chuckled.

"I'm not kidding."

Jacobs shrugged

"So basically what you're saying is that you don't care about the chart," Ty said.

"Basically," Jacobs said. "I figure either he works on the chart and stays out of my hair or he decides it's too much bullshit and doesn't bother coming back."

"Or he develops a helpful guide to tracking these bogies down."

"I suppose that's a possibility, but I don't have a dollar to bet on it."

"I'll spot you one." Ty shrugged and walked away.

Jacobs sipped his coffee and regarded the piles of manila folders on his desk. Maybe the chart *would* be helpful. He pulled the yellow legal pad from beneath the pile of folders. Scribbled down the left margin of the pad were the locations of the demon's visits. Moldavia. Portugal. Syria. The Democratic Republic of Congo. Belgium.… All out of the FBI's jurisdiction.

"Hey, Frank," Ty called from across the expanse of desks and working agents.

"What?" Jacobs called back.

"You kind of need to see it," came the response.

Jacobs groaned as he rose from his chair, feeling ghosts of high school football injuries, lack of sleep seeming to raise every ache and pain from their crypts. He walked toward the conference room, passing agents typing on laptops and talking on phones.

"You're gonna love this, Frank," Trent Isaac said as Jacobs passed his desk.

"Huh?"

"You'll see," Trent called as Jacobs walked to the conference room.

Ty and three other agents stood in the doorway looking into the room. Ty turned and, with a wide smile, said to Jacobs, "Check it out."

Jacobs pushed past the other snickering agents.

Callahan stood with a marker-drawn world map spreading across the back wall's expanse. Dozens of different colored strings spanned the map, crisscrossing like an insane spider's web.

"What the hell is this?" Jacobs said.

Callahan turned from the wall. "Oh. Good morning, Agent Jacobs. I'm almost done with what you asked for. I tracked the demon's movements worldwide. Instead of a chart, I made a map, color-coding it for easy reference. Day one is the red string. Day two orange. Day three yellow. Green. Blue. Purple. Of course I ran out of colors, so any more days and we're back to red, which is confusing, but we'll have to make do."

"It looks like a Pride flag exploded," one agent said.

"Where did you get all of this?" Jacobs asked.

"Agent Diaz was nice enough to help me find materials. You disappeared yesterday evening, so obviously I couldn't ask you."

"When did you do this?"

"Last night."

The snickering from Ty and the other agents turned into all out laughter. Ty said to Jacobs, "You forgot to send him home."

Jacobs spread his hands as if sizing up a heavy load to lift. He almost said something, but stopped. The whiteboard on the other side of the room caught his eye. There he saw photographs of victims and witnesses and the familiar composite sketches of the Nephilim. Included was a family-tree-type diagram of demons and angels and their hierarchy for the coming Apocalypse. "Jesus Christ," Jacobs said, looking at the diagram.

"Yes," Callahan said, grinning. He walked to the hierarchy diagram, pointing to an image of Jesus Christ at the top of the *Army of Light*. "I guess technically God should be at the top, but for all intents and purposes, Jesus Christ will be leading the charge, well, actually Michael will, but—"

"No," Jacobs said, twitching his head as if shaking off a punch to the nose. "Jesus Christ, comma, look at all this?"

"Is it going to be helpful?" Callahan said.

Jacobs looked at Ty, who'd stopped laughing long enough to shrug.

"You owe me a dollar," Ty said.

2

She didn't want to do many passes in the truck. It was too recognizable a vehicle for the townspeople not to notice it being driven around by a young girl. She did a sweep through the town's center, past municipal buildings. She heard sirens and watched as a police cruiser shot past her in the opposite direction. She had a pretty good inkling as to where it was headed. She chuckled, imagining Ira trying to press the phone's buttons with his giant fingers. She'd told him he needed to give her a five-minute head start before dialing 9-1-1 on the house's landline. She'd told him not to say anything into the mouthpiece, just leave the thing and Gray Zone his way out of there. That way the cops would find the girl's body. And the assholes that killed her.

She watched the cruiser in her rearview mirror and almost missed the sign for the Standish Public Library. She slowed and inspected the building: a big, brown blob of concrete, looking like something a giant rock monster had shit out. She swung the truck past the building, down a side road and onto the access road behind a strip mall. She parked the truck behind a supermarket, perusing the structure for video cameras. She saw one facing the opposite direction, directed at the building's loading dock.

She held onto the steering wheel for a moment, looking at her eyes in the rearview mirror, noticing again how much older those eyes appeared to be. She had already lived a lifetime of tragedy, and now a rampaging demon wanted her to do investigative research for him. On the bright side, she figured those rapidly maturing eyes looking back from the mirror couldn't see anything much more shocking. She figured wrong.

She stretched her sweater's sleeve over her hand and wiped down the truck, trying to remember everywhere she might have left a print. She preferred to let the authorities think she'd been killed and buried in the woods back at Chez Zippy. Why leave anything to make them think otherwise? She even checked the seat and floorboard for any strands of hair she'd left behind.

She heard more sirens in the distance. She imagined the first on-scene officer had found the carnage and, most likely after tossing his cookies, called it in.

She inspected the area surrounding the rear of the supermarket. She saw no one. The clock in the truck said it was just after 8am. She checked her backpack. The page from Ira's book was at its bottom, folded into a neat square among the remaining money from the vending machines and the money she was able to scrounge from Zippy's house—from the wallets of the bodies plus a pretty good wad of twenties from the nightstand beside Zippy's bed. She took a deep breath. It was time to do some shopping.

3

Raven relished the smells of bacon, eggs, hash browns, and coffee. Especially the coffee. It reminded her of her parents. And she cherished her immersion in the sounds of the restaurant. The scraping of forks on plates and the clanking of dishes emptied of their meals and the murmur of conversations. The greasy, savory tastes still lingered at the back of her throat, and she kept topping it off with the sweetness of a Coke. They had the glass bottles of Coke she'd always loved, and she relished the feel of the glass against her lips, a kiss of familiarity.

The waitress cleared the empty plate and said, "Anything else, hon?"

Raven looked up from the newspaper she was reading and glanced at the clock on the wall behind the counter. It was an old plastic thing, shaped like a cat, the clock face on its belly, its eyes the pendulum. Ten to eleven. Raven smiled and said to the waitress, "No, thank you. I think I need to get going."

The waitress dropped the bill in front of her. Raven reached into her new bag for her new wallet. In fact, she had a whole new ensemble, thanks to the consignment shop in the strip mall where she'd ditched the truck. There she'd bought the bag—a large, bright red, cross-body satchel—and a pair of Harley Davidson woman's biker boots (despite how badly her recent brush with biker chickdom had ended, she couldn't resist). She'd topped off the ensemble with a pair of black jeans, black shirt, and a pair of Jackie O oversized sunglasses. She wanted to stick to all black, try to stay unremarkable, but she couldn't resist the bright red bag in the consignment shop—a knockoff Prada for twenty-three bucks. In the dressing room, she'd pulled her hair into a tight ponytail. The wardrobe change added about ten years to her appearance.

She paid the bill for breakfast and tossed the newspaper on the table for the next patron. A headline caught her eye. OFFICIALS BAFFLED BY BUTCHERING OF IRAQI TERROR CELL. She didn't bother reading it. She knew more of these headlines would be popping up from now on. And she wondered how many more of these incidents the government was covering up. For how long would they be able to do so? She shouldered her bag and headed for the library.

In the library, Raven settled into a computer station. She placed a library card on the table and typed in the account's number and password, which, according to the library's homepage, was *NHLA* for everyone. She had lifted the card from a man in the Mystery section—he'd been perusing the Sue Grafton books—and, after slipping his library card from it, she'd dropped the wallet in the Romance section two rows down.

She navigated to *Google*, wondering where exactly one should start searching for worldwide priest abuse. She would need to look up individual cases, read countless news articles, determine if the priest was charged and convicted—she guessed it was only fair to unleash a demon on convicted pedophiles—and then try and determine where these guys ended up. She'd need to take notes to keep this all straight, but she had nothing with which to do so.

She looked at the people sitting in the other computer ports: An overweight woman with a scouring pad hairdo and thick Buddy Holly glasses. An elderly man struggling to keep the mouse quiet in his trembling hand. A hawkish-looking guy searching through pictures of Betty White with his hand in his pocket. Not a scholarly bunch, and not seemingly in possession of something she could use to take notes.

She spotted a kid sitting at a table in the corner, his head in his hand as he pored over a textbook. He looked about her age. He wore glasses and had shaggy black hair with the liquid sheen of Asian heritage. Raven approached him, hovering at an appropriate distance, hoping to get his attention without scaring the piss out of him. The textbook was for Latin, and she thought, *Good time to brush up, slick.*

He hadn't noticed her. She cleared her throat. Still nothing. She cleared her throat more forcefully. Nothing. She said, "Hello? Excuse me?"

He twitched violently, as if getting hit with a few thousand volts. "Christ-fuck," he squeaked and then glanced guiltily around the library.

Raven chuckled, breaking into her bright smile. She could see the boy melt immediately. In truth, he was in love before the smile had even hit her face.

"Sorry," she said.

The boy, trying to compose himself, said, "It's okay. You… are just…so…scared me. Shocked me. Startled me. You startled me."

"Don't you mean, expavescis mihi?"

The boy's face dropped. He looked down at his book and back at her, then at the book, and her again. "You know Latin?"

"Ita."

"What did you say?"

"Shouldn't you know?"

The boy's face wound up tight as he sputtered, "Obviously not. I have my finals this week, which is why, despite getting out early from school, I'm here on a beautiful day—" He took a breath, his voice slowing. "Wow, that was a lot of expository information. Anyway, my point is, I should be out doing…cool stuff."

"Cool stuff, huh? Like what?"

"Like…you know…stuff…that's cool?" He didn't intend a question mark at the end of that statement. "So what did you say to me in Latin?"

"I'll tell you if I can borrow a piece of that notebook paper and a pen."

The quickness with which he produced the pen and

paper—ripping the sheet cleanly from the notebook beside him—was magician-like. Raven took the sheet from one of his hands and plucked the pen from the other. She then said, in a low voice accentuated with her smile, "Expavescis mihi: you startled me," and she turned and walked back to the computers. She could feel him staring at her as she went.

She returned to her computer and typed in the search field: "priests convicted of abuse." She hit enter and picked up the pencil to start her vast research.

"Holy shit," she said under her breath. The first site that popped up was: *Database of priests accused of sexual abuse.* "That was easy," she muttered. She clicked on the link and a spreadsheet appeared, alphabetically listing names, notes on what happened, where it happened, and the current location and legal status of the priests. She read the fate (for now) of each priest: accused, accused, sued, charged, accused, accused, sued, convicted. She clicked on the first name with a "convicted" beside it. Thomas Adams. Miller, Minnesota. "100+ alleged victims. Ten legal suits filed in the 1990s. Transferred to three different dioceses. Removed from priesthood in 1994. Convicted in 2006 for abuse of a third grade boy. Completed ten-year sentence at Minnesota Correctional Facility, Shakopee. Currently residing at the Cure D'Ars Rehabilitation Center, Dorchester, Massachusetts."

She searched the "Cure D'Ars Rehabilitation Center, Dorchester, MA" and found it was a rehab for "wayward priests." Their motto: "Helping men of God rediscover their way since 1999." She wrote down the address, and then did a search for "database of sex offenders." A link came up for the *United States Department of Justice National Sex Offender Public Website.* She typed the rehabilitation center's address into the field. Thomas Adams, along with six other names, popped up as living at that address. Raven grinned. "Well, Ira," she said under her breath, "looks like you'll have your pick of assholes."

4

Ty sat down across the table from Jacobs in the conference room. Jacobs, with three empty Styrofoam coffee cups in front of him, was staring at the crisscrossing colored strings pinned on the wall. Ty glanced over his shoulder at the map and then back at Jacobs. Ty said, "No Callahan today?"

"I told him to go home and check in with his network. Goddamn that guy has a lot of energy."

"I believe the clinical term is manic."

Jacobs chuckled and rubbed his eyes. "I've spent hours on the phone with I can't tell you how many local authorities, revisiting I can't tell you how many reports from witnesses. They all say the same thing. Eight-foot-tall red giant with six fingers. The only variance in description is Molly Simmons that said he was painted black."

"Because of some sooty substance?"

"You think there could really be a demon out there? I mean, that's insane. Right?"

Ty shrugged.

Jacobs said, "I have to be right; this is all guys in rubber masks, right? Really tall guys in rubber masks? Several guys in rubber masks and on stilts. Spread out around the world. I mean, it can't be a demon. There are no demons. Right?"

Ty said, "Let me tell you a story. Growing up, I'd often stay at my grandmother's. Called her Mamsy." He paused, looking at Jacobs. Jacobs sat watching him silently. "No quip about me calling my grandmother Mamsy?"

"Too fucking tired."

Ty continued, "Anyway, Mamsy was old-school in her child-rearing. Old-school in everything I guess you could say. She still held to the notion of explaining things away with supernatural shit. So she told boogeyman stories. You know, if you don't behave, you can expect the boogeyman to be under your bed or to crawl out of the closet. She said he could tiptoe silent, so you'd have no way of knowing where he was, or if he was even there. Until it was too late."

"That's fucking horrifying," Jacobs stated matter-of-factly, staring at Ty with tired eyes.

"Yeah, no shit. For a kid, anyway. I mean, it sounds silly now, but back then I was pretty scared. I was, what, like six? But one day I took a dollar from her purse so I could buy a soda, which I wasn't supposed to have either. That night, I was freaked out. Stealing is not *being good*, and I knew the boogeyman was coming for me. So I took a bag of flour, spread handfuls of the stuff outside the closet door, all the way to my bed and around my bed. I figured that way, if I woke in the night, I could see if there were any footprints and I'd know where the boogeyman was. But it was like one of those *Three Stooges* bits, where they paint themselves into a corner. I'd been standing on the bed when I'd spread the flour all around it. And I needed to get the flour back to the kitchen. I was scared my Mamsy was going to notice it gone. I mean, obviously she was going to realize I'd used half the bag eventually and I knew she was going to 'skin me alive,' as she was known to say. But that fear of the boogeyman was enough to make a skinnin seem trite in comparison. So then I had to leap from the bed over the flour so I can get the bag back to the pantry without leaving footprints of my own. I jump, make it over the flour, but my socks slip on the wooden floor, and I go flying back, dumping the rest of the bag over my head."

Jacobs chuckled.

Laughing, Ty said, "My Mamsy comes in to find me, saying I looked like a goddamn photo-negative of Al Jolson."

They were both laughing now, allowing the laughter to run itself out into silence. Jacobs was looking at the wall again. "So what was the point of that story?"

"I don't know," Ty said. "I guess nothing."

"Well, thanks for nothing."

"No," Ty said. He laughed again. "I guess the point is that when you're a kid, stuff like that can seem so real that you do dumb shit, like pour flour around your bed. Now, as adults, the thought of a boogeyman is stupid. But for kids, that stuff is real. Not *seems* real. It *is* real. Something happens to us when we grow up. Makes us not believe. But people like Callahan can still see it somehow."

"So Callahan isn't the crazy one?"

"No, that motherfucker is as crazy as they come."

Jacobs said, "When I first split with Beth, I couldn't wrap my head around it. I didn't believe anything could have pulled us apart. And then I couldn't believe that we would treat each other like we did when things got bad. Then I didn't believe it when she actually went through with the divorce. Then I worked my ass off, changing my ways, not believing we'd stay separated. Then I couldn't believe it when the eighteen-wheeler knocked her out of my life permanently. Then I just stopped believing altogether."

The two of them sat in silence again. Jacobs staring at the wall, Ty looking at the hierarchy of angels and demons. Ty said, "So what was the point of that story?"

"I guess nothing," Jacobs said, still staring at the wall.

"Well thanks for nothing." Ty smirked.

Jacobs said, "Maybe it's time to start believing in something again."

"You're gonna start with a Nephilim?" Ty asked, grinning.

Jacobs shrugged. "It's something."

5

Raven folded the paper with the priests' names and addresses and placed it in her bag, mentally inventorying what she could do with the rest of the day, needing to kill time until 9:00pm, which was when the library closed. She strode across the library, almost to the exit, when she stopped. She was looking down at the pen in her hand. The boy's pen. While she'd been doing her research on the computer, he had walked by her three times. Feigning two bathroom breaks, although the bathroom was not close enough to warrant such flybys, and once perusing the bookshelves behind the computer bank. He'd picked out a book on gardening, nodding and weighing the book in his hands as if he'd been looking for it all his life. He'd then glanced at her and walked away.

Raven returned to the table where the boy was still buried in his Latin work, the gardening book untouched on the table.

Raven set the pen down and said, "Thank you."

The boy looked up, his face dropping and then rapidly searching for the right expression. "Uh…thank you. I mean, you're welcome…although I guess 'thank you' would actually have worked there, too."

Raven giggled, a light airy sound, and its tone surprised her. She hadn't heard herself giggle that way—like a carefree young girl—in years. She broke into her wide smile and said,

"You have no idea how important that pen was in the battle of good and evil." She turned and walked away.

After leaving the library, she went for a walk around the town's center. She glanced over her shoulder every so often to see if the boy from the library had followed her. She wished he had. Wished she had invited him. Or at least offered to help the poor bastard study. She explored different shops, enjoyed a large lunch in a sit-down restaurant, and even caught a movie in a movie theater—something she hadn't done since going with her parents. It was a horror movie, and she found herself laughing hysterically at all the wrong moments, bringing wary glances from her fellow moviegoers. She returned to the library around 8:00pm. The boy was long gone. She checked for hiding spots to slip into at closing time.

Around quarter to nine, when the librarian made her announcement that the library would be closing, Raven slipped downstairs to the bottom floor, which consisted of two unused conference rooms and a hallway leading to the back parking lot. It also had the room she figured to be least likely checked by anyone closing up for the night. "Elevator Machine Room" was written on the door, and to Raven's amazement, it was unlocked. She looked up at a camera in the corner of the hallway. She would have to gamble that as long as she didn't set off any alarms or cause any disorder to the place, there would be no reason for them to check the video.

She ducked into the room, nestling in among the whirring machinery and the stench of greased, metal mechanisms. She felt a jolt of panic as she thought of the machinery in the corner of Jimmy Wang's warehouse, but it quickly passed. She wasn't Jimmy Wang's property anymore. She was no one's property. And she had a demon friend to keep it that way. She dozed in and out, the machinery occasionally kicking on and off for the next hour as the custodial staff moved their equipment from floor to floor. But then there was silence. No more machinery. No more Doppler sounds of the vacuum creeping from room to room. No more sparse voices of the cleaning crew. The library was sound asleep. Raven hoped it stayed asleep for the night.

She slipped out of the machine room, listening for any signs of life. Nothing. The only light was the red glow of the exit sign and a band of streetlights peeking through the thin window of the exterior door. She crept along the hall toward the stairs, her heart thudding in her chest. She searched for triggered alarms and motion-sensors. The library slept on. She climbed the stairs to the back of the main floor. The reference desk was nestled out of view of any windows.

In a big, comfy office chair with her feet up on the reference desk, she sat waiting for Ira. The dim glow of emergency lights illuminated the page of the book she was reading. *The Bible*. She thought it a good time to catch up. She glanced at the clock as the minute hand edged toward 11:59. Putting the Bible down, she took the folded slip of paper from her pocket. The page from Ira's book looked unremarkable. Folded up as it was, it could have been a shopping list or someone's phone number or address. She unfolded the page, her fingers picking up an almost imperceptible vibration. Holding the page to her nose, she could smell the smoky, cooked-in stench of fire and soot. She wondered about the book. Whose names were in it? What power did it hold? Was it a history of the world? Could she flip back and trace world events through the names etched across its pages?

At exactly midnight, Ira appeared.

He stood on the other side of the reference desk from her, as if he had a question about obtaining a library card or where to find the periodicals. Raven peered up at him from behind the page of his book.

He regarded her silently for a moment before asking, "What are you doing?"

Raven lowered the page, revealing her wide grin. "Just thinking of a new cologne. Eau de Hell. We can target it toward the Emo crowd. We'll make millions."

"Emo?" The word coming from him caused Raven to burst into laughter. As if he were a confused father asking a toy store employee about a *Sesame Street* character.

"Never mind," Raven said, stifling her laughter. He stared down at her, still trying to figure out the conversation. She loved that about him. The way he attacked sarcasm like a puzzle. "Here," Raven said, sliding notebook paper across the reference desk to the demon. "This is a good place to start looking for your priests. You got seven of them, all convicted, all living in the same house."

Ira peered down at the page. "I do not recognize any of the names."

"Well, check the book. See if any names jump out at you."

He pulled the book from his pocket and flipped through the pages. "I don't see their names," he said. Raven detected a new tone in his voice. It was very slight, but it sounded almost like panic. He looked up from the book. "How do I find these men?"

"I wrote the address on the top of the page."

"I won't be able to find a location from the Gray Zone unless the sinner is in the book or I've been there before. These men need to be in the book for me to find them."

"Can't you just command your book to find them?"

"How, when the book doesn't know they even exist?"

"I printed you a map." She slid a street map toward him.

"Just command your book to go there."

"It doesn't know where *there* is," he said, pointing at the map. "The book needs the exact location, otherwise I could end up coming out of the Gray Zone anywhere. I could come out on the bottom of the Atlantic Ocean."

"Would you die?"

"No, but it would be very bothersome."

Raven giggled, but then cut her laughter short. She didn't like his expression. She could tell he was getting frustrated. And angry. *These priests have no idea what they are in for*, she thought.

Ira growled, "I cannot navigate any of this. I don't know where it is." His fists clenched into boulders.

He's going to smash up this place, she thought.

"It's okay," Raven said in a low, soft voice. "We can figure out a solution. Think we can ballpark it?"

"Ballpark?"

"Yeah. It's an expression. It means, if I get you close enough, do you think you can find it?"

Ira's fists were still clenched into boulders, but his brow loosened a little above his fiery eyes and his shoulders rose and lowered in a deep breath.

"I got it," she said, snapping her fingers. "Follow me." She stood and darted down an alcove to the computer ports. One of the monitors cast a blue pall over the room. She'd left the computer on, having caught up with world news and current events. She'd noted that all the sites were missing the top head-line: DEMON COMES TO EARTH TO FUCK UP BAD GUYS.

She sat at the computer and returned to the Sex-offender Database. She typed in Dorchester, MA. Several red dots pocked a map of the Boston neighborhood. Raven scrolled the map around to get her bearings. She found the priests' rehab and then scrolled to the nearest red dot and clicked on it. "Anthony Lynne," she said over her shoulder.

"Huh?"

"Anthony Lynne. Do you recognize the name?"

"Um."

"Check your book, dummy."

"Oh." Ira produced his book and flipped through the pages. "Yes. Anthony Lynne. He is here."

"And he is there," Raven said, pointing at the map. "Supposedly, anyway. Think if I drew you a map, you could get from this guy's house to this Cure D'Ars place?"

"Maybe."

"Maybe? It's only a few streets over."

"Yes. I will find it."

Raven took the list she had written for him and a pen she had swiped from the reference desk. She said, "Well, Anthony Lynne, looks like you're dodging a bullet tonight." She began drawing a map to the Cure D'Ars.

6

Raven hadn't included a compass rose on her map. But she'd told Ira the priests were north of Anthony Lynne's house. The religious order of the Cure D'Ars was on Gay Street, which, for some reason, Raven had found amusing. He didn't always get her humor. He thought perhaps she found the juxtaposition of the situation's levity against the gaiety of the location's name ironic in some way. He wasn't sure. But he knew she would certainly laugh if she saw him now—standing in the shadows of the street, squinting through the dark to see house numbers with her crudely drawn map hanging uselessly in his hand.

The air was electric, a blanket of clouds above the houses strobing with light. The first drops of rain peppered the street, each drop exploding into steam as it hit Ira's body. His stern countenance collapsed into one even harsher as he began trudging up the street.

Raven said that number fifteen should be on the left side of the street. "It should be a pretty big place, to house all these priests," she had told him. "Like maybe a multi-family home or something along that line." But they were all multi-family homes. In fact, Dorchester seemed to be nothing but multi-family homes. He looked down at the map, but the paper had become translucent, the ink of the pen-drawn streets smudging in the rain. The streetlights gave a golden-orange glow to the houses. He counted them to what should have been number fifteen. It was large and, like all the other houses along the street, seemed far too big for the lot it was built on, like a fat man crammed into an airplane seat.

Ira crept to the side of the house. There was a light on in one of the windows toward the back. He squeezed along the ribbon of grass, his butt flattened against a chain link fence. The window was about six feet up. The rain pounded on the pane, streaking and warping the light from inside like colorless stained glass. Ira balled his fist and squeegeed away the water in a circular motion with the side of his hand. It made a squishy, squeaking sound. Peering through the clear circle, he came face to face with a middle-aged woman sitting on a toilet. Her face was a perfect circle framed by a frazzled explosion of hair. Her mouth dropped into a silent, frozen scream. Her eyes, which had been the squinted half moons of the sleep-deprived, widened to half dollars.

Ira's eyes widened just as round as the woman's, his own mouth dropping open. He then attempted to smile—a pressed, crooked smile—and he raised his hand in a half-hearted wave. "Sorry," he growled, and turned to leave. He stopped and turned back to the window. "Do you know where number—?" But the toilet was empty—or, at least it no longer had a woman sitting on it. When he turned to leave again, a house caught his eye. It was set back from the rest of the homes. Set upon a large, sprawling lawn, it was a hulking structure connected to the street by a long, thin driveway, a hidden umbilical cord to society. Names in his book or no names, he knew that this was the place.

7

It wasn't the thunder that woke Fredrick Neil. It was the lightning: a moment of daylight flickering into the dark room. It was followed by one of those crackling, ripping reports of thunder, like the sound of wood splitting. This was followed by more thunder, a low rumble. Then came the rain's relentless attack of the roof and windowpanes, and the rushing spray of gutter water through aluminum spouts. Fredrick liked these sounds. "A lullaby of God's anger," his mother had told him when he was young, when he would pretend he was too afraid of the thunder to sleep in his own bed.

The truth was, however, he'd always loved thunderstorms. He was somehow comforted by God's anger. As a parish priest outside of Topeka, Kansas, his favorite thing to do had been to sit and watch thunderstorms with a rapidly diminishing bottle of Wild Turkey at hand. Here in Massachusetts, these Easterners thought they knew thunderstorms. He'd tell them, *There ain't nothing like a thunderstorm moving across the Kansas plains.* Some would argue there was nothing like a thunderstorm coming across an angry sea. He'd respond,

Do your thunderstorms become tornadoes? That generally shut them up.

In group therapy, when he recounted those days of watching thunderstorms in Kansas, he'd leave out the parts about drinking whiskey. He certainly left out the time he'd once tried to count off the seconds between lightning and thunder with gulps of rye. That experiment hadn't lasted long, and it had landed him in the Emergency Room. And then landed him here at the Cure D'Ars.

He still felt that longing for a drink. He wanted a swig of whiskey so bad. He curled into a fetal ball and began muttering the serenity prayer, his hands folded. Then came another flash of daylight and crackling rip of the air, and the hairs stood up on the backs of his arms and neck. That feeling the body gets just before a lightning strike. Or when it knows evil is near. He stopped muttering the prayer when he heard a rolling call of thunder—that low guttural growling—that didn't sound so distant. Fredrick Neil pulled the blankets close to his face and peeked over them.

"Darkness there and nothing more," he whispered, and resumed his prayer. The hairs on his arms and neck still stood at attention. The roll of thunder sounded again, but this time the sound had followed no lightning. And it *was* in his room. He sat bolt upright in his bed, whispering, "Who's there?"

This was the life of living with sex offenders. Always worrying someone could creep into his room. Granted, none of them were interested in adults, but they were in the house, and they were predatory. He willed his eyes to adjust to the dark. The light switch was across the room. If one of the pervs had entered the room, he would be situated between Frederick and the only light source.

The lightning illuminated the room again, revealing a form at the end of his bed. A wall of a being with harsh, stone features, made harsher by the flickering strobes of lightning. The thunder was perfectly timed, drowning out Fredrick Neil's choked, gasping scream.

The thing had him by the front of his nightshirt, its hand almost the size of his own torso. The darkness spoke in a sound he remembered those tornados making as they cut across the plains. It said, "Are you Thomas Adams?"

Adams? Did this monster just ask for Thomas Adams? The perv they kept in the attic apartment, where they'd blacked out the windows so he couldn't watch the neighborhood kids when they came out to play?

Fredrick tried to make a sound. Tried to answer the thing's question, but he could offer nothing but that choked, gasping sound again.

"Are you Thomas Adams?" the darkness repeated. "Or Harold Dillard? Or Robert Murphy?" The thing was listing off the pervs in the place.

Fredrick tried answering again, choking out, "Neil."

The massive hand tightened on his shirt, the fabric cutting into the back of his neck. "You tell me to kneel?" The horrific voice had become somehow more horrific.

"N-no. I'm Neil. My name is Neil."

The hand relaxed. "There is no Neil," the thing said.

Neil didn't know what it meant by that. But he didn't argue.

The hand tightened around the shirt again, but not as violently, and in a softer voice, the thing asked, "Where are these men I named?"

Frederick got his voice going again, choking out a whisper. "They are scattered throughout the house. Adams is in the attic room." Neil didn't know why, but he added in his choked whisper, "He's the worst one."

"The worst what?" the thing asked.

"The worst of the child-abusers. You're here for the perverts, aren't you?"

"These men have harmed children?"

"Yes."

"And you know this for sure?"

"Yes."

"Then why are they not in the book?" the thing asked.

"Book? What book?"

But the hand was gone from his shirt and there was nothing but the rushing sound of water through the aluminum gutters and the distant rolls of thunder, that now really were distant. And when the daylight strobes lit the room, the room was empty.

8

Old Yellah was whining. That's what woke Jacobs, not his phone buzzing on his nightstand. He tended to his dog, scruffing Yellah's head until the phone stopped. "Back to sleep, buddy," Jacobs said. "Whatever asshole is calling will leave a message." Old Yellah seemed to like this explanation, and he shuffled off to his sleeping spot at the end of the bed. Jacobs looked at who had called. Special Agent in Charge Thompson. "Shit," he said as the phone began buzzing again.

What followed was the typical dreamlike quality crime scenes take on late at night, or, he supposed now, early in the morning. The Dorchester neighborhood pulsated in the red and blue strobe lights of emergency vehicles, and the news crews' spotlights obliterated the darkness. The firemen and ambulance drivers were already packed up and ready to go, the heavy diesel engines droning in what should have been a quiet predawn. The fuel smell of the engines hung in the air, assaulting Jacobs's nose like ammonia. The police officers were wandering around, void of direction. The strobe lights made everything slow down in a kaleidoscopic way, and people seemed to just appear out of nowhere. SAC Thompson was talking to a small gaggle of reporters. Ty stood off to the side, talking on the phone. He turned and nodded toward Jacobs.

Jacobs started toward Ty, but Callahan stopped him, calling, "Agent Jacobs, Agent Jacobs."

Jacobs took a sip of his coffee, squinting against an errant news camera spotlight. He said to Callahan, "Number one, why are you here? And number two…I don't have a number two. Why are you here?"

Callahan looked as if he'd been goosed. Then he composed himself and said, "I am here as your advisor. I do believe that is the job I have been given. Is it not?"

"What I mean is, how are you, a civilian, at an active crime scene? How did you know to be here? And please don't tell me the Archangel Gabriel told you to swing by."

"I found out the same way the news crews did. A police dispatcher announced a demon was tearing up the Cure D'Ars. That type of thing gets the attention of people listening to radio scanners. One of my Knowledge Fighters alerted me to the situation."

"Knowledge Fighters," Ty said, appearing beside Jacobs. "What is that, someone who fights against knowledge?"

Callahan ignored Ty and said to Jacobs, "What is our next move?"

"*My* next move is to go in and check out the crime scene. *Your* next move is to stay here and not touch anything or talk to anyone. And for god's sake, do not talk to the press. Can I trust you to do that?"

"Nope," Ty said.

"Shit. You're right," Jacobs said, remembering his first order was to babysit this crank. "All right. You're coming with us."

Ty raised his eyebrows, "Seriously? You're bringing a civilian into an active crime scene?"

Callahan said, "Technically I am an adviser."

Jacobs turned to Ty and shrugged. Then he said to Callahan, "Do not touch anything. You're a civilian, and this is an active crime scene."

"I just said that," Ty said, throwing up his hands and following Jacobs and Callahan into the house.

The building inspector told them to avoid the back hallway. A load-bearing wall had been completely smashed through.

"Was it an explosive?" Jacobs asked him.

"Nope," the inspector responded without further explanation.

Walking through the place was like touring the haunted house attractions Jacobs would go to as a kid. It was barely recognizable as any kind of residence. The dust of smashed drywall blanketed everything, much of it kicked up into a low-lying fog like the dry-ice effect of those haunted houses. Splintered studs had broken free of the wall in compound fractures. Furniture hung out of the ceiling. Glass shards cracked and popped under foot. But there was no blood. No one had been killed.

"It's like a bull on meth threw a hissy fit," Ty said.

Jacobs turned to Callahan, who regarded the surroundings with a combination of wonder and satisfaction. Jacobs said, "Why didn't he kill anyone? Wouldn't killing priests be a good way of getting Armageddon going?"

"Most of these men are no longer priests. They broke their vows, choosing worldly vices over God. Frankly, they are no longer even men in my opinion."

"Then why wouldn't your demon kill them? Wouldn't they be powerful soldiers for the Wicked Army? Knowing the enemy's playbook, as they do?"

"Perhaps the power of Christ compelled him not to."

"But, like you said, most of these guys aren't priests anymore. Do they still have Christ Power?"

"As usual, I don't appreciate your tone, Agent Jacobs," Callahan said. "This is very serious."

"Well, not *as usual*, Mr. Callahan, I am being completely serious right now."

9

Jacobs and Ty entered the FBI office's interrogation room. Thomas Adams was already seated at the small rectangular table. Callahan was on the other side of a very large, very obvious two-way mirror. Jacobs did not want Callahan anywhere near this witness, but Thompson had insisted that Callahan, adviser that he was, assess the discussion. Callahan could communicate with Jacobs through an earpiece. Jacobs did not like Callahan speaking into his head like that—having a paranoid, delusional voice whispering in his ear was too much like schizophrenia.

Adams, although a large, burly man, looked somehow shrunken sitting at the interrogation table. He was bald with a ridge of closely cropped white hair encircling his head and a goatee that made him look more like a professional wrestling enthusiast than a priest. He no longer looked like the mug shot in Jacobs's hand. In that photo, he was a teddy bear of a man with a Santa-like twinkle in his eyes. Throw a clerical collar on that asshole, and who wouldn't trust him with kids?

Before Jacobs had even finished sitting down, Callahan said in his ear, "Ask him if it was a Nephilim. Ask if it was a Nephilim—"

Jacob's winced and whispered, "Stop it, not now."

Adams, who didn't realize Jacobs was speaking into a radio, dropped his jaw, his eyes widening.

Ty burst into laughter.

Jacobs stared at Adams a moment, about to offer an explanation, but didn't bother. Instead, he cleared his throat and said, "Mr. Adams, I am Agent Jacobs, and this is Agent Malone." Ty sat down at the table, not offering a word.

"I, uh, already gave my statement to the police," Adams said, his eyes shifting between the men.

"Yeah, I know. But when dealing with…" Jacobs opened the file and read aloud "…*the Devil, himself*, we tend to follow up."

Callahan was in his ear. "It wasn't the Devil. Ask if it was a Nephilim. He'll know if it was a Nephilim."

"I will," Jacobs growled into his collar.

Ty, watching the confused fear wash into Adams's eyes again, grinned and shook his head.

Jacobs said, "So why was the Devil in your house, Father Adams? Is it still Father? Or do you lose that moniker when you get caught molesting little kids? Whoa, actually"—Jacobs was looking down at Adams's file again—"you were a priest for a while after first getting caught, huh?"

"I have since been defrocked. *Mister* Adams will be fine. Or Thomas."

"Thomas?" Jacobs said, looking up at Adams.

Adams nodded.

"Tom? Tommy?" Jacobs asked.

"Thomas, please," Adams said.

Jacobs nodded and said, "I knew a cop named Tommy Adams; he was a piece of shit, too. Well, Tommy, why was the Devil in your house?"

"It wasn't the Devil," Callahan said in his ear. Jacobs ignored him.

Adams answered, "I don't know."

"You told the police that the Devil kept asking why you weren't in the book. What does that mean? What book?"

"I don't know."

"A book?" Callahan said in Jacobs's ear, his voice squeaking with excitement. "You didn't tell me about a book."

"Yes, there was a book," Jacobs said into his collar.

Adams nodded, expectantly.

Jacobs paused, waiting for Callahan to offer something.

Callahan offered nothing.

"Could it be a Bible?" Jacobs asked Adams.

"I don't know. He had a book with him. He was flipping through it and complaining that I wasn't in it."

"If it were a Bible, then it definitely wasn't the Devil," Callahan said through the earpiece. "The Devil could never read a Bible."

"Then how does he quote scripture?" Jacobs appeared to ask himself.

"Excuse me?" Adams said.

Ty was looking at the ceiling, trying to keep from laughing.

"Nothing," Jacobs said. "So you told the police that the Devil spoke in Latin?"

"Yes."

"Any other languages?"

"He spoke English once."

"What did he say?"

Adams shifted in his seat and took a deep breath. "He became increasingly agitated with my answers. And finally he said, 'What the fuck.' Then he began smashing up the place. He just went on a rampage. I don't know how no one was killed."

"Was it a questioning 'What the fuck?' or a statement, like, 'Eh, what the fuck'?"

"Question. He seemed to be in disbelief."

"What answers was he becoming agitated over?"

"He asked if I was guilty of the sins I was accused of."

"And what did you say?"

"I think we all know the answer to that question, Agent," Adams said, glancing at Ty and then back at Jacobs.

"Wouldn't the Devil know if you were guilty or not?" Jacobs asked.

"It wasn't the Devil," Callahan screamed in his ear.

Jacobs winced and ripped the earpiece from his ear. He threw it on the table and looked at Adams as if nothing happened. "Please, continue," he said.

Adams stared at the earpiece a moment and said, "I don't know. I told him I'd been absolved of my sins. The bishop himself had absolved me. And then he asked, 'What bishop?'"

Jacobs glanced at Ty. Ty raised his eyebrows. Jacobs looked back at Adams. "What bishop?" he asked.

"Bishop Truss, back in Miller, Minnesota. He is the one who transferred me from Saint Christine's to Saint Theresa's."

"And what did the *Devil*"—Jacobs glanced over his shoulder and winked at the glass, and then turned back to Adams—"have to say about that?"

"He said, 'He knew?' I assumed, referring to the bishop, and I told him they all knew. Right on up the line. They all knew about all of us. We were all guilty, but we were all absolved of our sins, and they moved us on to do it all over again."

"And that's when he said 'What the fuck?' and started tearing up the place?"

"It's when he said, 'What the fuck?' I said one more thing to him before he tore up the place."

"What was that?"

"I told him, 'It's not my fault.'"

Jacobs stood up. Ty followed suit. Jacobs said to Adams, "Well, Tommy, thank you for your help."

"That's it?" Adams said. "What is going to be done? What if he comes back?"

Jacobs shrugged, "I don't know…pray?"

Ty added, "Sounds like you shouldn't tell him it's not your fault."

The two agents were about to leave when Jacobs turned back. "By the way," he said to Adams, "could this devil have actually been a Nephilim?"

"What's a Nephilim?" Adams said.

Jacobs chuckled and left the priest alone in the room.

10

It's hard to get a good night's sleep when a demon keeps interrupting your slumber. About an hour after Raven sent Ira on his way to find the priests, he was back. She'd found a pile of beanbags in the children's section and curled up on them like a cat. She woke from a deep sleep when she felt the hairs on her neck prickle—a feeling that had signaled danger in the past, but now brought her comfort. She opened her eyes and, in the streetlights that sliced through the front window, she saw Ira's hulking form—even more hulking among the child-sized tables and chairs.

"Forget something?" she asked, stretching her body.

"I need a bishop," Ira said.

Raven and Ira returned to the computers and found his bishop in Miller, Minnesota. He was in an old folks' home now—one Ira had never needed to visit, and thusly, couldn't figure out the address of. But Raven played the odds: one of the residents of the nursing home had to have, at some time, harmed a child, so she read the names of the residents, and sure enough, one was in his book. With the nursing home's location in hand, he was gone.

He was back an hour later.

"Archbishop," he said.

Raven found an approximation to where the man was and drew Ira a map.

An hour later, he was back.

"Cardinal," he said.

"Look, Ira, I think I see where this is going." Raven typed on the computer's keyboard and hit enter. She said, "This is where you need to go."

Ira squinted at the picture of the Vatican. "That is the home of the Holy See," he growled. "Thomas Adams said it went all the way to the top. To the Sovereign Pontiff?"

"Goes beyond that, buddy. One of the Popes who oversaw this thing is already canonized. So, you could say that when it goes to the top, it goes to the *top*." She nodded at the screen and said, "Need me to draw you a map?"

"No," he said. "The book can find all holy sites. I will need no map." His hands were balled into boulders again, and his shoulders rose and fell in deep breaths.

Raven said, "I'm sorry, Ira. I don't know why these priests are not in your book. But they are guilty. Want me to print out more names? We can take your punishing into the digital age."

"No," Ira said. "I can only follow the book. Human justice systems are too fallible."

Raven said, "Looks like maybe there's some fallibility in your book system, too."

Ira looked at her a moment, his mental cogs turning. His attention returned to the picture of the Vatican on the computer screen, and then he was gone.

"You're welcome," Raven called into the empty room.

11

Ira stepped out of the Gray Zone and into the Holy See's office. It was a large room with ornate carpets. Tall windows on one side. On the other side, a large wooden chest and bookcases filled with old volumes. Toward the front of the room was a wooden desk that looked more like a dining table, and in the back, between two gargantuan bookcases, was the Pope, genuflecting on an ornate kneeler facing the wall.

The Pope raised his head, recognizing that someone, or something, was in the room. He stood and turned to face Ira. His expression was blank. A kind of what-took-you-so-long look. He clutched his Rosary tightly in his fist in what Ira took as defiance.

Ira held up his book. "Why are there no priests?" he demanded in Latin. He knew the See's language was his own.

The Pope did not answer. He stood regarding the demon with his cool eyes, his fingers twisting the beads.

"You're in charge of them. Why are they not in the book?" Ira shouted, striding toward the Pontiff.

The Pope didn't flinch.

There came a knocking on the room's thick wooden door. A muffled voice called, "Are you well, Your Holiness?"

Ira flung the large, wooden chest across the room. It crashed in front of the door, blocking it. "Why no priests?" he shouted, waving the book.

The Pope's fingers tightened on the Rosary, but still he said nothing.

The banging on the door intensified. There came banging on the windows as well. Ira turned to see faces peering through the heavy glass. Ira threw the bookcases one after another, books scattering like flocks of birds, the bookcases jamming into the windows' frames with explosions of glass.

Ira's face was now inches from the face of the Pontiff. The man's expression remained blank. Ira held up his book. "Did you know about them?"

There was a stalemate moment as the two regarded one another, the only sound the banging and shouting outside the door.

The Pontiff opened his mouth to speak, the rosary breaking apart in his tight fist, and a high breathy word escaped his mouth, "Mama." Then urine crept from beneath the man's robe as his eyes rolled back in his head and he dropped to the floor in a faint.

"Um…" Ira said. He crouched, lifting the man's head from the floor. He gently slapped his face a number of times, saying, "Um…hello? Hello? Wake up, I have questions about…."

The Pope was out cold.

"Um, do you…um, know about…" Ira tapped his face a few more times. The Pope opened his mouth and let out a loud snore. "…Um, priests…in my book…?"

The banging from the door turned into thunderous thuds. Someone had commandeered an axe and was coming through one way or another.

The Pontiff snored again. Ira stood, looked around the

room, grumbled, and with his shoulders slumping, returned to the Gray Zone.

12

Something woke Raven. Stretching, she murmured, "So did you get to meet the Pope?" Then she realized that what had woken her was not the buzzing, electric feeling of a demon materializing nearby, but the heavy click of a lock unlocking. She opened her eyes. Morning daylight streamed through the library's window.

"Shit," she whispered. The lights in the main library flickered on and she heard the murmur of the librarians' morning greetings. She wriggled under the beanbags as someone strode into the room.

"Late start this morning, Joan," a woman's voice called from the main library.

"I know, I know," said Joan, her voice too close for Raven's comfort. There came the sound of books sliding on a shelf.

The distant voice called, "There is already a gathering of cherubs outside. Are you ready for them?"

"Let them in," said Joan with breathless annoyance. Raven heard the woman shuffle off quickly.

Cherubs? Raven hoped she meant the order of angels—lately that wouldn't have been out of the realm of possibility—but the sound of high-pitched voices and padding feet squashed that hope. The padding grew louder. And then something heavy dropped onto her. Raven said, "Oomph." There was movement above her, and then a corner of the beanbag was peeled away to reveal the library's ceiling—Raven thought back to her peeling back the sheet to see Zippy's staring eyes from behind the couch—and then a small child's face was peering down at her.

It was a boy with freckles and a shock of red hair. "What are you doing?" the boy asked.

"Resting," Raven said casually.

A little girl's face appeared next to the boy's face. A pretty girl with frizzy pigtails. "Hello," the girl said.

"Hello," Raven said. Raven craned her neck to see where the librarian was. She heard women's voices discussing something toward the back of the room. Raven climbed from beneath the beanbags. She sat on one of them with her hands folded on her knees. Two little girls ran up to her.

"Hi," said one of the girls. The other one began climbing on Raven's back.

"Hi," Raven said. "Um, I think we should be sitting and waiting nicely for the librarian, right?"

"Nah," the little girl climbing on her said. She had long bangs and piggy cheeks.

"Sally, get down," an adult voice said. Raven looked up and saw the librarian with several other children in tow. "You're all supposed to be sitting and waiting for me."

"Told you," Raven whispered over her shoulder at Sally.

Sally stuck out her tongue.

The librarian regarded Raven. "Hello, I didn't see you come in."

"Yeah, I'm stealthy like that," Raven said.

"She's too old for story time," Sally said.

Raven shot the little girl an arched eyebrow and then she hopped up to her feet. She held out her hand to the librarian. "Hi, I'm Raven. I'm a grad student at UNH, studying Early Childhood Development. I'm staying in Standish this summer with my aunt and, seeing as how I'm doing my thesis on the use of story time to develop social skills, I figured I would sit in on a few of your story times. If that's okay?"

"Who did you say you were staying with?" the librarian asked.

"The Jacksons," Raven said, taking a shot at a random name.

"Ella Jackson?"

"Yup."

The woman stared at Raven a moment. Raven, realizing the woman was trying to fit some square piece of information into a round hole, added, "I was adopted."

"Okay," the librarian said. More children padded into the children's section. "You are certainly welcome to join us. Let me know if you have any questions."

"Thanks," Raven said, returning to the beanbags.

"I want her to read," Sally said, pointing at Raven.

Raven arched her eyebrow at the little girl again and said, "Oh, no thank you."

"Yeah, I want her to read," said the boy with the red hair.

"Would you like to read?" the librarian said to Raven.

"No thank you. I'll just observe."

"I want her to read," Sally said more forcefully. And then all the children joined in, calling in a chorus. "I want her to read."

Raven, with her back to the librarian, scrunched up her face at Sally. Sally smiled. Raven stuck out her tongue. Sally laughed and pointed at Raven. Raven turned to the librarian, and with a wide smile, said, "Sure, I'd love to read."

"Wonderful," the librarian said, handing Raven the book and gesturing for her to sit in a chair facing the beanbags.

Raven took the book. It was one of her childhood favorites. E.B. Richardson's *The Smell from My Brother's Room*. Raven grinned, looking down at the cover, almost transfixed as memories of her past flooded into her with a wave of nostalgia. She sat in the chair and flipped briefly through the book, relishing the familiar artwork.

"Aren't you going to read it?" Sally said in a tone of disgust.

"Oh, I'm supposed to read it to you?" Raven asked the group in exaggerated confusion.

"Yes," the children called in unison. The children laughed. Raven glanced at the librarian and saw the woman's subtle nod of approval.

"She's not very smart," Sally said.

"Sally," the librarian scolded.

"Nope, she's right," Raven said in a sing-song voice. "I'm not the smartest. But I do know how to read, and this is one of the first books I learned to read. Along with *War and Peace*."

"Huh?" the kids said in unison and then laughed. The librarian chuckled at the absurdity of the joke, even though Raven was telling the truth.

"And I used to have to try and figure out what the smell from my own brother's room was," Raven said. That part was a lie. She held up the book with the pictures facing the children and she peered around the side of the back cover so that she could see it, too. She didn't actually need to read the words, as she remembered almost every sentence, but she wanted to travel back to a simpler time in her distant memories of the pictures. She began to read: "'What is that smell from my brother's room? It's eerie and frightening like impending doom. What is that smell? What is its host? Dead leaves? Rotten eggs? Old cheese? A wet bag? Whatever it is, it smells gross!'" Here Raven scrunched up her face and held her nose. The children laughed.

As Raven continued to read, the children leaned forward, listening intently. Sally also watched intently, although her expression was one of someone daring another to impress her. Raven said, "'What is that smell? I simply must know. I'll muster my courage, I'll muster my strength, and into my brother's room I will go. But wait! I don't know what's behind that door.

What if it's a monster with bad intentions at its core? I could knock, and then, *Come in—*'" Raven said this with the proper monster growl. "'—it might hungrily implore. Or...what if it's a giant dragon in there today, whose mouth fills up the entire doorway? I could walk through that door into certain death. That smell I keep smelling could be its bad breath!'" Here Raven frantically checked her eyebrows, saying to the kids, "The dragon didn't singe my eyebrows with its bad breath, did it?"

"No," the kids screamed with laughter. Sally scoffed.

Raven read, "'What if it's a troll looking to deposit missing kids into my brother's closet? I could scream all I wanted, I could cry and stomp all aflutter. They'd never find me, not in that closet's clutter. What is that smell? I've got to know. Is it a body he's hiding? My brother does like Edgar Allen Poe.'"

"Who?" some of the kids asked.

"He's a very important scientist," Sally said.

"Writer," the librarian said.

"Scientist," Sally said more forcefully.

"'So...'" Raven continued, "'is it a dragon's bad breath? Or a monster's BO? My brother's untimely death? Ah, that's wishful thinking, I know. Is it a flatulent ghost? Or some gobbledy goo? A diseased host? Wait, don't vampires smell, too? That's it! The suspense has become much too thick! I'll just peek in the door. I'll just look real quick. Here I go for the doorknob... did I just hear a clatter? I'm going to open it...I hope I can hold onto my bladder. I'm opening the door. Boy, it smells foul! I'll slam it shut again, should anything howl. And there we have it…'" here, Raven smacked her knee and paused with the proper dramatic effect "'…the source could be no other; the smell in the room is only my brother.'" Raven said this last part while scrunching up her face and waving her hand in front of her nose. The children laughed and cheered.

The librarian said, "Wasn't that wonderful, children?"

"Yeah," all the children said. Except for Sally. She sat with her arms folded and said, "It had to be her brother. There *are* no monsters. People that think there are monsters are stupid."

Raven smiled brightly, looking down at Sally, and she said, "Oh no, you're wrong, little girl. There are monsters. Big, scary monsters that do horrible, horrible things to those who aren't nice. If you do bad things, these monsters will crush your skull and pull out your guts. So you be nice, Sally."

Raven stood and, still smiling brightly, handed the book to the librarian. "Thanks," she said, walking out of the room without looking back.

13

Raven was bored. She'd wandered to both ends of Main Street, read the newspapers (*The New York Times* and *The Standish Sentinel*), then decided to return to the library. Partly to surf the web. Partly to see if the boy from the day before was there. Raven strode into the main library and spotted him right away. He was seated at the same table across from the computer stations. She crept up behind the boy and said in a low voice, "Bene fecisti exem?"

The boy gripped the table and made a small squeak deep in his throat. He turned and looked at her, a new spasmodic convulsion taking his face as he tried to find the right expression to wear. He settled on one of mature stoicism and squeaked the word, "What?" He cleared his throat. "Ahem—what did you say?"

"I guess you didn't," Raven said. She tilted her head to read the book open in front of him. "What do we have now? Yikes,

Chemistry. Ooo, balancing equations. Is this a school you go to, or an inquisition?"

The boy's eyes narrowed as he tried to balance the equation of who this girl was and why she wanted to talk to him. "You don't have final exams?"

Raven smiled. "Private school. We're done already."

"So you just come to the library for fun on beautiful summer days?" the boy said. Realizing he may have been rude, his eyes widened as if he'd burped, but when Raven broke into girlish giggles, his face relaxed.

"No, smartass, I'm getting an early start on researching colleges. Something, from the looks of your understanding of chemical reactions, you won't have to worry about." The lie about researching colleges came so easily to her lips, and she realized that had fate been more kind, now would be the time she would be researching colleges. And studying for final exams. And going to parties and the prom.

"You know how to do these things?" he asked, gesturing to the equations.

"It's pretty easy," she said. "It's one of the most fundamental laws of nature. The universe needs balance. Balancing chemical equations is bringing chaos back to its desired state. They pretty much do it themselves, you just have to recognize it."

"I'm sorry, I think you just had a stroke or something. You were babbling some kind of Zen gibberish," the boy said.

Raven smiled and sat down beside him, grabbing his pencil and paper. "I didn't think I'd be spending this beautiful summer day helping some dumbass figure out basic equations," Raven groaned. "But I'll do it for the sake of the universe's balance."

"Really? You'll help me?"

"Why wouldn't I?" she said. Glancing up, she saw the children's section librarian, Joan, talking to one of the other librarians, the squat, bull-dog-looking one with the thick glasses. Raven thought her name was Helen. They were whispering while regarding Raven. No doubt discussing her performance of *The Smell from My Brother's Room*. "You know what?" Raven said. "I'm hungry. What time is your exam?"

"Eleven," the boy said.

"Okay," Raven said, gathering up the books and standing. "Let's do this studying over some breakfast. I can't balance equations on an empty stomach."

14

Jacobs needed to get out of the office. He needed to walk, get into the sun and fresh air. Maybe it would help him organize the jumbled mess that was his thoughts. Besides, he needed coffee, and he could only take so much of the Bureau stuff. Ty asked if he wanted company. Jacobs told him no. Ty told him to get him some Starbucks. Jacobs told him, "Right, Dunkin Donuts it is."

Coffee in hand, he walked down to the nearby mall, found a bench and plopped down onto it. The early summer heat radiated off the asphalt and concrete and metal. He watched the people walking by. Smelled their sweat and perfume mixed with the fried food smells wafting from the restaurants. He sipped his coffee. Still too hot. Hot as Hell one might say, and in a delirious shift in rationality, he began to wonder what the actual temperature of Hell was. Now that there could actually be a Hell, the statement took on a new meaning, because it wasn't just an idiom; it was something quantifiable. He shook his head, reeling these thoughts back to rationality. There was no Hell. There was no demon. Rather, there was a group of highly motivated demon impersonators, and they—

Jacobs suddenly realized there was a man sitting next to him. The man had his own Styrofoam coffee cup, and Jacobs recognized him from the Dunkin Donuts he'd just been at. And he only remembered him from Dunkin Donuts because the guy had been outside the FBI office before that. The guy was nondescript. Average height. Lean build. Handsome, but not too handsome. The guy leaned forward, elbows on his knees, suddenly wanting Jacobs to recognize he was there. He watched the people whisking by, then looked over his shoulder at Jacobs. "How're you doing?" he said.

"Fine," Jacobs said.

"Nice day."

"Not bad," Jacobs said. There was a moment of silence. Jacobs broke it by asking, "You a reporter?"

The guy flashed a smile. A gleaming lightning-streak of teeth that looked almost dangerous. "Nah. But I am interested in your demon."

"I don't know anything about a demon," Jacobs said, sipping his coffee. He watched a mother pushing a stroller and towing a squirming toddler.

"Sure you do," the guy said. "You've been chasing him for days now. You and Callahan."

Jacobs felt as if he were deflating. Callahan. He knew he'd blab. "The fucker blabbed, huh? You newspaper or magazine? You aren't one of those blogger twerps, are you?"

That dangerous smile flashed again. "I told you, I'm not a reporter."

"Please tell me you're not Gabriel."

That smile again. "Nope. Name's Thayer. CIA."

Jacobs groaned. "So now the CIA's involved, huh? Are you like Deep Throat or something, Mr. Thayer? Here to tell me I'm in danger of uncovering something too big?"

"Hill."

"Excuse me?"

"It would be Mr. Hill," the man said. "Thayer is my first name. And I'm certainly no Deep Throat. You had to know there would be other agencies involved."

"The CIA? And who else?"

Thayer shrugged. "All of them."

"What does that mean?"

"CIA, NSA, Military Intelligence, Russian FSB, Mossad, even the Vatican Intelligence Network."

"The Vatican? They don't think this is an actual demon, too, do they?"

"They've been following it for some time. Right up to the attack there today."

"What attack?"

"Well, the news reports are saying it's a gas main explosion, but all Vatican Intelligence chatter went dead afterward."

"Anyone hurt?"

"'Pope overcome by incident,' was the official report, but no injuries."

"Interesting," Jacobs said.

"Why is that interesting to you?"

Jacobs looked at him sharply. "What do you want, Mr. Thayer?"

"Hill. Mr. Hill. And I want help. As I've said, there's a mad dash to find this thing. And you have the advantage."

"Advantage? I don't have any clue what the fuck I'm doing."

"Yeah, I've kind of gathered that," Thayer said, "but you do have Callahan."

"Callahan is nuts."

"Maybe. But we also think he knows something. Like legitimately knows something."

"What, like Gabriel's phone number? He's nuts."

"You mention Gabriel again. Why is this?"

"Guy claims he talks to angels. Nuts. Remember?"

"So 'the angel' *is* a real angel?"

"What are you talking about? Have you been talking to Callahan?"

"No," Thayer said. "In fact, Callahan is probably the tightest part of your operation. And the most productive, it would seem."

"Well he does have a lot of energy."

"I think the clinical term is manic," Thayer said with a smile.

Jacobs twitched. "Huh?"

Thayer continued, "We've been following Callahan's communications. He became a person of interest when we realized he was writing blogs about demon attacks, and it turned out there was a level of veracity to his reports. Then the blogs suddenly stopped. And we found he's working with you. Asked for you specifically, did he?"

"Wait. Following his communications? Isn't that illegal?"

"You're not one of those naïve idealists, are you?"

"Apparently."

"In a few emails to key followers of his—"

"The Knowledge Fighters?" Jacobs said.

"Yes. He mentioned an object he is to obtain from the demon. Said the Angel ordained him to get it. So the Angel *isn't* a codename for a person?"

"No, I told you, he thinks it is a real angel. Gabriel, to be exact."

"Well, I guess that makes sense."

"It does?"

"In the context of the information we've been given, yes. I guess we need to start taking things more literally."

"Information you've been given? From who?"

"You said, 'interesting,' a moment ago when I said no one was killed at the Vatican. Why is that?"

Jacobs glanced at Thayer, sizing the man up, then shrugged. "Look, from the apparent information you're being given, you should know I don't think this thing is a demon. I don't think it is a *thing*. I think it is a group of people killing child abusers. And I find it interesting that for some reason they're sparing priests."

"All the victims were child abusers?"

"Yeah, that much seemed pretty obvious."

"So far you're the only one to have made that connection. And Callahan believes this theory, too?"

"No. He believes it's a demon sent to kick-start Armageddon. I already told you, Callahan is completely irrational. He's a religious nut."

"So is half the United States Government. More than half, actually. None of them are rational. And they all have their own theories as to what is going on, and what they want done about it. Many follow the same theory as Callahan and want to start amassing troops in the Holy Land. You never wondered why Thompson let a civilian tag along on an investigation like this?"

"Thompson says Callahan knows people in high places."

"I'll say. Two congressmen and a senator have asked Thompson to extend Mr. Callahan every courtesy."

"I thought you said Callahan was airtight."

"He is. They had no idea what he wanted, they just follow his website and believe the things he says."

"You're telling me members of Congress follow conspiracy theorists and believe this bullshit?"

"That's nothing. There are some who suspect your supposed demon is really an alien. Others think it's some kind of Sasquatch. A handful have the more rational belief that it is a coordinated government or terrorist attack, even though most known terrorist organizations have been the target of at least one strike. As for the military, they don't care what it is, they just want it."

"For what?"

Thayer sat back and sipped his coffee as a couple walked past. When the couple was out of earshot, he said, "To weaponize it."

"Weaponized demons?" Jacobs said.

"You've watched movies. What's the first thing the military wants with something that kicks ass? They always want to find some military application. This thing, this demon, somehow got onto a US military base and killed a detainee."

"I heard about that. News said it was a serviceman who killed the detainee."

"That is what you might call a cover up."

"So what do you want with me?"

"Let's help each other," Thayer said. "Let's find this thing first."

"You want to find the thing first? Go ahead. Sounds like you know more about my operation than I do. I'm not sure why you're asking me what you already seem to know, or how you know it all. So I'm going to continue following the evidence to what I think it is: a group of vigilantes punishing child abusers, and you can hear about the rest of my investigation on the play-by-play."

"C'mon, most likely it'll be the FBI that nabs this thing. They want to take it in the U.S. Avoid as much foreign involvement as possible. Let me tag along."

"Sorry. I have my assignment, and I'm moving forward on it. If you want to keep buying coffee where I buy mine and giving me information like this, then I'm all for it. But

Callahan is needy enough, I don't need some spook over my shoulder, too."

"Then let me have Callahan. I think he knows something that he's not saying."

"Callahan ain't a commodity. He's a private citizen who chose to work with me. Or, scratch that, it was ordained. He may be a religious nut, but he's *my* religious nut, and he's going to lead me to whoever is doing this all. But I can assure you, he's never mentioned some object he's supposed to get. Just read his emails if you need more info."

"His emails have all stopped. I think he's on to us."

"Yeah, well, he's a paranoid insane person, so that makes sense."

"I think you're making a mistake. The people who are *really* in charge know it's only a matter of time before the media gets a hold of this. The higher-ups aren't going to let that happen. They're going to take this over and you'll be cut out. No one will know who you are."

"That's what I'm hoping for." Jacobs finished his coffee and stood. "It was nice to meet you, Mr. Thayer."

"Hill."

"Whatever." Jacobs began walking away.

Thayer stood and called after Jacobs, "Don't you want to know how I knew Callahan was working with you?"

Jacobs turned. "You said it was in his emails."

"No I didn't," Thayer said and walked away.

15

Raven sat with the boy from the library. They were in what was becoming her favorite breakfast place, at a table with chemistry books and notebooks spread out before them, along with empty plates. Raven glanced past David's shoulder at the television hanging over the breakfast counter. No volume, but on the screen was the shaky camera work of a breaking news video. It was a close-up of a huge window set in ornate stone. Several people in hardhats inspected a large object poking out of the broken glass. The crawl underneath the scene read: "Gas main explosion at Pope's residence. No injuries. Pope overcome by incident."

"Uh-oh," Raven said.

The Lost

1

Her name was Raven Mijares, and David Lee was in love. He felt like a marionette, and his puppeteer wouldn't let his feet touch the ground. With a string attached to his heart, the puppeteer carried him through the most hectic two days he'd ever had. The girl had just come up to him, two days in a row, in the library. Just started talking to him. Offered to help him with his studying. A final-exam angel sent to get him through sophomore year of high school. Although, when all was said and done, she wasn't really helpful at all. He almost skipped his chemistry final just to have more time to hang out with her. She finally got him to go, saying, "I just helped you study for this test for almost two hours and you're not going to take the thing?" And by agreeing to meet up with him after the test.

Like a miracle, she was actually waiting where he had told her to meet him. At the skate park. He figured the skate park was the best place for an audience of kids to see him with a beautiful girl. Plus, most of the cool kids were someplace else, so she wouldn't have a comparative basis of just how lame he was by high school standards.

He was going to bring her flowers—picked fresh from the town hall's front steps—but he figured that would be corny. He wanted to bring her something, however, so he grabbed a couple of ice cream sandwiches from the school cafeteria and darted out to find her. By the time he got to the skate park on the hot, late June day, the ice cream looked like explosive diarrhea in a wrapper, and he was forced to throw them away. He walked toward her, wiping his hands on his shorts. She was sitting on a bench, watching the little-kiddie park next to the skate park. This was good. He at least had more athletic ability than the toddlers on the jungle gym (most of them, anyway).

"Hey," he said to her.

"Hey," she said with a smile like a fireworks display.

They went to Plymouth Rock Pizza for a couple of slices. Another place to be seen by classmates, from which he could still usher her out—like a president during an assassination attempt—should anyone of any coolness arrive.

"Is this place even remotely near Plymouth Rock?" she asked.

"I think it's within 200 miles," David said, paying for two pizza slices with the ten-dollar bill he'd bummed from Barry Nguyen earlier. And, as fate would have it, when they turned from the counter, there was Barry sitting at a booth with Gary Ong and Petey Ramirez. Actually, it wasn't really fate, as David had told Barry and Gary and Petey that he was going to be hanging out with a gorgeous babe, and they called bullshit. So he told them: be at Plymouth Rock Pizza and he'd produce her.

When he brought her over to their table, there was silence as their faces dropped. David introduced them to Raven, and Raven said, "What are you, like the whole Asian population of New Hampshire?"

"That's kind of racist," Barry said.

"I'm Puerto Rican," Petey said.

"I'm kidding," Raven said. "I'm Asian, too. I'm a Flip."

"Flip?" Gary said.

"Filipino," she said.

"You don't look Filipino," Gary said suspiciously.

"I'm half Russian."

"Ah," Barry said, "Ty govorish po-russki?"

"Da," Raven said, laughing.

David's face dropped. "You speak Russian?" he asked Barry.

"I got an app," he said.

"All right, we gotta go," David said, ushering Raven out the door like a president during an assassination attempt.

David took Raven on a tour of the bustling metropolis that was Standish, New Hampshire. It basically consisted of a diner, a sit-down restaurant, a pizza shop, a movie theater, a skate park, and a library. All places Raven had already seen. "There is a lake," David said. "Do you want to go swimming?"

Raven shrugged. "Maybe."

They went to David's house to see if any of his older sister's bathing suits would fit. She tried them on in the bathroom, and David stood outside the door in the hallway, pacing and sweating and doing all he could not to peek in through the keyhole. The bathing suits didn't fit, and Raven came out of the bathroom, saying, "Your sister might be the one girl with smaller boobs than mine."

"Your boobs aren't small," David said. "They're...." He didn't say what he wanted to say, which was that they were perfect. Instead, he said, "They're normal for...a girl. Your age." Even though he still wasn't sure what age she was.

They went to the family room in the basement and played video games and channel-surfed. Then they went outside and shot hoops in his driveway.

"What time do your parents come home?" Raven asked him, sinking a swish.

"Around five," he said, clanking his shot off the rim. "Want to stay for dinner?" The thought struck him suddenly with excitement. Sitting at the dinner table with this perfect girl, showing her off to his family. Catching the jealous glances from his sister. *Suck it, Janie. See? You're not all that.*

"Nah," Raven said, "think I'll pass on the family time. I should be going soon. I have to get back to the library at some point."

"We don't have to eat here. We could go out to dinner. Want to grab something more to eat? I got some money. We can go for a sit-down meal." He then shrugged casually, realizing his voice was winding up with a little too much excitement. "Or something like that. I was thinking of having a nice meal tonight. Treat myself for a job-well-done on my exams."

"Don't you have more exams to go?"

"Yeah. But, you know. I got the toughest ones out of the way."

She actually said yes to going to dinner, and the note he left for his family on the kitchen table read: *I won't be home for dinner tonight. I'm on a DATE!* He scratched out the part saying: *Suck it, Janie!*

They enjoyed dinner at a place called Slappy's, which was the name of Standish's "fancy" restaurant. Even with their constant conversation, David still knew nothing more about Raven, other than she was a Filipino-Russian with a Spanish-sounding last name.

After dinner, Raven said she needed to get back to the library. David tried to talk her out of it, but she wouldn't relent. They arrived at the library around seven. "Wait, why are the windows dark?" Raven said, running up the library's front steps. She yanked on the glass doors, which rattled stubbornly in her grip. "Why are the doors locked?"

"Oh, shit," David said, "I forgot, it's Friday. They close early on Fridays in the summer."

"But it's not summer," Raven said, still rattling the door.

"Well, I guess…" David looked up, counting on his fingers, "I guess not technically for a few days, anyway. But the summer hours have begun."

"But that.…" Raven rubbed her face, seemed to compose herself, and calmly said, "That kind of sucks."

"Why? What did you need in there anyway?"

Raven let out a breath and said, "Nothing. It's fine." She pulled a folded piece of paper and studied it as if it were going to tell her what to do. She then put it back in her pocket and came bounding down the steps. "Forget it, let's go." She grabbed his arm and ushered him away from the library.

"You still want to hang out?" he said, realizing just how shocked his tone sounded.

"You might be stuck with me for longer than you think," she said.

She told him, however, that it was imperative that he tell her when it was 11:30. She had to jet by midnight, she said.

"Why?"

"The whole turning back into a pumpkin thing."

"Got it," he said, amazed that she seemed to be the only girl in the world without a cellphone. He was also amazed at just how much fun being with another person could be when the person didn't have a fucking cellphone. And he never felt the need to look at his own cellphone either. Which is why time seemed to fly by, and he had no idea what time it was when they ended up on the banks of Standish Lake. Which, Raven had noted, was more like a pond.

"Men and their exaggerations," she'd said.

It was one of those perfect postcard nights. Calm. Not a ripple on the water. Moon reflecting off its surface. The moonlight caught the dim, distant forms of two swans making their way across glass. David and Raven sat on the edge of large, sloping slabs of rock, their bare feet buried in the shoreline's sand. It was the first break in their conversation, and they looked out over the water, trying to keep track of the swans. Raven suddenly let out six breathy, rhythmic huffs. "Che-che-che-ha-ha-ha."

"Are you okay?" David asked. For a moment, he thought she was hyperventilating, or was gulping air before lunging into the water.

Her smile flashed in the moonlight. "*Friday the 13th*? The lake. That sound…. No? Nothing?"

"I've never seen it," he said. Then he smiled. "How do you know so much useless shit?"

"Lot of time on my hands," she said.

"C'mon. How does a girl like you have a lot of time on her hands?"

She looked at him with an expression of sarcastic earnestness. "Well, if you must know, smart guy, I was kidnapped a few years back and sold into a sex-slave ring." She shrugged. "You have a lot of spare time when held in bondage."

David laughed. "Ha, okay. And they let you watch old movies in bondage?"

Raven shrugged. "Sure. Movies, television. I even surfed the internet, with a lot of restrictions." Her voice changed to a more serious tone. "I hacked through the restrictions once, but no one responded to my pleas for help. In the real world, no one cares."

The smile slipped off of David's face.

Raven began laughing. "You should see your expression."

The smile returned to David's face and he said, "Well, then, smart ass, how did you end up here?"

"A rampaging demon came and wiped out my captors, then I followed him through an interdimensional portal, and now I am helping him track down bad guys. Mostly child abusers. A lot of priests."

David shrugged. "All right. Sounds reasonable."

"How about you?" Raven said. "How did you come to know so little useless shit?"

David said, "I was kidnapped by aliens, and they put me in an intergalactic zoo for years, so I was unable to catch up on my pop culture. Or any culture, really."

"Billy Pilgrim in the flesh?"

"See, I have no idea what you're talking about."

They were watching each other now, instead of the lake.

Raven said, "Are you sure the aliens didn't give you an accidental lobotomy during an anal probe?"

David was silent a moment, his eyes drifting up over her head. Raven smiled as David blurted out, "Because my head is in my ass. I got that one."

Their eyes met again. David felt the gravitational field of her smile overwhelming his apprehension, and he began to lean toward her. He was really going to kiss this specimen of perfection. This was really happening.

"What time is it?" she said.

Or maybe it wasn't really happening.

He leaned back and pulled out his cellphone. It said it was 11:59.

"10:59," he said, putting the cellphone back in his pocket. The moment was too perfect to let anything get in the way of its completion. Not his approaching curfew, or her pumpkin-whatever. The gods would just have to understand. This perfect kiss needed to happen, here and now. Their eyes locked, and he leaned forward again. She didn't lean away. He sensed her lips, awaiting his, and then their lips met, and the clichés were true. Fireworks, butterflies, electricity spreading across his skin, that weightless, rising, floating feeling.

But then he realized that he really was rising. Her lips were gone. His shirt was tightening around his armpits. He opened his eyes and saw he was about eight feet off the ground, and before him was the face of Hell—though he, of course, didn't realize it was literally the face of Hell. To him, it looked as though the sloping stone slab had come alive and was holding him by the nape of his shirt, his feet dangling in the air above the sand.

"What are you doing to her?" the thing said, its voice pretty much exactly what David would imagine a rock monster to sound like.

Raven called out in shocked embarrassment, "Ira, stop." Her tone was like a daughter mortified by something her father was doing.

"Who is this?" the thing bellowed, and there was fire in its eyes.

David tried to wake himself up. Thinking, *See? I knew she was too good to be true, this day really was just a dream.*

"Ira, this is David. Put him down. He's not in your book. Go ahead and check. Go on."

The fire in the thing's eyes was not as intense, but there was a skeptical sneer on its granite features. "Hmmph," the thing grunted. David felt its breath wash across his face like the draft from a heated furnace. It smelled of burning coal. David closed his eyes. His armpits were becoming numb, and he could hear the slow, tearing sound of his shirt stretching.

"He's my friend," she said.

David's feet were on the ground again. He opened his eyes just enough to see the thing looking down from a height unfathomable for a human being. "Sorry," the thing sneered. David turned and looked at Raven.

"I truly am sorry, David," she said. "I had a really fun day with you. But I think I need to be going now."

"Uh-huh," David said, relieved that his voice still worked. And that he hadn't had a heart attack. Or peed himself.

"C'mon, Ira," Raven huffed, starting up the sloping rocks.

The thing that had lifted David grumbled and climbed the rocks after her.

"I can't believe you did that," she said.

"It looked like he was hurting you," the thing retorted.

"No, Ira, it was a kiss, and he's my age, not in your book."

"How was I to know?"

"And, by the way, I saw what you did to the Vatican…"

Their voices faded into the surrounding woods.

David stood on the edge of the lake, looking out over the water. He stood like that for twenty-two minutes before snapping from his daze and heading home.

2

Jacobs was sitting in the conference room, sipping his coffee and leaning back in one of the chairs with his feet up on the table. It was 2:30 in the morning. He was watching Callahan, who was standing before his rainbow map, trying to find some kind of pattern in the demon's movements. Oddly enough, Callahan's attempt to find order in any of this was the only thing offering comfort at the moment. The crazy guy was starting to sound more rational.

"If only we could figure out how to head the thing off," Callahan said, looking at the map. "Stake out who he is most likely to strike next."

"Do you have any idea how many pedophiles are out there? How would we know which one was next?" Jacobs didn't want to mention what Hill had told him about the Pope. The explosion at the Vatican couldn't be their guy. Hitting something that big? For the time being, he'd just believe the official reports of a gas explosion.

Callahan said, "Could we get one on, like, loan or something, and follow him?"

"Are you suggesting we get a known pedophile and send him out for children?" Jacobs said. The crazy guy was sounding irrational again.

"Could work," Callahan said, turning back to the map.

Jacobs was going to mount an argument when Ty burst into the room, waving a folder and saying, "You are not going to believe this one."

Callahan did not turn from the map to acknowledge Ty.

Jacobs said, "Do I need to remind you we are in the conference room of an FBI building, trying to find a pattern in the movements of a demon? What normalcy am I clinging to?"

"I was manning the cuckoo line," Ty said, referring to the job of fielding phone calls regarding tips on the case. "We got a witness who saw the demon."

"Okay. We got lots of them."

"This one says it's got an accomplice. A girl."

Callahan turned from his map as Jacobs dropped his feet off the table. "Where is this?" Jacobs asked.

"New Hampshire," Ty said. "And there was an attack in the same town the day before. We must have missed it because it appeared to be part of some biker turf war, but it fits the criteria for our demon."

"Two sightings in consecutive days in the same place?" Callahan said.

"Who's the witness?" Jacobs said.

"Some kid. Get this: kid is late for curfew, and when his parents are reaming him out and grounding him, he tells them he was attacked by a giant monster. Parents naturally think he's bullshitting them, but he won't relent, so they tell him they're going to call the police. Then the kid spills this story about meeting some girl, spending the day with her, and she tells him she escaped from a sex-slave ring after a demon rescued her. The kid thinks she's joking, but then a demon shows up. So the parents call the FBI to report this girl. Kid's demon matches our bogey. And there's more."

"What is it?" Jacobs said.

"We got a name for the thing."

Jacobs's mouth dropped. Callahan stepped forward a few steps, transfixed, as if about to give Ty a hug. The silence hung in the room for a few seconds before Jacobs and Callahan said, "What is it?"

"Ira," Ty said.

"Ira?" Jacobs and Callahan said.

3

Raven woke with the feeling of pins and needles. Ira had just left. The sky was rapidly lightening, the chirps of crickets loud in the bushes. There was a chill in the air, but the breeze hinted at a hot day ahead. She sat up on the aluminum bleacher and regarded the little league diamond in the brightening gray.

She thought back to their conversation the night before. She and Ira had stumbled across the diamond after cutting through the woods surrounding the lake. That had been after scaring the shit out of poor David Lee. And after her giving a proper scolding to Ira for doing so. When they'd found the field and bleachers, Raven suggested she hang out there for a while so she didn't have to wander around the town at night like a homeless person, even though technically that was what she was.

"Is it safe for you to spend the night here?" Ira had asked her.

"Probably not. So maybe you should hang and talk for a while."

Ira had looked off at the trees. Raven knew he was feeling the pull of the book's names.

She'd sat on the bottom bleacher. "C'mon, I want to hear about the Pope. I saw your handiwork on the news." Ira looked down at her, and Raven strained her neck to look up. She patted the bleacher beside her. "Sit. You got some explaining to do."

Ira took his typical moment of working things out in his brain as he peered down at the seat and then sat, his back hunched, arms pinned between his thighs, his knees almost shoulder-high. Raven thought he looked like a grizzly bear trying to perch on a sapling branch.

"So what happened that caused you to smash up the Vatican?"

Ira took a deep breath. "It doesn't matter."

"Yeah, it does. I helped you find those priests; I deserve to know what happened."

"The Holy See…he wasn't helpful. None of them know why the priests are not in my book."

"Is it that they don't know why priests aren't in the book? Or is it that they have no idea what the book is? Your communication skills aren't the greatest."

Ira stared off into the dark. His only response was a growling, "Hmmf."

"Is there anyone who would know?" Raven said.

"Yes."

"Can we go talk to that person?"

"He…" Ira narrowed his eyes. "He wouldn't be helpful."

He took a deep breath and said, "It is as it is. I don't know why the priests are not being punished for their sins. Or why they are not in the book. Or why…." He trailed off. "I guess not all names are in the book."

Raven said, "Who puts the names in the book?"

"I don't know."

"You keep talking about sanctioned deaths. Who is sanctioning these deaths?"

"I don't know."

"Who is in charge?"

"It's just…the way it is," he said.

"The way it *was*. You came up here. Was that sanctioned, as you say?"

"Nothing stopped me," Ira said, not unlike a child justifying a wrong. "It is more efficient for me to do it this way." He stood and looked down at her, his fists clenching, his voice taking on more of a growl. "They've forgotten my name. I need them to remember who I am. They need to realize their fates *before* they take innocence." He pulled the book from his pocket and held it up. "They need to accept the blame. And the consequences of their actions."

"It's okay, Ira," Raven said. "C'mon, sit down."

He sat.

"I get it," Raven said, her voice calming. "You got a job to do, and you want to do it the best you can."

Ira, scrunched up like the bear on the branch, stared off toward the unseen horizon again.

Raven scooted down a little and laid her head on the aluminum bleacher. She could feel Ira's heat radiate through the metal. She looked up at the stars. So many stars. And she noted that this was the first time she'd really stopped to look up at them. She'd been held captive for so long, and now that she was out, she never bothered to look up at the sky. Her eyelids were getting heavy. She hadn't had a good night's sleep in…about three years now.

"Is there a Heaven?" she said.

"I told you, I can only assume so."

"Don't you wonder what it is like?"

"No."

"I do," she said, her eyelids shutting. "I wonder if my parents are there together. I wonder if I'll see them again. Do you think we'll all be together again?"

"Who?"

"Me and my parents."

"I don't know."

Raven shifted onto her side, putting her hands under her head. She said, "You're supposed to say, 'yes, I will be with them again.'"

"But I don't know."

"It doesn't matter. You can still say it to me."

"You want me to lie to you?"

"It's not lying. It's comforting."

"What's the difference?"

"The difference is making someone feel better. You're allowed to lie to someone if it helps the person. If it makes them feel comforted. If it gives them hope."

Ira didn't say anything.

Raven said, "So do you think I will see my parents again in Heaven?"

"I don't know."

"You really suck at this comforting thing, Ira." She nestled a little more into the warm metal of the bleacher. "So, what are you going to do about the priests?"

"Nothing."

"Don't you care about why they aren't in your book?" Raven felt her thoughts begin to elongate and twist as they climbed toward slumber.

"I care," Ira said.

"What are you going to do now?" Raven said, her voice only a murmur as sleep took her.

"My job," Ira said.

She slept peacefully on the bench, waking occasionally to sleepily open her eyes and see the demon, unwavering, standing guard over her. When she saw him at these moments, he'd be looking down at his book, watching the names steadily appear, and when the sun came up, Raven knew he'd gone to try and catch up with the names.

4

In the back room of the Standish Public Library, Jacobs sat in front of a monitor as the town's "tech guy" fast-forwarded through grainy video footage of the library's different rooms. Callahan stood behind them, biting his index finger's nail and jiggling his foot up and down with bottled excitement. Beside Callahan was Joan, the children's librarian.

"Wait, I think that's her," Joan said. "The girl with the red bag on her shoulder." The tech stopped the fast-forward, and the four of them watched a girl dressed all in black with a bright red bag stroll through the library. "She was such an odd little creature," the woman said.

"How old was she?" Jacobs said. "I can't get a bead on her age from this."

Joan shrugged. "She said she was a graduate student, but she looked young. Except in the eyes. She looked old in the eyes." Joan shrugged again. "One of those people you can't tell the age of. She could have been anywhere from twelve to thirty."

"Helpful," Jacobs said.

The woman shrugged.

On the video, the girl began strolling along the bookshelves. She disappeared behind one of the shelves in the Mystery Section. A few minutes later, she could be seen in the Romance section. She casually dropped something on the floor and walked away.

"What is that?" Jacobs asked, squinting at the monitor.

Joan leaned forward. "I think that's a wallet. Someone found one in the Romance Section the other day."

"Did anyone claim it?"

"A gentleman did. He seemed confused as to why it was found in the Romance section."

"Do you know if anything was missing from the wallet?" Jacobs asked.

"I don't think so. Nothing reported."

Jacobs narrowed his eyes and watched the different video feeds follow the girl through the library. Jumping from room to room and camera to camera as if watching Hollywood's worst film editor at work. Something didn't sit well with him about the wallet, but he wasn't quite sure what it was yet. This girl found or stole a wallet and didn't take anything?

The girl walked into the computer section and sat at one of the ports. She produced a card from her bag.

"What is that?" Jacobs said.

"Looks like a library card," Joan said. "She's logging onto the computer. You need a library card to do so."

They watched Raven type into the fields. She stopped. Rubbed her face. Typed again. Looked around at the other people. Typed again. Stopped and sat watching the screen.

"Can you get her login information from that computer to get more about who she is?" Jacobs asked the tech guy.

"Yeah," the guy said. "Won't tell you who she is though."

"Why not?"

"It's not her library card. She still hasn't logged in yet. See? She's reading the instructions on the home screen. She's probably trying to figure out the password."

"Obviously the card's what she took from the guy's wallet," Callahan said.

Jacobs turned toward Callahan and said, "Well, yeah, obviously."

Callahan grimaced.

"She's in," the tech guy said, nodding at the monitor.

Jacobs returned his attention to the monitor. "She figured out a password? Isn't that, like, impossible?"

"All library accounts have the same password, unless it's changed. Whoever lost this card probably hadn't changed it, and she figured it out."

"She's crafty," Callahan said.

"Well, it *is* written right on the homepage," the tech guy said.

Raven got up from the computers and walked over to a table with a boy seated at it.

"That's the kid," Callahan said. "The kid, David. The one who reported this. He was telling the truth. She did approach him in the library."

They watched the rest of the scene unfold, David giving her paper and a pen and Raven writing down information and then leaving the library.

"There she goes," the tech guy said. "Want me to fast-forward again to see when she returns?"

"Yeah."

The video footage fast-forwarded through several hours,

taking over half an hour of real time, until Joan squawked, "There she is."

"What's the time-stamp?" Jacobs asked.

"8:02pm," the tech guy answered.

They watched Raven wander around the library, checking doors and peeking into rooms.

"What's she doing?" Joan asked with a hint of disgust in her voice.

Jacobs shrugged.

They fast-forwarded through her sitting and reading, stopping when she got up from the table and exited the library's main room. They then saw her appear in the downstairs hallway, striding toward the back door. She stopped and ducked into the elevator machine room.

"I'll be damned," Joan gasped.

They fast-forwarded through the cleaning crew's cleaning, and stopped when Raven emerged from the elevator machine room and climbed the stairs back into the library. She sat at the circulation desk reading a book.

"What book is she reading? Can anyone make that out?" Jacobs asked.

"It's the Bible," Callahan said.

"How can you tell?" Jacobs asked.

"I've read it enough to recognize it."

Jacobs pursed his lips and turned back to the monitor. "Wait, what's wrong with the feed?" he asked the tech guy.

"I don't know. That's weird," the tech guy answered.

The area of the video on the other side of the circulation desk was warped into a writhing spectrograph of colored peaks and valleys.

"It looks like she's talking to someone," Callahan said.

"There was no one else in the building. We watched the

cleaning crew leave and set the alarm," Joan said.

"Whoever she's talking to is blocked by this stupid squiggly thing," Jacobs said. "Can you clean this up?"

"I'm trying to," the tech guy said, fiddling with buttons on the monitor.

"She's moving," Callahan said.

They watched Raven go to the computers and look up something.

"We need the search history of that computer," Jacobs said.

"Uh-huh," said the tech guy, who stopped fiddling with the monitor and was now watching the video of this girl talking to what looked like a walking blob of static. Under his breath, he said, "How the fuck is the static following her like that?"

"Arnold," Joan snapped, "watch your mouth."

"He's right, though," Jacobs said. "It looks like she's talking to that static. We need to get this to the FBI computer lab to see if they can fix it up."

"You won't get anything, Agent Jacobs," Callahan said.

"Why not?"

"Demons can't be filmed. They have no soul."

"Demon?" Arnold asked.

Joan gaped at Callahan like he had just used some extreme profanity.

Jacobs took a deep breath and offered a feeble chuckle, "Yeah, ha, 'demon' is a nickname for a wanted fugitive."

"Wanted fugitive is a redundancy, Mr. Jacobs," Joan said, "and I would like to take another look at your credentials, please." She held out her hand.

"This is like that wicked old show about the FBI agents chasing ghosts and shit," Arnold said.

"Jesus, it's called *The X-Files*, and it's not that old," Jacobs said, standing and handing Joan a business card. He said,

"Here is the number for the FBI's Boston field office. Call them, they can confirm who I am. And someone from the bureau will be by to get this video for analysis." He turned to Callahan. "We should be going, Mr. Callahan."

"We still need to find this girl," Callahan said. "She is the key to finding the…." He stopped and glanced at Arnold and Joan. "This Ira fellow," he said.

Jacobs looked down at the girl on the television monitor. "I'm sure she's long gone. Like a needle in a haystack."

5

Outside the library, Callahan and Jacobs walked down Main Street toward the Denali. "I don't suppose you know how to find a needle in a haystack," Callahan said.

"Asks the guy whose followers tracked a demon across the planet?" Jacobs said.

"Demons leave a bigger footprint than little girls. Especially girls not wanting to be found. When David Lee initially reported her name, I contacted my associates to research her. There was nothing. Her digital footprint is zero. Raven Mijares doesn't exist."

They arrived at the Denali and Jacobs stopped at the vehicle's back bumper. He looked earnestly at Callahan. "No more communications via the internet."

Callahan looked shocked. "You think me obtuse enough to use a computer?"

"No phone calls."

Callahan chuckled. "Agent Jacobs, do you really think I'd use phone calls? I use a secure encryption app. In the past, you have made fun of my apparent paranoia, but I can assure you, no one outside of my Knowledge Fighters will ever know about any of this. And those men and women are impermeable."

"Aside from you blabbing about a demon in the library," Jacobs said as if to himself. He was looking across the street at a small breakfast joint.

"You have to believe me, Agent Jacobs, I will tell no one about any of this."

Jacobs returned his attention to Callahan. "Actually, I do believe you."

"Is that why Agent Malone hasn't accompanied us? You think someone is leaking information?"

"I don't know," Jacobs said. He started walking across the street.

"Where are you going?" Callahan called.

"Coffee."

"Impossible man," Callahan muttered, watching Jacobs mount the far sidewalk and open the breakfast joint's glass door. "Doesn't even ask if I want...." His voice trailed off when a girl stepped out of the restaurant's door as Jacobs, staring at his feet as if deep in thought, stepped in. The girl had black hair pulled in a tight ponytail and a bright red handbag over her shoulder.

It was the girl from the library. And Jacobs, the FBI agent, hadn't even noticed. Callahan strode across the street to intercept her.

When the girl spotted him, she began walking faster.

"Hey," Callahan called, waving his hand. "You, young girl, there. Wait."

The girl cut into an alley.

Callahan trotted after her. "Stop," he called. She didn't stop. He grabbed her arm and yanked her around to face him.

"Back off, dickhead, I'm not one to mess with," the girl hissed.

Callahan snatched the Jackie-O glasses from her face.

"Hey," she squeaked.

"It is you. The witch."

"Who you calling witch, bitch?"

"You're the demon's witch. Can you summon him, is that it?"

Understanding came into Raven's eyes. "I'll summon him right now, if you don't let go of me."

"You aren't going anywhere. I'm taking you back to headquarters. And you're going to answer some questions."

"Headquarters? Look, Inspector Gadget, you want answers?" She bit his hand. He grimaced and let go, but he was quicker than she thought and snagged her bag, reeling her in for a better grip.

"You will pay for this, you little demon-whore," Callahan growled. "Do you know what they do to witches?"

"Probably nothing, this being the twenty-first century."

"I wouldn't count on modernism to save you from my crew. I'll burn you myself."

Raven shut her eyes and began muttering. "Diabolum voco hominem ad necandum stultum et deformem." She opened her eyes and stared into Callahan's eyes. His grip on her loosened. The girl said, "Et diabolus, qui libenter audit verba mea, faciet sicut dico." Her eyes left his and focused on something behind him. A sly smile crept upon her face.

Callahan turned to look over his shoulder, cringing, sensing the bulk of the demon behind him.

But there was nothing there.

He turned back and felt an explosion of pain in his crotch. A pain so bad it numbed the lower half of his body and stole his breath. He dropped to his knees and looked up at her. She grabbed his collar and said, "Next time I'll summon him for real, motherfucker." She brought her palm square into the center of his face. With an explosion of light, he felt a soft snap in his nose and another burst of pain. "We'll see who's going to burn, asshole," she said.

Callahan fell onto his side, coughing and taking shallow gulps of breath through his mouth, trying to stave off the pain in his nose and crotch. Through a prism of tears, he watched the girl walk off through the alley. Despite the pain, he feebly shouted, "You'll burn, you little cunt." He broke into another fit of coughs and gasped, "I'll burn you myself." He collapsed back onto his side as he heard footsteps approaching.

"Callahan, Jesus, what happened?" Jacobs said, putting his hand on Callahan's shoulder.

"Girl," Callahan gasped. "The girl. Raven. She's here."

"Where?"

Callahan pointed down the alley. Jacobs trotted to the end of the alley, looking both ways at the end. He dropped his shoulders and, sipping his coffee, walked back to Callahan. Jacobs said, "She's gone." He looked down at Callahan. "Shit, man, are you okay? What the hell happened?"

"She attacked me," Callahan growled. "I need a hospital. Take me to a hospital."

Jacobs took out his cell phone.

"No. No," Callahan said, rising to his knees. "I don't need an ambulance."

Jacobs chuckled and said, "I'm not calling an ambulance. I just thought of how to find a needle in a haystack."

"How?"

"Burn the haystack."

6

Raven had been riding with Carl for only twenty-two minutes and she had already heard his entire life story. How he was a star athlete in high school with a full athletic scholarship to Brown University—"You know, that Ivy League school in New Jersey?" "You mean Princeton?" "No, Brown. The one in New Jersey"—but it didn't pan out because of a "horrific knee incident" (his words), so he was hired as an engineer straight out of high school—"Like a train engineer?" "No, like the building designing kind"—because of his "mad skills" building displays at Nashua's Lego store. He built a replica of the Taj Mahal that was so sound they couldn't even damage its structural integrity with a quarter-stick of dynamite. "And believe me, we tried."

It was on a worksite in New York City, building a twenty-story high-rise in a "Deco-Gothic motif," that he had a "horrific back incident," which led him back to Ayres, New Hampshire. Luckily, he just happened to be in Standish, checking out a bid to redesign the Standish Library—had she heard of it?—when he came across her looking for a ride because her car broke down and she needed to get to a job interview. Now, driving down I-95, he was on about politics. How no one paid attention to facts and news or anything anymore. But not him; he paid attention to everything. He wasn't going to be taken by shyster politicians. "Live free or die," that was the state motto, and if there was anything he hated more than fags and wetbacks, it was some shyster politician who was going to take away his benefits. "You gots to be informed," he said.

A rhythmic screeching cut through the radio's music. Carl stopped talking as a voice on the radio said: "This is a message from the Emergency Broadcast System. An Amber Alert has been issued in the state of New Hampshire. Be on the lookout for Raven Mijares, who has been missing for a week. Raven is a sixteen-year-old female with black hair and brown eyes. She was last seen in Standish, New Hampshire—"

"Hey, Standish," Carl said, pointing at the radio.

"—Wearing a black shirt, black jeans, and carrying a red handbag—"

Raven scrunched her bag between her body and the passenger door.

"—She is considered to be in extreme danger. Please contact New Hampshire State Police or the FBI with any information regarding the whereabouts of Raven Mijares."

The high-pitched sub-diving alarm sounded again, and then the music returned.

"How about that?" Carl mused. "We was just in Standish. Anyway, like I said, it's important for people to be paying attention to what's going on around them…."

Raven glanced out the window at the passing New Hampshire landscape, wondering if she could talk Carl into getting her all the way down to Nashua.

7

She cut the ride short, stopping in a place called Berry, not far from Nashua. As Carl had become more comfortable, his sexual advances had grown more emboldened, until he'd made a very thinly veiled request for a blowjob—if she was tired, he said, she could put her head on his lap, and if she wanted, could give him "lap kisses." They passed the "Berry, one mile" sign on the highway, and Raven said, "Berry, here we are. That's where I need to be."

"Thought you said Nashua."

"No, I said near Nashua."

They pulled into a strip mall parking lot, and Raven quickly hopped out of the truck, saying, "Thanks, Carl, good luck with your building designing."

"But what about my lap kis—"

She shut the door and walked toward the Berry Post Office with purpose, figuring he wouldn't follow her into a federal building. She was almost to the door, reaching for the handle, when she heard the squealing tires of Carl's exit. She stopped.

Her picture was on the post office's front door. It was a grainy picture pulled from the library surveillance cameras. They'd had reason to check the video after all. Obviously, David had told them he'd met her there. The sign had the same information as the radio announcement: Amber Alert, girl in danger, Raven Mijares.

Why had she given David her real name?

Because she liked being Raven Mijares again. She liked being a teenager again. She liked being normal again.

You'll never be normal again, she thought, *not when you have a demon come and scare your boyfriends away.*

But how did they get my age? she wondered, gawking at the sign. She didn't think she'd told David that. They must have estimated it, maybe? She read the phrase: "Please contact the FBI." The FBI was after her—was that the headquarters that creep in the alley was talking about? Did the FBI really want to charge her with witchcraft?

Someone came up behind her. Raven ducked her head and strode away from the post office. On the far end of the strip mall was a supermarket.

She scrounged her final quarters from her purse and bought a *New York Times* from a dispenser. She lingered outside the store for a while, reading the paper and glancing toward the post office to gauge how many people stopped to look at the poster on the door. No one did.

The *Times* was filled with headlines of chaos and mayhem. There was even an editorial asking: COULD THIS BE THE

END? The editorial focused mostly on the increase in panic and conspiracy theories coinciding with the uptick of violence and tension in the world.

Raven glanced up from the paper as a woman passed her with a full shopping cart and two young children in tow. Blowing a strand of her black, bobbed hair out of one of her large, dark eyes, the woman stopped at a minivan and tended to one of her whining children. Raven tossed the newspaper into a trashcan and moved toward her.

8

Raven stared into the mirror of a gas station restroom. She figured it would offer the most privacy, and not be as noticeable when she left it a mess. The walls of the place were like the hands of a mechanic, streaked with the ghosts of black grease that no soap could ever quite cut through. The toilet bowl was coated with a substance that looked like yellow cake uranium.

She now wore a simple, floral sundress—wanting to look as sweet-suburban-mom-like as she could. The biker boots didn't go with the outfit, but she wasn't ready to part with them—she thought of them as a trophy for overcoming Benjamin's biker gang. She had reluctantly downgraded to a simpler brown bag, rather than the bright red Prada knock-off. The license she'd lifted from the mother in the supermarket's parking lot was propped up against the bathroom mirror. The woman's big, brown eyes stared from the photo. There was nothing Raven could do about their difference in weight— according to her license, the woman was about forty pounds heavier—but the haircut…. Raven took the scissors she'd bought and began cutting her hair into the same bobbed style.

With a pang, realizing she could probably have sold the hair for a few bucks, Raven scooped as much of it as she could into the trash can. She then returned the key to the gas station attendant, whose face betrayed confusion—not quite grasping why this girl looked different than the girl to whom he'd given the key. There was a motel across the street from the gas station, and she darted to it with her final new purchase: a small suitcase on wheels.

Raven pretended to struggle as she hefted her suitcase through the door. In fact the suitcase was empty except for her red bag, which, like the boots, she hadn't been willing to part with. The girl behind the desk shifted her gaze from her smartphone to a television in the corner of the lobby, as if her eyes needed to be locked on a screen at all times. "Yeah?" the girl huffed.

"I need a room, please," Raven said cheerfully, placing her bag on the desk and pulling the mother's wallet from it.

The girl regarded the cheap bag as though it were roadkill. She huffed again and said, "I need an ID and a credit card."

"I'm paying cash," Raven said. She'd used the credit card to buy her new clothes and bag—keeping a running tab in her mind, assuring herself that someday she would pay Sarah Watson back for all this—but she didn't want to push it. There was a good chance Mrs. Watson had reported the card lost or stolen by now, and Raven still had a pretty good wad of cash from Zippy's.

The girl seemed to chew gum that she didn't actually have in her mouth and said, "Fifty dollar room deposit."

"What are your rates?"

"Hundred a night," the girl said, still watching the television.

"I'll take one night," Raven said.

Raven heard her name being spoken and fought the urge

to turn. "Once again," a voice on the television was saying, "An Amber Alert has been issued for sixteen-year-old Raven Mijares. If you have any information, please contact the FBI."

The girl behind the counter was typing away on a computer, seemingly oblivious. "Better make it two nights," Raven said. It would clean her out financially, but she needed to stay out of sight for as long as possible. Let that creep from the alley and the FBI think she was still on the road somewhere.

The girl sighed heavily. "Two?" she said, without looking up from the computer.

"Yes, please."

"It'll be 268. ID?" The girl didn't look up from the computer as her hand sprang out.

"Excuse me?"

"I need your ID."

"Oh, of course," Raven said, handing her Sarah Watson's license.

The girl snatched the license, paused to glance at it, and kept typing. She looked at it more closely as she typed the information into the computer. The girl's hand sprang back with the license. Raven took it and returned it to Sarah Watson's wallet. "268 dollars," the girl said.

Raven dug out the wad of money, counting out $268 and handing it over to the girl. She had six dollars left.

The girl handed Raven a key on a cracked plastic keychain and said, "You're in room 6. Out and to the right. Enjoy your stay at The Berry Motor Lodge."

"Thank you," Raven said, wanting to say, *That's it*? She'd thought she was going to need more of a con. Explain why she didn't look 31 years old, or 142 pounds. Why a sweet looking woman like Sarah Watson was staying two nights alone in a seedy motel. But the girl didn't ask.

Raven rolled her suitcase to the door, pretending again that there was some heft to it, then rolled it across the parking lot toward her room.

The girl behind the counter, however, did have a rudimentary understanding of the world outside her phone—maybe because it was posted all over her phone. She *had* wondered why Sarah Watson didn't look 31 years old, and why she wasn't 142 pounds, and why sweet Mrs. Watson looked like she'd just chopped off all her hair in a gas station restroom. The girl behind the counter was going to call the FBI—she just needed to post it on her social media feeds first.

9

The phone's ringing brought Callahan into the connecting doorway between the motel rooms. With his black eyes and the tape across his nose, he looked to Jacobs like a cross between Jake LaMotta and Jake Gittes. Since being discharged from the hospital, he'd spent his time sticking Post-its all over the wall, trying to recreate a rudimentary map like the one in the FBI field office.

Jacobs had been standing at the window of his room, watching the breeze dance through the leaves of a large maple tree beside the Mayflower Motel's parking lot, wondering why everything in this town seemed to be Pilgrim related. He answered the phone. "Yeah?"

"You're supposed to identify yourself, Agent Jacobs," Thompson said on the other end of the line.

"This is Agent Jacobs, how may I direct your call?"

"Direct yourself to Berry, New Hampshire. The girl has been spotted at The Berry Motor Lodge. You are to meet your strike team at Berry PD."

"Strike team?" Jacobs said.

Callahan stepped further into his room.

"Avoid any press," Thompson said. "Someone posted online that they'd found Raven. The FBI has stated to the press that this is factually inaccurate. You're to stay out of the way of the strike team, but I was able to get you and Callahan first access to the room after it's cleared."

"What do you mean first access? It's our case."

"There are other agencies in the game now. Play this one for real. Those people in white buildings are taking this very seriously."

10

It was almost midnight, and Raven was on the motel room's bed, propped up against the pillows and the headboard. She flipped through the reality television rejects and infomercials and late night talk shows. If her demon friend wasn't a sign of End Times, then what was on television certainly was.

She felt twinges of hunger mixed with the start of menstrual cramps. Not the best time for her period. With all that was happening, she hadn't even realized it was that time. Her captors had all shunned her during this time, mostly because they couldn't use her for what they'd paid for, like she had some kind of defect a company had not disclosed. The sheik had gone as far as saying she was unclean and an abomination in that condition, segregating her. She hadn't minded the segregation. It was a nice respite from having to deal with the sheik. Sometimes Ahmad would bring her meals, even though he was not supposed to. One of the other "harem" girls was the only one allowed any contact with her during this time.

Now, in hiding, she needed supplies. And money. But with her face splashed all over the news, it was best to stay put. If she didn't go shopping soon, however, she would be spending the next few days rigging maxi pads out of toilet paper, or taking a perpetual shower.

Her channel surfing landed on a news broadcast. The talking head—a woman with a heavily highlighted hairdo so perfect it looked like it was poured from concrete—was saying, "Police are still investigating the brutal deaths of three fraternity members at FSU. The three boys allegedly drugged thirteen-year-old twin sisters as part of an initiation pledge. Police say the boys were found with drastic injuries to their heads and torsos. Officials offer no further descriptions."

The Gray Zone doorway appeared beside her and Ira stepped into the motel room. He seemed almost shocked when he realized where he was.

"Speak of the devil," Raven said.

"What about him?"

She smiled. "They were just talking about you on the news. Well, about your handiwork. At least, it sounds like you."

Ira looked at the television. "Oh, yeah. Them." He looked around. "Where did this room come from?"

"I spent the last of the money on it. And FYI: I'm wanted by the FBI. So I'm kinda stuck here." Raven's smile fell. She winced with a wave of cramps.

"Are you all right?"

"Yes, I'll be fine. I have cramps."

"Are you sick?"

"No, it's just cramps."

"Did you eat something poisonous?"

Raven grinned. "No, dummy. Cramps. It's that time of the month."

"Time of the month for what?"

"You know. Woman issues."

Ira still regarded her with confusion. "What is a woman issues?"

"Menstruation," Raven said.

Ira twisted his face.

Raven's grin turned to a sneer. "What is that for?"

He said, "The blood…it's…."

"It's what?" Raven said, standing and putting her hands on her hips.

"Disturbing."

Her voice was rising, almost to the menace Ira was capable of. "Why is it fucking disturbing?"

Ira looked guiltily at the floor and shrugged. "It is uncomfortable to bleed from someplace so delicate."

"You're telling me that you have a rising body count of dismemberment, but this is the blood flow you can't fucking stomach?"

"But it's your blood, and…."

"And what?"

He stopped, his eyes focusing on a distant idea. "I feel bad for your discomfort."

Raven, still with hands on hips, looked him up and down. The anger leaving her voice, she said, "I don't know if that's sweet or fucking stupid. But regardless, you know what this means, right?"

"That you are not pregnant," Ira said.

"Well, yes, genius, but also that I need tampons. And food. Tag, you're it, big guy, you're gonna have to go shopping."

11

The supermarket was empty at this hour. Silent and dimly lit. The few illuminated fluorescents casting shadows of the shelves. Standing in the dimness was Wrath, punisher of the wicked, destroyer of armies, shopper of tampons. Having Gray Zoned into the deli department, he stood tentatively at the back of the store. To him, the place smelled like the Third Ring of Hell. He saw a sign reading, "take a number," so he, struggling with his giant fingers, took one, not knowing if he'd need it for some reason later. Raven had said the main item she needed would be in an aisle containing "feminine products." Ira looked up and saw those words emblazoned on a sign above Aisle 9, all the way down the other end of the supermarket.

He strode in that direction, passing rows of meats on display. She'd said he should grab food, too. He thought meat would be the best food, but she had specifically said nothing that had to be cooked, or would spoil, or wasn't easy to carry. She said to get something called "Power Bars" in the breakfast section. At the end of the meat display was a rack of dried meats in sealed plastic. He read the label: "Jerky." He shrugged and grabbed a handful (which for him was almost the whole display). It was meat, it didn't need to be cooked, and it was easy to carry.

Medicine lined the racks of Aisle 3. He detoured down the aisle. Raven said that he should get something called Ibuprofen. He regarded the countless boxes and bottles. When he found a bottle labeled "Ibuprofen," he nimbly plucked it out with his giant fingers. He also took a bottle called "vitamins," which she had also said she would need.

In Aisle 4, he found the breakfast foods. He took five boxes of "Power Bars." At the end of the aisle, he came across jars of peanut butter. Raven had said that peanut butter paired with bread, something she called a P, B, and J, would be a great source of easy protein. Ira picked out five jars, realizing she had never told him what the J stood for. He was beginning to realize that this all was not as easy to carry as she had insisted, and he shifted the items into the crook of his elbow. In the next aisle, he found the bread. He took three loaves. Whole wheat, as Raven had instructed.

Next came the bottled water. "Can't live without water," Raven had said. Ira piled three one-gallon jugs into his arm. He saw cases of bottled water beside the jugs. That might be better. He maneuvered one of the cases into his armpit, hanging two of the gallon jugs from his fingers and abandoning the third. He turned and saw the fruit juices. Raven had said that cranberry juice would help with her "vaginal health." When he'd winced at the word, she'd said, "You've got a problem with vaginas?" "No," he'd sulked. "It's just a lot of information."

He now walked down the aisle, inspecting the labels on each bottle. There didn't seem to be cranberry juice. Grape-cranberry, cherry-cranberry, pomegranate-cranberry. There was something called cranberry cocktail. Was that the same as cranberry juice? He picked up the bottle. "Real cranberry juice," he said, reading what was printed in big letters on the front label. He put the bottle on his pile of items in his arm. He picked up another one, but he noticed in finer print on the back, *27% juice.*

"Twenty-seven percent? That's not real juice," he said.

The bottle of cranberry cocktail on his arm began to roll. He deftly returned the other bottle to the shelf and caught the bottle falling from his arm, placing it back on the pile in one clean motion, but the bottle on the shelf teetered and fell. Ira bent to catch it. To keep the bottle on his pile from falling again, he had to shift his weight, and he turned and scooted, keeping everything in place, but bumping the row of shelving with his rear end. The entire row tilted and fell, crashing to the floor with thunderous reports of glass and metal on linoleum. Ira looked down at the mess, his shoulders drooping. The cranberry cocktail bottle on top of the pile in his arm rolled and fell, breaking at his feet. He growled and turned toward Aisle 9, still holding the final cranberry juice in his free hand.

He came to Aisle 9.

"Tampons, not maxi pads," that had been Raven's strict instructions. "Say it back to me, Ira. *Tampons, not maxi pads.*"

"Tampons, not maxi pads," he had growled back.

But there were several different boxes of tampons. Which was he supposed to get her? He saw one that claimed it had "The Best Protection." That must be the one.

He placed the cranberry cocktail down carefully on the floor, and, looking sheepishly up and down the aisle, as if someone might see him, he plucked the box from the shelf. Turning to leave, he saw another box claiming that it was the "Ultimate Protection."

Wasn't ultimate better than best? But how could anything be better than best?

He returned the boxes to the shelf, still trying to calculate the virtues of best versus ultimate, when he saw another box claiming it was "Protection You Can Count On." That sounded not as good as the best or the ultimate, but he picked it—in his experience, superlatives were the claims of the false-hearted.

Bending to pick up the cranberry cocktail, the items in his arm shifted again. As he scrambled to catch them, he kicked the bottle on the floor. It shattered, creating a puddle of sticky redness, into which all the other items fell.

Ira groaned, looking around the store. Toward the front was a row of shopping carts. He imagined what Raven would say to him at that moment, and the word spilled from his mouth. "Duh."

12

Raven was above Benjamin. The butter knife held in both hands. She drove the blade into his face, between the eyes. His eyes crossed comically toward the hilt sticking out of his head like a demented unicorn horn. Blood spilled out of the wound, streaking his face red. But then there was suddenly a hand over her mouth. She didn't need to turn to know it was Zippy. Below her, Benjamin's eyes uncrossed and he looked straight at her. A smile spread beneath the gore, and he said, "Nice try."

Raven's eyes opened. She was in the motel room. Holding the folded page of Ira's book to her face, she inhaled the smoky scent, and sat up on the bed. She unfolded the page and stared at it. Then she snatched the pen from the nightstand and wrote on the page: *Are you there? Can you hear me?*

The space beside the bed split open and Ira came through it, pushing a full shopping cart.

"Did you get my message?" she blurted.

"What message?" Ira said, sounding as if out of breath.

"I wrote—" she began, but stopped, taking note of his expression. "You okay?"

"Do not ask me to do that again."

Raven hopped off the bed and looked into the shopping cart. "Nice job." She picked out the sticky box of tampons, stained a deep red. "Is this blood?"

"It's cranberry cocktail. There was an…incident."

"Oh good, you got cranberry juice. Where is it?"

Ira growled and looked at his feet.

"Okay, that's fine," she said. "Looks like you got everything else." She opened the box of Power Bars and the box of tampons, snatching a bar and slipping several tampons into her pocket. She turned to face Ira. "Thanks, big guy," she said. A wave of cramps hit her and she winced, grabbing her stomach.

"Are you okay?" Ira rushed forward and put his giant hand on her shoulder, his six fingers draping over her back. It was the first time he'd shown any real affection toward her. She pushed past his hand and grabbed his waist, gripping him in a hug, her ear against his stone-like stomach. She listened hard and thought she detected the faintest echo of a heartbeat. His hand, tentative and unsure, patted her back. She could have stayed there for some time, could have even fallen asleep standing against that stone wall, but his hand stopped patting and hung in the air. His comforting could only go so far.

Raven pulled away, still holding her stomach. "Anyway, thanks," she said and shuffled into the bathroom. "Maybe you can find a place for the groceries," she said before shutting the door behind her.

She had Ira's Book pressed to her stomach. Why she had lifted it, she wasn't sure. Curiosity, she supposed. Or maybe just because it was there, and she could.

The book felt alive in her hands, vibrating with energy, as if at any moment it would squirm out of her grip like a cat no longer wishing to be held. She lowered the toilet's lid and sat down.

She held the book up, her fingers tingling as she inspected the ancient, worn leather. There was no writing anywhere on the outside of the volume, and it smelled old. And burnt. She opened the Power Bar and began to eat it, hesitating before opening the book's cover. For a moment, it felt like the thing was locked shut, like she needed to be as strong as Ira to open it. But then she realized it was just her apprehension, and, when she mustered the courage, it opened easily.

The pages seemed to glow, backlighting the names burnt into the pages with sweeping calligraphy. She flipped through the book, pages fluttering in a blur. And they kept fluttering. She should have reached the last page long ago, but still the pages kept passing, the names moving like etchings in a demented flip book. The effect was nauseating and she snapped the book shut.

She finished her breakfast bar and threw the wrapper away. She looked at the book again, sliding her fingers along the volume's spine, coming to the leather place-marker. She lifted the blade. It was heavy and tarnished. Raven waved the blade in the air and felt it catch. A gray slit appeared in the air and then shut again. Remembering the shade from Sheol's fingers in her mouth, she let the blade fall. She opened the book to the pages held by the place-marker. A page and a half of names. The last one being Ungar Lundquist. As she traced the name with her eyes, she saw a new name burn into the page. Ahmet Akdağ appeared as if written by an invisible hand. And then another name. Abílio Borge. And then another name. She shifted her gaze up the column of names, and saw the phrase: *Are you there? Can you hear me?* But it was not in her writing.

Raven shut the book. Who was writing these names? How many were there? How many more were on their way? They came so relentlessly; how could anyone keep up? How much punishing would Ira have to do? What did this punishing do to him? How much of his human half was left?

A lot, she thought. More than should be. This demon was still outside the bathroom putting away groceries and waiting to see that she was all right, despite his duty to dispatch the climbing number of names in his book.

The book she had stolen from him.

Raven stood and placed the book on the back of the toilet. She took a tampon from her pocket and took care of what needed to be done. When she was finished, she caught her reflection in the mirror.

She noticed movement.

In the mirror's corner was the reflection of the window behind her. It was high in the wall, about three feet by four feet. Had she seen someone out there? The window would be about seven feet up on the building's outside wall. No one was tall enough to be peeking into it without a ladder. Except Ira. Did he know about the book? Was he spying on her? But he wasn't the spying type. He was definitely more the direct-approach type. If he'd realized she'd stolen the book, he'd have let her know it by now.

She turned to look at the window as something came crashing through the glass. Raven was out the bathroom door, screaming Ira's name, by the time the clanking metal thing bouncing across the bathroom floor popped with its firecracker report and began hissing thick smoke.

13

Given that the FBI was unsure whether the girl was an accomplice or a kidnap victim, the teargas was supposed to drive her into the bedroom so the main entry team could apprehend her and the suspect at the same time. Sargent Jedediah Leonard, second man in, was to follow the point man, B.J. Philips, through the front door, keeping his left hand on Philips's back until he was inside and could cover his Area of Responsibility. But as soon as he crossed the door's threshold, everything went what he'd call FUBAR. The point man screamed and was gone from beneath his hand. He had the sense that Philips was flying across the room. Leonard knew that he had to keep to his AOR, but he couldn't help looking at Philips disappearing into the fog of teargas in the bathroom. Leonard heard his own breathing quickening in his gas mask and the girl was screaming, "Ira, Ira." And then he heard her hacking coughs as the teargas took hold of her.

Leonard still felt Steven Lloyd's hand on his back as he led Lloyd and two other men further into the room. The AR-15 came up by instinct, butt against his shoulder, sightline searching for the target, his right finger slipping in through the trigger guard—but then he went momentarily weightless before hitting the back wall of an open closet. He popped up to his feet, but the closet door shut and knocked him back on his ass. His weapon went off, hollow tapping of rounds puncturing the wooden door, swinging it open again as splinters sprayed. David Dumille, the rear entry man, was now in the bathroom's doorway. Dumille raised his weapon, only to be knocked back into the bathroom by an airborne Lloyd.

A man screamed and the front window crashed. Then Leonard heard only his own confused, racing breathing. He scurried to get his feet under him and was halfway into a crouch when he spotted the target standing in the center of the room. It was a huge, red man, and it was holding the final member of the entry team, Rick Grimes, from the strap of his AR-15. The giant turned and looked at Leonard, who was almost to his feet, and it said to him in a deep growl, "Sit."

Leonard sat back down on the closet's floor. Grimes came tumbling down upon him, and the closet door swung closed, bounced off Grimes's foot, and opened again. Grimes's weight had knocked the air out of Leonard's lungs, and he'd felt something pop in his shoulder, but with the adrenaline rushing through him, he felt no pain as he heaved Grimes off of him and climbed to his feet. He brought his weapon up and peeked around the edge of the closet door.

The giant now stood outside the motel room's front doorway, cradling the coughing girl in his arms.

Over the crackle of a PA, Sterling Morrow, the operation's commander, was saying, "Put the girl down and put your hands up."

The giant stepped out into the night.

Leonard swept over to the front door, spotting the giant, which was lit in a blinding spotlight. The dissipating tendrils of teargas gave it the appearance of standing in fire.

To the left was the G-Men's unmarked SUV. To the right the tactical team's van and two State Police Interceptors. In the middle was the M1117 Armored Vehicle. Bill James was situated in the top hatch with the fifty cal. trained on the giant. The rest of the motel was silent, all the guests having been evacuated.

"Put the girl down," Morrow called over the M1117's PA.

Leonard raised his weapon again, his finger slipping into the trigger guard. The giant turned his head, its fiery eyes falling onto him. The unsaid implications were deafening: *I told you to stay in the closet.*

Leonard lowered his weapon and backed up a step.

The giant put the girl down.

With a final coughing fit, she stood a little wobbly.

Morrow called over the PA. "Okay, honey, you're okay. Come to us."

The girl paused a moment.

"It's okay," Morrow called over the PA. "Come to us."

The girl looked at the giant and then began walking—not toward the M1117, but instead toward the tactical van.

Why is she going that way? There's no one there, Leonard thought. *No, little girl, go the other way.*

Morrow called out, "No, honey, the other way."

The girl ran for the tactical van.

There was a moment of silence before FUBAR somehow went worse. The giant charged at the M1117. James opened up the 50 cal., the sound thundering over the small town. But the giant didn't stop. *How the hell are those rounds missing at that range?* Leonard thought, but then he realized the rounds weren't missing.

The giant hit the M1117 with his right shoulder. The vehicle tilted on its tires, then righted like a boat taking a rogue wave broadside. The giant pushed again. James ducked inside the hatch as the armored vehicle tipped over with a loud crunch of metal.

The popping of the AR-15s rang out as Leonard squeezed off a burst of rounds. Amidst the gunfire, a screaming girl's voice called, "Ira, Ira, come on."

The target ran for the tactical team's van. Leonard followed with the barrel of his weapon. He fired off another burst as the giant squeezed through the open back doors of the van and disappeared inside of it.

A male's voice fought through the chaos, "Hold your fire. Hold your fire."

Leonard stopped firing and turned to see the G-man waving his hands. Machine gun fire continued and the G-man scrambled for a walkie. Leonard's earpiece crackled. "Hold your fire. Hold your fire," the G-man said. "The girl is in the van. This is still a hostage situation."

The gunfire stopped. The parking lot was ultra-quiet. Leonard trained his weapon on the van's open back doors. On his right, Logan was leaning against the wall beneath the broken window through which he'd been thrown.

Morrow called over the radio, "Meet at CP 1."

"Here we go again," Logan said, climbing to his feet.

Grimes, now standing behind Leonard, said, "Hooah."

The three men made their way toward the M1117 with their weapons trained on the van's back door. Phillips, Dumille, and Lloyd exited the motel room, their weapons raised. Leonard was almost to the overturned armored vehicle when they all stopped.

The engine of the tactical van started—it was common practice to leave the keys in the ignition during a raid. The team stood in the silent parking lot and watched as the van, with a rev of the engine, smashed past the two State Police Interceptors and sped off into the night.

14

Raven had expected the van's tires to spin dramatically, as had happened when Ahmad taught her to drive stick on the sheik's Lamborghini. But instead, the van lurched and barreled forward, the engine revving. The impact with the police cars was more jolting and louder than she had expected—more violent than the cars crashing through barriers on television and movies—and she let out a small, girlish, scream. Promising herself she would not ever squeal like that again, she shifted into second gear and swung the van onto the main road. She knew that the highway was about two miles away. Maybe she could lose them on the open road. It was as good a plan as any until she heard the thump-thump-thump of helicopter rotors.

Damn, she thought as she groped the instrument panel for the headlights. She popped them on, swerving around a car taking a left turn. She glanced in the rearview mirror, seeing only Ira's broad back as he took up almost the entire rear of the van. He sat calmly watching the road behind them through the open back doors, like a child watching television. Raven glanced in her side mirror to see the State Police Interceptors pull onto the road with emergency lights flashing. She heard the sirens cut through the pounding of the helicopter rotors.

"We need to get rid of this company, Ira. Can you do something about that?"

A car pulled out in front of the van. Raven swerved wildly to avoid it, jerking the van into oncoming traffic and then yanking it back into her lane before almost hitting another car head-on. The maneuver should have sent a passenger in the back pinballing, but Ira didn't budge.

"What do you mean, get rid of?"

"Can you stop them somehow?"

Ira regarded the objects scattered around the back of the van. Kevlar vests and helmets hanging from the wall, rifles nestled into a gun rack, and, on the floor, a duffle bag filled with equipment.

"It would be very unwise to employ aggressive actions on these people at this speed. I don't want to kill them."

"We don't have to kill them. Can't we just…I don't know—" Raven swerved again, narrowly missing a police cruiser coming from the other direction. "Shit," she said. "Can't we just, like, hamper their efforts? If they catch up to us, it's gonna get real ugly real quick."

The police cruiser spun in a 180 and joined the pursuit. Another coming from the opposite direction pulled into her lane as a barricade. "Oh, you asshole," Raven said. "Hold on," she called to Ira, although it was more to herself than to the demon in the back.

She veered, clipping the front end of the police car. The impact was deafening, jolting through her arms and rattling her teeth, but this time she didn't squeal. The police car spun away from them into a twisted metal heap, but the van kept on trucking. "C'mon, Ira, what can you do for us here?"

Ira looked beside him and saw a cluster of tactical helmets hanging from the van's wall. He picked one from the bunch and inspected it. "These look like Nazi helmets," he said. "I dealt with a lot of wearers of such helmets."

"Now's not really the time for reminiscing," Raven said, spotting the sign for the highway onramp. "Let's do this quick. Be good to lose them before the highway."

The police Interceptor was gaining on them. Raven was familiar with the PIT maneuver. Ahmad had once explained it to her. The pursuing car was going to come up beside the rear quarter of the van and nudge it into a spinout, cutting the engine or—the more likely scenario for this top-heavy vehicle—flipping it.

"How far to the highway?" Ira said.

"About a hundred meters." She had no idea why she was using metrics all of a sudden. Maybe because she felt like she was back East with Ahmad, opening up the Lamborghini, or the Ferrari, or her favorite, the Shelby Cobra. "We need to do it quick, Ira. I have to slow for the turn, and he's about to PIT me." Up ahead, she could see the onramp lit in the helicopter's spotlight. "Ira?" she called, letting impatience into her voice.

"Make the turn," he growled.

"Jesus," Raven muttered and down shifted, the engine revving violently, the tachometer jumping. The Interceptor made a last-ditch effort, racing to the side of the van. Before it could get there, Ira threw the helmet at the front of the car, embedding it like a cannonball deep into the grill. The Interceptor lost speed, steam pouring from the hood. It spun out, wedging itself between the onramp's guardrails, creating an instant barricade for the other pursuing cars. "Holy shit,"

Raven screamed, watching the pileup in the side mirror as she negotiated the turn.

The highway was dark, no other headlights, only the dim glow of the moon and the slicing spotlight of the helicopter. "Ira, we got one more guest we need to unload."

Ira peered out the back doors, glancing up at the helicopter. He groaned, looking around the back of the van.

"Is there a way of bringing them down without killing them?" Raven said.

Ira took a grenade from the duffle bag. "I could throw this at them. Is this the one that makes you cough?"

"No, I think that's the one that goes boom," Raven said, hoping the depictions she'd seen of grenades in movies were accurate.

He reached into the duffle bag again and brought out a teargas canister. "This?"

"That's teargas. At least I think it is. It's either teargas or smoke. Either way, it won't blow them up. Can you reach them from here?"

"Yes."

"Then pull that little ringy thing and throw it at them," Raven said.

"Will they be able to land safely engulfed in gas?"

"Sure," Raven said with a reassuring smile. "They're trained for stuff like that." When Ira turned away, she rolled her eyes and grimaced.

Ira tried to fit his finger into the ring, but his finger was too wide. In the rearview mirror, Raven saw his face set in concentration as he tried to pull the pin. "Give me that thing," she said. Ira held the canister out to her. She pulled the ring. He looked at the thing as if trying to figure out how she'd done it. "Throw it," Raven screamed.

"Oh," Ira said. He leaned almost his whole body out the back doors. Raven felt the front tires lose traction as his weight shifted the van's center of gravity. She was afraid the vehicle was going to do a wheelie, or even flip over backward.

Ira threw the canister.

Raven leaned forward to look in the side mirror. The helicopter wavered, then began to spin in sweeping circles, sliding from her view. "That doesn't look good," she mumbled. She called, "What's going on up there, Ira?" The helicopter came back into view, a stream of smoke erupting along its spotlight. Then it spun away again.

"Um, it looks like maybe he is having some difficulty flying straight," Ira said.

"That's not good," Raven said.

"What did you say?" Ira called.

She called back to Ira, "They train for this stuff all the time. I'm sure they're fine." She turned off the headlights and negotiated the road by moonlight. She slowed, sticking to the left lane of the highway. Up ahead was the ghostly shape of a no left turn sign. She downshifted, the engine revving violently.

"They look like they've landed," Ira said.

"Did anything blow up?" Raven called.

"No."

"Any fire?"

"No."

"See, I told you they'd be fine," she said before rolling her eyes again and letting out a huge breath. She downshifted again and hit the brakes, yanking the van left onto the unpaved, packed dirt of a utility turnoff. She swung the bouncing van into another left turn and shot down the opposite highway with the headlights still off.

"Where are we going?" Ira said.

"Whichever direction they think we aren't," she said. She pressed her foot down steadily on the accelerator and shifted back up through the gears. "We'll dump the van and try to find something a little less flashy." Raven could see the heap of the helicopter ditched on the northbound side. The crew scrambled around in the moonlight. She hoped all of them were coughing too violently to notice the dark van drive past.

15

Callahan followed Jacobs past the tipped M1117 and past the strike team, which looked like a Little League team that had just lost the big game. The parking lot was washed in strobes of red emergency lights from a fire truck and two ambulances. The first news van pulled up. This covert operation had gone very non-covert when the 50 cal. began ringing out.

Jacobs led Callahan up to the motel room where Sargent Phillips stood in the doorway, a dejected look in his eyes. All piss and vinegar before, Callahan thought, now ragged and defeated. Pride goes before the fall. Or before being thrown through the air like a football by a rampaging soldier of Satan. Callahan wanted to laugh. You think you are part of Christ's Army? Only Christ's chosen can vanquish the Beast's beasts. And I am one. Ordained by Gabriel himself to stop this embodiment of evil.

Philips said to Jacobs, "The place is clear. We didn't touch anything. It's all yours. Believe me, we're glad to hand this one over." He shuffled off to join his team.

Callahan followed Jacobs into the room.

"With the press here and other agencies alerted to this clusterfuck, we don't have much time to find something," Jacobs said.

"Find something, like what?"

"You're the expert. You tell me."

Callahan took in the room. The damage wasn't as bad as he'd imagined. It looked more like an out of control frat party, rather than a brutal attack on a heavily armed tactical team. The front window was broken. There were bullet holes in the closet door. A thin fog of teargas lingered in the corners. A supermarket carriage full of food was parked beside the bed. Jacobs stood at the foot of the bed looking up at where the wall met the ceiling. A few bullet holes punctured the area, continuing on their path after punching through the closet door. Jacobs's phone rang. He answered it.

Callahan wandered further into the room, glancing into the shopping cart as Jacobs talked into the phone. "Uh huh, uh huh, yup. Okay. See if they can get it back up in the air, or at least bring in another bird," Jacobs said. He turned the phone off and said, "Damnit."

"What?"

"The thing took out the entire pursuit team."

"Killed them?" Callahan said, trying to mask the excited glee in his voice.

"No. Amazingly, no one was harmed."

Callahan frowned. What kind of killer demon was this? He wandered over to the bathroom, praying: *Please, Lord, help me find what you want me to find.* He caught his reflection in the mirror. Looking tired. Beat up. Literally beat up. Is this what he got for fighting the Lord's battle? Beat up by a little girl? While inspecting his black eyes and swollen nose, he realized that his prayer had been answered. In the mirror's reflection, he saw a leather-bound book sitting on the back of the toilet.

Callahan stopped himself from darting over to it, praying: *Jesus, give me the strength to not betray my excitement.* He turned to face Jacobs, who was watching him from the bedroom. Casually, Callahan said, "So two officers were thrown in here"—he gestured around him—"and then how many were thrown out that window?"

Jacobs turned to inspect the smashed window. "Just the one."

Callahan snatched the book off the toilet as Jacobs went on. "The thing tossed a 190 pound man, loaded with equipment, out the window like he was nothing."

Callahan felt the book tingling in his fingers and he slipped it into his jacket's inside pocket. He returned to the bathroom's doorway. He said, "And he tossed two other officers in the closet?" His voice sounded higher in his own ears. He could feel the book in his pocket. It felt alive somehow. That side of his abdomen tingled from the thing. He was afraid Jacobs would be able to see it moving around in his jacket. He took a deep breath. "And the rear-entry man said the girl was initially in the bathroom, here?"

"Yeah. Said she was alone in there. After the teargas was sent in, the girl ran out to the…suspect. The de…." He took a breath. "Ira."

Callahan chuckled. But he wasn't sure why. "Yeah, right, our friend, Ira."

Jacobs looked Callahan up and down. Callahan was sure Jacobs knew about the book. The way he looked at him screamed, *I know you're guilty of something*. Callahan held the book tight to his abdomen, looking like a man with indigestion. He turned and pretended to inspect the bathroom mirror. "So what do we do now?" Callahan said.

"I was about to ask you the exact same thing," Jacobs said. "I briefed Thompson on the situation. He's putting together some help for us. A few more agents. He's also set us up with some rooms at a motel. I say, let's get a couple hours of sleep.

We can attack this thing with fresh minds when the other agents arrive."

"Can't we just stay at this motel?" Callahan said. Still with that underlying nervous giggle in his voice. He tried to will himself to sound calm. Normal.

"It's not generally acceptable to sleep in an active crime-scene. Which this entire motel is now."

Callahan broke into laughter.

Jacobs looked at him in that knowing way again. "You all right?"

"Yes," Callahan said, stifling the giggles. "Just tired. I think the lack of sleep and the excitement of it all is getting to me."

"And the fact of being right?"

"What do you mean?"

"The thing that came out of this motel room certainly looked like a…demon." He looked pained to say it.

Callahan considered Jacobs for a moment. Part of him wanted to embrace the man's humility, the other part wanted to smack him across the face for his stupidity and weakness. He felt the book buzzing against his side. "I think sleep is in order, Agent Jacobs. Let's take a break and attack this with fresh eyes."

16

His panic had started in the quiet after the pursuit. As they drove through the dark, Ira began saying, "Where's my book? Where's my book?" His questioning increased in intensity as he began to smash the inside of the van, throwing things out the back door, tearing metal apart in his search. Raven could barely keep to the road. Finally she pulled off the highway.

They got out and Ira started smashing the van with his fists. He then lifted the thing over his head and heaved it down an embankment.

"Feel better?" Raven said, looking at the twisted heap of metal.

When he turned to face her, his shoulders were rising and falling in deep breaths, his hands in fists, his brow gnarled above the bonfires of his eyes. The flames weren't of anger, but of frustration, and panic, and loss.

She hadn't thought he'd be able to lift the thing, but he did, and as he threw it, she wasn't sure if she should laugh or cry. That maelstrom of anger, and its out-of-control manner, was childlike. He was throwing a hissy fit, and she thought to herself, *Ira, mad. Ira, smash.* But then she was filled with terror. Because suddenly she realized that his out-of-control hissy fit was just that: out of control. And she was to blame.

"We need to go, Ira," Raven said, looking down at the van's corpse.

"Not without my book."

"We don't know where it is. It must have…." Her voice faded off, then she took a deep breath and said, "It must have fallen out of your pocket during the chase. We need to get going. Sun will be up soon."

"How could I have lost it?"

Raven swallowed hard. There was something in his voice she'd never heard from him before now. Something she'd never imagined could be in his voice. Anguish.

"I don't know, Ira. But we'll figure it out."

"I need to go back."

"You can't now."

"I have to."

Raven swallowed hard again. "If you go back, you *will* have to kill innocent people. We're lucky no one was killed already. C'mon. We need to calm down and make a plan." She looked over her shoulder at the dark road. "But first we need to get out of sight. When we got off the highway, a sign said there was a town about a mile that way. We get some new wheels, and we figure it out."

Ira's fists unclenched and his breathing eased. "Okay."

She watched him. Wondering if he'd throw another fit, but he was calm. Surprisingly so. "I'm…sorry about your book, Ira," she said.

"Why are *you* sorry?"

She let out a breath. "It's just something you say to someone, when they've lost something important to them."

"Why?"

"You just do. Let's go," she said, cutting across the street and into the woods. Ira followed her.

17

They stuck to the shadows, creeping around the backs of buildings. Raven had no idea what time it was, but she heard a couple of delivery trucks off in the distance, so she figured it was almost sunup. The front of the U-Haul building was lit up, but the back was dark. They crept up to one of the ten-foot box-trucks. Raven glanced at Ira, sizing him up beside the truck, then waved him on to a fifteen-foot box truck. She inspected the driver's side door, then walked in concentric circles around the parking lot, her attention on the ground.

"What are you doing?" Ira asked her.

"Looking for something to jimmy the door open. We're taking this truck, and I need to get into it."

Ira smashed the window. "Will that work?"

Raven winced, looking around to be sure no one heard him, then said, "Yup. That should just about do it."

She reached through the window and unlocked the lock.

"How will you start this vehicle?" Ira said.

"I'm going to hot-wire it."

"What is this, hot-wire?"

"I'm going to bypass the lock on the starter," she said. "I need you to remove the plastic from the steering column."

"Did you learn to do this, too, from Ahmad?"

"I looked it up online. I was going to hot-wire one of the sheik's cars and make a break for it. But I never got the chance." Raven climbed in the driver's side door, scooting along the seat to peek at the steering column.

Ira watched her. "You don't need tools to do this hot-wiring?"

"Nah; it's easy enough, I just need to…oh, here we go."

The truck started.

"That was fast," Ira said. "It is easy, this hot-wire."

"Especially when the keys are in it. Hold on…." She opened the glove box, rummaged through papers, and pulled out a map. Then she darted to the back of the truck, opened the rear door, and climbed up. "C'mon," she called.

Ira stooped and climbed in behind her, the vehicle's suspension groaning. Raven snapped on a dome light on the ceiling and sat on the floor, unfurling the map. Ira squatted and then plopped onto the floor behind her, with another groan from the truck's suspension.

"All right, where to next?" she said. "We're in this town." She pointed to a spot on the map, and Ira leaned down closer. She said, "We should probably head west, toward more rural areas. If we—"

"We head here," Ira said, pointing at the map.

Raven squinted at where Ira was pointing and she said, "Mystic Island?"

"That is where we go."

"But it's an island."

"There is a bridge."

"Yeah, that may be, but the last place you want to be, when on the run, is an island. We'll be trapped."

"If we are to find the book, then that is where we need to go."

"The book is there?"

"No. But there is someone there who can tell me where the book is. We go there." He pointed at the map again.

"All right, hopefully the FBI realizes just how dumb it is for us to go to an island and they don't bother to look for us there." Raven folded the map and went to the back of the truck. "Enjoy the ride," she said with a smile. She hopped up and grabbed the door handle, slamming the door shut.

18

Jacobs was looking up at the demon. It wasn't eight feet tall, it was ten at least. Twelve, maybe. Its flaming eyes glared down at him. It lifted its hand and brought it down onto Jacobs's head. He heard more than felt the impact. A sharp smacking sound, distant but also too close.

Jacobs opened his eyes. He was still wearing his clothes, including his shoes. He'd arrived in the motel room—he looked at the clock—about three hours ago, and dropped onto the mattress, face first. Now he woke in the exact same position. He'd been awakened by a sound. A metallic smacking sound. Why was some deep part of his brain telling him that the sound was important?

He heard an engine revving and realized the sound that had woken him was a car door slamming. Why was that important? He climbed off the bed with a grimace. His entire body and mind screamed for more sleep. He peeked out the window, but whatever car it was had gone. He shuffled to the door connecting his room to Callahan's room. After rubbing his hair and yawning, he knocked.

No answer. With another yawn, he knocked again. Still no answer. "Callahan," he called. "Callahan," he called louder. Nothing.

Jacobs opened the door. "Callahan? You awake?" he said.

But there was no sign of Callahan. No bags stored neatly in the corner. No toiletries in the bathroom. No clothes in the closet. No maps and Post-it notes on the wall. Jacobs walked to the bed. Two maps were folded neatly and left on the bedspread. Jacobs picked up one and spotted the *Property of the FBI* stamp on the corner. "Motherfucker," he muttered.

He jumped at the sound of his phone ringing. It was Thompson. Perfect.

"Yeah," Jacobs said into the phone.

"You're supposed to identify—"

"I'm not in the mood. Give me the update."

"They found the tactical van," Thompson said.

"Good for them," Jacobs said.

"They're in Massachusetts. Or at least they were in Massachusetts when they ditched the van. Dracut."

"I thought they were heading north?"

"They must have turned around. You and Callahan need to come home."

Jacobs regarded the room again. "That could be a problem. Looks like Callahan flew the coop."

"Why?"

"How the fuck should I know why that guy does anything he does."

"Does he have the book?"

"What book?"

"Tactical team said there was a book in the bathroom during the raid. Old looking, leather book. The NSA agents said it's not with any of the evidence logged from the room?"

Jacobs straightened. "Why would NSA agents have access to *my* evidence?"

"Your boogeyman has been deemed a threat to national security. You're out. Come home to the Boston Field Office for debriefing."

When he arrived at the field office, Jacobs paused in the doorway, glancing over the room at the other agents buzzing about. He was sure news of what happened had already spread through the office. Were they going to bring him back into the fold as the tragic hero—one who had fought against the odds? Or was he seen as the Prodigal Son returning after squandering his, and the Bureau's, chance to stop a serial killer (or, let's face it, a killer demon)? A few agents looked up at him—he couldn't quite read the expressions washing across their faces—and then they returned to their work. Ty wasn't one of the agents that had looked up. Jacobs walked over to Ty's desk.

"Any word on Callahan?" Jacobs said.

Ty still didn't look up. "How would I know?"

"Wasn't sure if you heard anything," Jacobs said.

"Why would I?" Ty finally looked up. "You apparently took me off the case. Imagine that. I got dumped from a case I was never actually assigned to."

"Look, Ty, I had to be careful. I was tipped to a possible leak in the Bureau."

"And you thought it was me?"

"The tipster used the exact phrase you said. I'd said Callahan had lots of energy, and this CIA spook said 'the clinical term is manic.' You said that exact thing. I thought it was him trying to tell me you were the leak."

"So why are you telling me anything now, if you think I'm the leak?"

"I don't know, maybe because it doesn't matter anymore."

"You really thought I'd be a leak?"

"I guess not. I don't know."

Ty said, "I told you I didn't want to get involved in the first place."

"I didn't want to be involved either. But I am. Something fucked up is going on. Be happy to be done with it."

"You should be, too."

Jacobs nodded and left Ty to his work. He knew how Ty felt. Jacobs had dragged him into this thing, then pulled him off the case, just as Jacobs was being pulled now. Ty was right, he should be happy to be done with it, but he needed to know what that thing at the motel was.

Diaz came out of the break room, a smile on his face. "Must suck having a case taken away like that, huh, Jacobs?" Diaz said. "You must have pissed someone off? Or did you just fuck it up that bad? I know I wouldn't have. I would have played by the rules and had this case solved by now."

"No you wouldn't," Jacobs said.

"Your clusterfuck is all over the news. It's being reported as a terrorist cell hiding in New Hampshire. But it wasn't terrorists, was it? What was really in that motel?"

Jacobs ran several fantasy scenarios through his head. String Diaz up by his tie? Knock the hot coffee into his face? Throw him through the conference room door and over the table? Or just smash him in the nose? "It *was* a terrorist cell, from the GOFY region of Iraq," Jacobs said. "Callahan was most disappointed. I have work to do, now, so if you will excuse me."

"There is no GOFY region. I heard there was a demon in that motel."

"You heard wrong."

"Where's Callahan?"

Jacobs took a step closer to Diaz, saying, "You have five seconds to clear this hallway before I waterboard you with that coffee."

"You can't—"

"Five.... Four...."

Diaz started walking. "You—"

"Three...."

Diaz kept walking.

Jacobs looked into the conference room, eyes lingering on Callahan's map still on the wall. His eyes narrowed as a thought came to him.

He walked to the map and focused on the New England region. There were the bikers slaughtered in Standish. The kid in the Standish Library. But then there was the Vatican. Maybe the damage at the Vatican was what it had been reported to be: a gas line explosion. Then there was Berry, New Hampshire. And Dracut. He then followed an imaginary line a short distance to the East. A direct course to Mystic Island. Hadn't Callahan said something about a church? A doorway to Hell or something, wasn't that what he'd said? And it all began there. It all began on that damn island.

Agent Trent Isaac popped his head into the conference room. "Thompson is looking for you," he said.

As if to himself, Jacobs said, "'Vizzini said go back to the beginning.'"

"Whatever," Trent said, leaving.

Jacobs walked out of the conference room, not stopping at Thompson's office.

19

They parked the U-Haul in the woods. Raven said they should probably hide it a little better, but Ira told her that no one would find it. People didn't travel these woods.

Raven soon saw why. Something about the woods seemed very wrong. They were thick with tall, wide, gnarled, ancient looking trees which would have looked more at home in an Eastern European forest than they did on a New England island. As they traveled among the trees, she kept catching things from the corner of her eye, only to turn and see nothing there. Several of the trees had bark patterns looking like human faces, like something from a William Blake painting. She felt increasing anxiety, but not because of these tricks of the eye or the sunlight being swallowed by the thickening branches and leaves. Rather because of a train of thought she just couldn't shake. Maybe it was the quiet of the woods, or something else about the place. She stopped walking.

"Ira?" she said.

Ira stopped and turned to look at her. "Yes?"

"I lost your book," she said.

"I don't understand."

"I took it. I stole it."

Ira stepped toward her, then stopped. His stoic expression seemed to burst invisible seams. "What do you mean?"

"I was curious about it. I wanted to see what was in it. So I picked your pocket. I was going to give it back, I swear. I just…."

Ira's shoulders raised and lowered with his deep breaths.

"I left it in the bathroom when they raided the motel room. I thought I could figure out how to get it back. I figured it would just work out. We'll find it, right? Wherever we're going, we'll figure out how to find it?"

Ira's shoulders continued to rise and fall. He turned and looked deeper into the woods, then back at her. "You lied to me?"

"I thought it was one of those comforting lies. If you thought it was just lost, then you wouldn't be mad at me, and we could figure out how to find it. Which we have, right?"

He looked deeper into the woods again. He didn't say anything.

"It wasn't fair to make you think it was your fault," she said. "I'm sorry."

His shoulders rose and fell with one more sigh. "We are almost there," he said, and resumed his trek through the woods.

20

He knew it was impossible, but Jacobs could have sworn he heard a sucking sound as the fog engulfed his car. He'd never been in a full-blown car chase or anything as heart pounding as that, but he'd been in some hairy situations on the road; this was by far the most nerve-racking driving he'd done. And he wasn't quite certain why. Sure, the fog was dangerously thick, to the point that a car stopping short in front of him would have a very unpleasant surprise, but it was more that the fog was—

"Horror movie thick," Jacobs said aloud, startling himself.

He had the radio turned completely down, trying to use all of his senses while driving through the soup, and he could hear the tires' occasional thump-thump as they passed over ruts or joints—he wasn't quite sure which because he couldn't see a goddamn thing. He had the sense that something could leap out of that fog at any moment. Something with suckers that would latch onto his windshield or something with claws and teeth splattering saliva on the hood. This is what made it—

"Horror movie thick." He'd repeated the words out loud, startling himself again. "And apparently it has me talking to myself, too," he muttered.

The tires thump-thumped over a final larger joint, and the fog instantly cleared. "There we go," he said. He was off the bridge. He was on Mystic Island. He glanced in his rearview mirror, watching the fog swirl around where his car had broken through.

The sunlight made him feel better, and he finally dared to reach for the coffee in the cup-holder, taking a long sip as something caught his eyes in the mirror again. A black SUV broke through the fog behind him. He was glad he'd had no reason to stop short on the bridge.

He drove through neighborhoods of converted fishing villages toward the road that cut past the high school, toward the eastern part of the island.

The Keeper

1

The ground had begun to rise a while back. Ira was walking some distance ahead, never looking back to see if Raven was following. She called to him, "You know, friends are supposed to forgive each other."

"Are friends supposed to steal from each other?" he said.

"No," she called, "and that's a really good point, but—"

"But nothing," Ira said. "You stole my book."

"I wanted to see it. I wanted to see who was in there. I wanted to see if a message I wrote on the page you gave me would show up in it."

Ira stopped. "Did it?"

"Yes. See that? You learned something new about your book because of what I did. That's cool, right?"

"And now it is lost."

"Misplaced. We'll find it. I promise."

Ira growled, climbing up through the woods again, the land becoming steeper in a final rise to where the thickness of the trees subsided slightly. Shafts of light pierced the ceiling of leaves. The ground leveled off, and here stood a dilapidated, stone house, its façade crumbling and weather-worn. Ira broke stride only long enough to take a deep breath before plunging through an open doorway and into the house.

Inside were stone walls and a wood floor stained with

time. A table stood at the center of the room. An antique iron lamp with a never-diminishing candle spilled light in a gold, flickering wash across the walls. A chair was positioned at each side of the table like compass points. A figure was seated in one of them, writing in a book similar to Ira's.

It is here that your humble narrator directly enters this story. I was the figure sitting at that table.

It was strange to view myself through their eyes. Raven saw me as a hooded figure, hunched at the table, my face in the shadow of a cloak's cowl. My fingers, thin, impossibly long, impossibly white, holding a black quill. What Ira saw was a repugnant reptile deserving to be squashed.

I smiled and welcomed them with a wave of my hand. "Ah, Kharon," I said, referring to the demon by his Hebrew name. "Come in, come in. And bring your young friend, Raven."

Raven's eyes narrowed. "How does he know my name?" she asked.

"He knows everything," Ira growled.

"Except decorating tips, apparently," Raven said, glancing around the room.

I chuckled. "There's that Raven wit I've come to know so well," I said. "Please, have a seat." I gestured to the chairs.

They approached the table.

"Sit," I said, smiling. Raven heard that my voice had a low whispering, hissing lisp. Saw, in the light of the lantern, that my skin had a greenish tinge and that my teeth were pointed pearls.

She looked up at Ira. Ira nodded. Raven sat in the chair across from me.

"Demon?" I asked, gesturing to another chair.

"I'll stand," he said. "Where's my book?"

I grinned, and Raven noted my sharp smile again. I said,

"Wow, right to business as usual, I see. All in time, demon. Your friend here has questions she wants answered." I gestured at Raven.

"No I don't," she said. She was trying to make out my eyes, still hidden in the shadow of my cowl.

"Oh, you do, my dear. You do. Among many other questions, you want to know who I am, why Ira hates me so, and mostly, is there a Heaven and will you find your parents there?"

Her eyes grew wide. Not much shocked her anymore, and few intimidated her, but I had managed to do both.

"And your friend, Kharon, has his own questions." I looked at Ira. "Least of which is your book's location. You want to know why *are* those pesky priests not on your list? And who is that silver-eyed man?"

Raven looked at Ira.

I smiled at her. "He hasn't told you about him yet. But don't feel bad. He's not the loquacious type. You've already figured this out about him, have you not?"

"Loquacious?" Ira said, the word like a wad of peanut butter in his mouth.

"It means talkative," Raven said.

"Hmmph," Ira said.

Raven returned her attention to me.

I said, "You wonder how I know all this. I am happy to tell you. The answer actually involves your friend here. We shall sit a moment while I decide if I tell the demon where his precious book is. As I decide, I will tell you how I came to see all." Here, for dramatic effect, I lifted back my cowl to reveal my eyes.

Raven gasped, for my eyes had been crudely sewn shut.

2

Jacobs stood beside the priest who was unlocking Saint Sebastian's wide wooden front doors. Jacobs studied him, wondering if *this* priest might get a visit from the giant vigilante.

The priest said, "These locks had to be replaced recently. Someone broke them open, but there was nothing out of place inside the church. Not a thing touched." There was a loud click and the priest pushed open one of the doors. "Here we are, agent. If there is anything else you need, please let me know. I will be in the rectory; it's down the street some, just beyond the cemetery."

"You're not coming in with me?" Jacobs said.

"Oh no, agent, I would only be in the way. Besides, I don't want…. I generally don't go down into the basement."

"Why?"

"I just…don't. Don't have a need to. We have a maintenance man who deals with anything down there. My place is at the pulpit."

"Has the maintenance man been down there recently?"

"I don't believe so. To my knowledge, no one has been down there for some time. There has been no need."

"Even after the break in?"

"There is nothing down there to check on, agent."

"Father, is the doorway to Hell in this church's basement?" Jacobs asked this question so bluntly that the priest seemed to struggle with deciphering the words.

Finally, he said, "What exactly are you investigating again?"

"Missing person," Jacobs said.

"The girl? The Amber Alert?"

Jacobs nodded.

"And you think she's in our basement?"

Jacobs didn't answer. Instead he said, "What's in the basement, father?"

"There is a door," he said. "Where it leads, I do not know. It has always been bolted shut." And with that, he excused himself.

The church, like many churches, seemed much bigger on the inside than the outside, the space intensifying each step on the ancient wooden floor into echoing groans and squeals. A stained glass window filtered the moonlight through images of saints and sinners alike, and in the church's corners were the usual plaster statues. Jacobs noted how those type of statues always seemed the opposite of certain Renaissance paintings; where the Mona Lisa would always seem to be watching an observer, these figures always seemed to look away. He stopped under the crucifix. He regarded Jesus's look of accepting deference to the situation he'd found himself in. The thorns, the punctures, the abs. Jacobs continued on through the church, rubbing his own belly.

He cut across the protesting floor and found the door to the basement. The priest had left some of the church's lights on, but not here. The stairway was dark and foreboding, but became more ominous when he clicked on his flashlight. He crept down steps that were more ancient and more groaning than the floor.

The basement was a cavernous stone room with high ceilings. There was nothing else down here for his flashlight's beam to hold onto, not even a boiler, which he assumed was installed somewhere else, ensuring that no one—not even the priest's maintenance man, would need to venture below the church. On the far wall, there was a door, but it was not bolted shut. It was gaping open, black in his flashlight's beam.

He took a deep breath and began walking toward the door, feeling very much like he was in the bridge's fog again.

As if at any moment something was going to spring out of the dark. Only this time it would not latch onto his windshield; it would latch onto him.

Arriving at the door, he detected the smell of sulfur, and his breathing shallowed against the stench. He crouched and inspected the sheared bolts on the floor. He was no forensics expert, but it didn't look like those bolts had been cut by any tool. They looked like they'd been snapped off.

He placed his hand on the door's edge to help himself up, but pulled it away suddenly. The door was hot. Or maybe it wasn't. It was more a jolt, not so much of electricity or heat or…he wasn't quite sure of the *or*. He just knew he did not want to touch it again.

He shined the flashlight through the doorway, but nothing beyond its threshold seemed to illuminate, as if it were a black hole robbing the universe of photons. He took a deep breath and stepped over.

Immediately, thoughts crawled into his mind, ones he couldn't quite follow. He deliriously labeled them guerrilla thoughts. They slipped into his mind, hit hard, and slipped out before he could recognize them. Whatever they were, they were unpleasant. Fire. Dismemberment. Agony. These words remained like fingerprints after the thoughts slipped away. He heard distant screams like hurricane winds blowing past a steel wire, but he couldn't tell if they were parts of his thoughts or a part of reality.

He sensed movement. He raised the flashlight's beam, but it blinked out. "Are you kidding me?" he muttered. What a time for the batteries to fail. He wanted to vomit. But a rush of adrenalin washed that nausea away as he realized there was something in there with him. He could feel its bulk. Sense its gaze upon him.

He turned and darted back into the church's basement, leaving the door behind him, wanting to look back, but really not wanting to look back. In the basement, his flashlight came back on, and he used it to quickly find his way back to the stairs.

3

"Just tell me where the book is, Keeper," Ira growled.

"I will," I told him. "But the girl deserves to know what she is involved in, does she not?"

"I should have left you tied to that tree," Ira said.

"Believe me, I wish you had," I told him. "But, no, you had a better idea for my punishment, didn't you?"

Ira stepped forward, his fists clenched, and growled, "Plenty of trees here, if you want to try me."

"Um, excuse me," Raven said. "If you don't mind, I need to be brought up to speed here. Can someone tell me what the hell is going on?"

"Go ahead, Keeper," Ira said. "Hurry up and tell your tale, and then you tell me what I need to know."

"Oh, believe me, demon, there's nothing I want more than to tell you what you need to know. So I suggest you listen carefully to what I say." I turned my attention to the girl. "I was not always known as The Keeper. I was once known as Nachash."

"Is that supposed to mean something to me?"

"It means Serpent."

The girl cocked her head. "Serpent, as in *The* Serpent? Like the Garden of Eden?"

"She is quick, isn't she?" I said to Ira.

He grunted.

I said to the girl, "So you know the story. The two kids

and their nakedness, eating the fruit, exiled from Eden, et cetera, et cetera, et cetera."

"I've heard it once or twice," Raven said.

"Well it was your friend, Iratus, here, who was charged with punishing me for my taking of Adam and Eve's innocence."

Raven looked up at Ira and said, "Wow, look at you. What did you do to him?"

I answered for him. "First, being the brute that he is, he tied me to one of the tree's branches, making a rather intricate knot out of my serpentine body. And then…" I sat back and lifted my hands, "…he did this to me."

"Wait…" Raven said, cocking her head. "I thought the Serpent's punishment was that God created a hated creature in his image, something to crawl on its belly and strike fear in the hearts of men."

"Impressive," I said to her.

Ira looked down at her with his eyebrows raised.

"What?" she said, shrugging. "I read the Bible at the library."

"You are right," I told her. "God did at first punish me in this manner. But as it was then, and still is, Iratus had the real knack for punishment. He convinced God that I would enjoy having a hated animal in my likeness. Of course, he was right. So Iratus convinced God to instead give me the body of a man and, seeing as I was such a bad guardian of the Tree of Knowledge, make me the tree, so to speak. He had God turn me into this wretched thing before you, then shove all knowledge into my mind. And to cap it off, Iratus sewed my eyes shut, so I would have to see everything, but never through my own eyes."

"It wasn't enough, if you ask me," Ira said.

"Not enough?" I snapped at him. "Can you imagine what it's like to know everything at once?" To Raven, I said, "I was exiled here to be the Keeper of Knowledge. A surrogate forced to know everything so that God doesn't have to."

"I thought God knew everything," Raven said.

I chuckled, "Oh, no. God actually knows very little. In fact, he's able to do very little. He's more a figurehead than anything else." I looked at Ira and said, "Do you remember the day you tied me to that tree and God shut down Eden?"

"Of course," Ira said. "Michael came with the cherub with the flaming sword and...." His voice trailed off. "Michael. Michael with the silver eyes."

"You didn't recognize him in his human disguises. He can only be in all his glory at the sacred sites he's been endowed to protect. In fact, he had to convince Gabriel to visit Callahan, that it was the Word of God he was delivering."

"Who is Callahan?" Ira said.

"He's your friend from the alleyway," I told Raven.

"The FBI creep?"

"He's not actually FBI. The creep part is up for debate. Regardless, he has the book."

"Michael orchestrated this Callahan stealing my book?" Ira said.

"Oh, no, Callahan was instructed to keep an eye out for the book. Michael never thought he'd actually get it." I looked at Raven. "Raven stealing it was purely coincidence. It couldn't have worked out better, to be honest. Like it was ordained. I suppose deus ex machinas really can happen."

"Hold on," Raven said. "Before you start pointing fingers at me again. None of this makes sense. First off, aside from Gabriel and this silver-eyed Michael guy—and I can only assume you mean the Archangels—your Garden of Eden story doesn't fit." She gestured toward Ira, saying, "If he's a Nephilim, then how could he be in the Garden of Eden?"

"He was around long before Eden," I said.

"But Nephilim are part human," Raven said. "How can he be part human if there were supposedly no humans before Eden?"

Ira stared at her, his mind working overtime now. If he'd been in a cartoon, smoke might have been spilling from his ears. The fact is, Ira didn't have an answer to her question. But I did, and what I was about to reveal, Ira did not know about himself. In fact, God didn't even know what I was about to reveal. There were only two other beings that had this information; one because he remembers, and the other because he begged me to tell him—but more on that later.

I said, "The truth is, Kharon is no Nephilim. He's not even a demon."

<h1 style="text-align:center">4</h1>

Jacobs wanted a coffee, but when the first place he found was a bar, his desire soon changed. The bar was called The Dutch Horse Pub. A dimly lit structure, the primary decorative factor of which was wood paneling. A man who looked like he'd just answered a casting-call for "bartender" stood behind the rectangular bar, leaning against a beer cooler and texting on his phone. Seated at the bar was an obese man with thinning hair and haunches that dripped over the barstool. He sat beside a skinny woman with thick makeup. They both watched a muted television over the bar. Down the bar from them was an old-timer of an indiscernible age, one of those people that has been eighty for the past sixty years. Across from him was a man in his mid forties with shaggy hair and a beard. Jacobs sat beside the man with the beard.

Without looking up from his phone, the bartender held up his finger, finished his text, and then came over to Jacobs.

"What you got on tap?" Jacobs asked.

"Beer," the bartender said.

"Any specific kind?"

The bartender took a folded piece of cardboard that was positioned in front of Jacobs and slid it closer to him. A list of beers ran down its side.

Jacobs looked at the list. It seemed to him every beer now had adjectives attached to it, not to mention hometowns. Ambers from Portland and Stouts from Vermont. Jacobs said, "You got Budweiser here?"

"This is a bar. In America. Yes, we have Budweiser. You needed a beer list for that?"

"Just give me a Budweiser," Jacobs said. The bartender went off to pour the beer. Jacobs snorted and turned to the guy beside him. "You live around here?"

"What're you, a Fed?" the man said.

Jacobs flinched. "Why do you say that?"

"It's written on your forehead."

Jacobs's hand went unconsciously to his forehead.

The guy chuckled.

"Why's the goddamn FBI here?" the old man down the bar called toward Jacobs.

"Take it easy, Fred," the bartender said, finishing his pour and bringing the beer over to Jacobs. "Here you go, agent," the bartender said to Jacobs. "Start a tab?"

"Sure."

The bartender walked away.

The man with the beard said, "This about that missing girl in New Hampshire? Or the terrorist cell they raided? Or are those two things connected?"

"Missing person," Jacobs said.

"And you thought you might find a missing teenager in a bar?"

"Just resting. Been driving all over this island."

"You're allowed to drink on duty?"

"Nope. But I've never been one to follow rules."

"Sounds like you're in the right profession."

Jacobs took in the man's unkempt hair, the beard, the over-the-hill surfer-dude style. He read the man's T-shirt out loud. "Heavy D. needs an Irish car bomb."

"Long story," the man said.

"And what is it you do?" Jacobs asked the man.

"I work at a T-shirt shop."

"Sounds like you're in the right profession."

"You really looking for that girl?"

"Yeah. Any ideas?"

"You been to Parson's Woods?"

"I drove past it. Woods look pretty thick. This girl is resourceful, but I don't think she'd rough it in deep woods."

"What is she, like a witness in a case or something?"

"Can't say."

"There's a house in the woods."

"Really? Anyone live there?"

"Nah. In fact, I'm not even positive it exists. No one goes in those woods. But legend is there's a house in the center of them. And if you're looking for missing people, Parson's Woods is the place to go."

5

"What do you mean, he's not a demon?" Raven said.

"Well, I suppose you can say he is now," I said, "but this demon standing before you is very young in the grander scheme of things. You know the old tree falls in the woods adage?"

"Yes," Raven said.

"Well your friend Ira is the tree. Or, more accurately, he's the sound."

Raven noticed Ira's fists clenching. I noticed it, too. There was a good chance I was about to be tied to another tree, but it was worth it for the moment.

I told them, "It's not unlike a Delayed Choice experiment in Quantum Physics. Think of it this way: if you are looking at a distant star in space, and there happens to be a galaxy between you and that star, the gravity of that galaxy will bend the light of the star. Are you with me?"

"Maybe," Raven said.

"No," Ira said, clenching his fists tighter.

"That doesn't matter," I said to Ira. "As you will see, it only matters if *she* understands. Anyway, the light from the star can go several paths around that galaxy. It only chooses which path to take when it is observed. Perception forms the path of that light, and, frankly, the universe around us. If there is a large concentration of a particular perception, it can actually manifest into reality."

"A perceptual concentration? Like a religion?" Raven said.

"Can't get much by her," I said to Ira. I then said to Raven, "Exactly like a religion. Some call it the Tinkerbell Effect in Peter Pan, where the large concentration of wishes brought the fairy to life."

"So you're saying religion is a fairy tale?"

"I'm saying the concentrated perceptions fostered by religion gave more familiar forms to the abstract forces of the universe. Good and Evil manifested into a God and a Devil. Along with all the other metaphysical aspects of nature. Love, Hate, Kindness, Pride, and Wrath. Kharon. Iratus."

Raven's attention snapped to Ira.

"What?" Ira said.

"He doesn't get it," I told her.

"Get what?" Ira said.

"You're not really a Nephilim," Raven told him, her voice tender.

Ira's brow lowered. "What do you mean?"

"He's saying you're the physical manifestation of wrath."

"I don't understand."

I smirked. "He's not going to get it. Or accept it. It's hard for one to discover what one really is."

"He's saying you're not a Nephilim," Raven told the demon in the kind manner with which one might explain something awful to a small child. And I can assure you, it wasn't because she was afraid to set him off. It was because she cared about him and wanted him to understand. "You are actually Wrath. You are literally Iratus."

Her attention snapped back to me. "But that doesn't make sense either. Most people have never heard of a Nephilim. How is there enough of a concentration of perception to bring one into being?"

"Think of it as a dream," I told her. "Dreams are merely the mind's attempted understanding of random thoughts. Synapses firing off as information is sorted and stored throughout the brain. Your brain is wired to process things in an ordered sense, so it strings these random thoughts into a story form, filling in the gaps with sequential information. The metaphysical world does the same. The story of what happened to me after giving the fruit to Eve, and my association with the big guy, here, those were all just offshoots of the larger perceived story. Something had to happen to the Tree of Knowledge, so this thread of the story developed. I am the manifestation of the metaphysical concept of Knowledge. If, say, the Hindu religion had developed as a larger concentration of perception,

I may have ended up with an elephant's head. And I would be a whole lot more well-liked than I am now."

"There are millions of Hindus, why didn't that manifest?"

"There are more Christians, and, let's face it, Christianity got the jump on going mainstream. This is all one reality, mind you. There are countless realities, but this is the one that matters at the moment."

Raven said, "So it's like, if you got enough people to believe it, Schrodinger's Cat could turn into a dog."

"Exactly," I called out, laughing—something I hadn't done spontaneously in a very long time. "A portion of Wrath had physically manifested itself, and a backstory manifested along with him. He became a Nephilim, and his book was another offshoot of that development. Think of the book as a kind of leash. This manifestation of Wrath," I motioned to Ira, "had to be given very specific quarry, otherwise, he could potentially wipe out all of humanity."

"But he doesn't have his book anymore," Raven said.

"Yes, that's right, isn't it," I said, steepling my fingers and grinning broadly.

"Where is my book?" Ira growled.

"We'll get to that," I said. "The young lady still has more questions. And frankly, you do, too. Questions like why weren't the priests in your book? How is the Archangel Michael involved? Why have you been set loose on the Topside?"

"Set loose?" Raven said.

"I came Topside on my own," Ira growled.

"Did you?" I said. "Or were you goaded into it by the man with the silver eyes?"

"By Michael?"

"He knew the inadequacy you were feeling, the frustration of facing the rising numbers of sinners each day."

"How did he know that?" Ira said.

"I may have told him," I said sheepishly. "He'd been asking me all kinds of questions lately. He seems to be the only one who cares that I am here. All it took was a little push from him to set you loose. In fact, I was somewhat surprised how easy it was. But you have always had that single-minded sense of duty. Your devotion to the book. This devotion put a kink in Michael's plans, actually. He thought for sure you would start slaughtering the priests, but you stuck to the rules, didn't you?"

Raven was watching Ira. Studying him. Waiting for when he would finally snap and tear down the building. Wondering if he would try to kill me. When she was sure he had a grip on his emotions, she said to me, "Why are there no priests in the book?"

"They'd been absolved of their sins. By the Pope covering up the sins and keeping the priests in the fold, so to speak. Thanks to Papal Supremacy, it was as if the crimes had never happened."

"Why would Michael want Ira to kill priests?" Raven said.

"To start the Apocalypse." I said.

"How would that start the Apocalypse?"

"If enough people got wind that a demon had come to Earth and was killing clergy, and enough people *believed* that this was happening, then you would get the Apocalypse. Right down to Horsemen and Raptures and armies of the undead."

"Michael wins the Apocalypse," Raven said to herself, coming to understand.

I said, "You are a fast reader. From Creation to Revelation in one night."

"I may have skipped a few begats," she said.

"Michael is the hero that leads the powers of good into battle, vanquishing the Devil and trapping him in exile.

Michael wants the Devil gone because he wants to be God's favorite angel."

"Why? Who is his favorite now?"

"Lucifer," I said to her as if she should know.

"I thought Lucifer *was* the Devil."

"He is."

"Then why is he his favorite angel? I thought he was his great adversary?"

"I suppose technically, yes. But they are from the same fabric. In the beginning, as this all began to take shape, Lucifer volunteered to become the representation of evil, but he is still very much a direct part of God. They work in tandem, and the balance of positive and negative energy needs to be maintained. Think about it: if the Devil really wanted people to be bad, then why would he deter their wickedness by punishing them in Hell? Why would they even need Punishers?" I gestured to Ira, who still looked confused. "Souls need to be distributed fairly evenly through Heaven and Hell, otherwise the balance will be thrown off and the universe will pull apart."

"How?" Raven said.

"Everything in the universe is spinning. All rotating at a tremendous speed. Think of it as being like a giant washing machine on the spin cycle. You've seen what happens when a load of laundry is not evenly distributed and goes off balance. It begins to wobble, and then it becomes so powerful that it can walk a two-hundred pound machine across the floor. Now imagine if the sides of the washing machine were to vanish. Well, that is what will happen if enough believers bring about Revelations and the Rapture. The instantaneous influx of every Christian, whole, into Heaven, and the Devil's counterbalance gone…? It will throw the balance off, sending out shock waves that will tear not only this universe apart, but also all the universes, having a domino effect that will essentially end all reality."

"Why would Michael want the Apocalypse then, if he knows it will tear apart the universe? He won't be the hero if there is nothing to be the hero of."

"Because Michael doesn't know it will tear the universe apart."

"Why not?"

"Because I didn't tell him."

"But why?"

"Because the end of the universe might not seem so bad to me."

"Won't you be torn apart, too?"

"Yes. I'm banking on it. Do you have any idea what it is like to have all knowledge in your head? The world is an ugly place. And I see all of it. All the time."

"But it is a beautiful place, too. Don't you see that?"

"Yes, I do." I smiled in spite of myself. "But good and evil are already out of whack. Have been for years. We've already begun our wobble. Religions and their loopholes. The bad getting to Paradise with eleventh-hour absolution, the good shoved into Purgatory for not believing in the right deity. The universe needs a reset. Destroy itself and regroup back into its balance. I'm okay with that. All of our energy will be recycled, and I won't know a goddamn thing."

"Where's my book?" Ira growled.

Raven looked up at the demon. "Ira, do you understand what he is telling you? You being on Earth could lead to the destruction of the universe."

"I understand what he is telling me. Where's my book?"

"Ira, you're too dangerous on Earth, even with your book. But without it, you're like…." She didn't know how to finish her statement.

"A walking genocide," I finished it for her. "Too bad the book is gone. And you'll never get it back."

"What do you mean?"

I then took the time to recount what had happened to the book. I gave them an abridged version, but for you, I will be more exact.

6

We need to go back a little in the story. Back to Agent Jacobs hearing the car door slam outside his motel room. The car belonged to a man named Jimmy Coogan, one of Callahan's Knowledge Fighters. Coogan was taking Dennis Callahan to Canada—the demon he was following was supposedly heading north. Why it was heading north, Callahan wasn't sure. But it meant Callahan needed to head north, too. The government would be looking for him, so he had to get out of New Hampshire. In fact, with federal agents after him, he had to get out of the country. As far from the Deep State as he could get. Although he'd found that if Jacobs and his cronies were any indication, the Deep State was not as imposing as he'd thought.

Coogan enacted what they had some time ago dubbed "Plan J" (named for John, the writer of Revelation; Coogan had suggested Plan A, for the Apocalypse, but Callahan told him Plan A sounded dumb). Coogan's job was to go to Callahan's house, gather his fake passport, his stash of cash, and his family Bible. Then Coogan was to arrange lodging. Something better than the motor lodge shit the feds had been putting him up in. A place in which Callahan could "disappear for a few days" from the New World Order. A place to do some "research" on the coming crisis.

Coogan would have driven cross-country if ordered to do so. He was more than willing to help the cause. Coogan wanted to be on the front line when The Rapture went down. And helping Callahan help the Archangel Gabriel was an excellent start toward obtaining that goal.

Parked now in front of the hotel, Callahan took the room key from Coogan and got out. "If you need anything else," Coogan said, "you have my number, I can—"

"Go home and prepare," was all Callahan told him, and shut the car door behind him.

In his hotel room, Callahan dropped his bags on the floor. He didn't even bother with his usual routine of hanging his clothes neatly in the closet or placing them in the drawers.

He removed the book from the inside pocket of his jacket and went straight to a small desk in the room's corner. The book had literally not left his side since he'd obtained it. He placed the volume onto the desk, removed his jacket, hung it on the back of the chair. The place where the book had been nestled still tingled like a rectangular patch of skin that had been numbed with Novocaine. He rubbed it absentmindedly, and sat in the chair.

He stared down at the book, not entirely sure what to do with it. Gabriel had told him to find it. But now that he had found it, why had Gabriel not come to collect it? Was Gabriel's intention for Callahan to hand it over to him, or was Callahan supposed to do something with it? He couldn't exactly remember if Gabriel had given him instructions. After all, he'd been a little distracted by the fact that he was talking to an angel.

Callahan's hand hovered over the book. He took a deep breath and then picked it up, feeling that buzzing in his fingers again. He inspected its ancient cover. He hadn't done this earlier, waiting in his motel room for Coogan to pick him up, worried that Agent Jacobs, or the strike team, might barge in. But now he had the privacy to do what he wanted, the time to feel the worn leather, to smell its charred stench. His heart pounded. His mouth was dry. What would happen if he opened this thing? His mind slipped back to the Indiana Jones movie he'd seen as a kid—that heathen film, using something as holy as the Ark of the Covenant as a movie prop—when the Ark was opened and ghosts came flying out of it. Could that happen here with this book? Could he unleash demons? Unleash Hell?

He was absently rubbing the blade attached to the leather place marker when he realized he had already opened the book.

Nothing spilled from it. No ghosts. No demons. No Hell. Just names. The left page was only half-filled with names. The right page was blank. Why was that? Was that the last person the demon killed? Callahan jerked as another name suddenly appeared in the book. He shut it. Sat there a moment. Breathed heavily. He opened it again. Another name appeared. He ran one finger along the letters. There was no ink to smudge. As if the name was just seared into the paper. He turned to the next page. It was blank. He flipped more pages, they were all blank. And despite the fact that he should have come to the end of the book, the pages kept coming. He returned to the marked page and flipped back the other way, hundreds, thousands, millions of names sweeping by. He shut the book and opened it again to the first page. But it wasn't the first page. He always opened to a page of names, and there were always countless pages of names before it.

Maybe it was the place marker that determined where it started? He gripped the blade and moved it to the beginning of the book. As he did so, he noticed an odd distortion in the air. The blade seemed to buzz in his fingers. He moved it the other way, and the same distortion occurred. He rubbed his face and let out a deep breath. Was the book doing something to him? Was this a hallucination? Maybe the book was dipped in LSD. Or it was giving off electromagnetic pulses distorting his brainwaves. He moved the blade again, better inspecting the line it created in the air. He reached out and felt it. His finger slipped inside, the tip disappearing then returning when he yanked his hand back. The line was still there. He placed his hand into it, lifting, and peeked into a grayness beyond.

Callahan gasped and stood from the chair, stepping back, not realizing he was still holding the book. The line in the air vanished. He took a deep breath. Let it out. He took the blade again and made another cut into the fabric of the space before him, this time vertically, from eye height to his ankles. What appeared to be a thin chasm of grayness lay before him. He slipped his hand into it, then widened the slit as though finding his way through stage curtains. He saw a larger space hidden inside the slit. A space of gray fog. Another world. But what world? Was it Hell? Holding the book tightly, his heart hammering, he leaned into the grayness, which was thickening in a slow, whispering crawl. The book's buzzing intensified. Callahan was compelled to open it. Two words appeared in the center of the blank page: LOOK UP.

Callahan looked up. He saw only the gray fog thickening. He tried to squint through it. Could this be a message from Gabriel? Could this be where he was supposed to find him? Could that be the reason Callahan was supposed to get the book in the first place? The whispering seemed to be calling to him.

"Hello?" Callahan called into the fog. He leaned in farther, trying to see through the grayness. "Hello?" he called again.

"*Hello?*" a whispering voice answered.

Callahan saw movement in the grayness. He called, "Gabriel? Is that you?"

An arm shot out of the fog. A thin, skeletal appendage of gray death. It gripped him by the throat and yanked him into the grayness. Several emaciated figures were upon him. He tried to scream, but their hands were already pushing down his throat, tearing him open to find his life-light.

7

Raven had her face in her hands by the end of the story. "So the book is lost in the Gray Zone for good?" she said.

"That is the case," I said.

"Who wrote: 'Look up' in the book?" she asked.

"I did. I write all the names in that book. I even transcribed the message you wrote on the page Ira gave you," I told her. I then added, "But, alas, the book is gone. The demon needs to either destroy the universe as we know it or slink back to Hell. And with his leash gone, not even Hell will be safe from his rage."

"We're leaving," Ira said.

"What?" I said. "No rage, demon? No tying me to trees? It was your book that was taken, not your balls."

Ira said to Raven, "We give this coward no more of our time. He may be able to see all that is happening, but not all that will be."

"No, you're right. Not all that *will* be. But all that *could* be. I play the odds."

"He is a manipulator, who only thinks he sees all. He doesn't understand choice because he has none. He had it and lost it. And now he'd rather destroy everything than accept the consequences of that choice. He hates that we still have free will."

"Correction, demon," I said. I pointed at Raven. "*She* has free will."

Ira stood still a moment, those slow cogs of his mind turning. "We leave," he said.

Raven stood from her seat and turned to go, but I stopped her, saying, "Didn't you want the answer to your question, Raven? Your parents? Heaven? Reunion?"

Ira, about to exit the doorway, turned, a low growl rising from his chest. "Don't listen to him. He is up to something."

"I'll find out on my own," Raven told me, she and Ira turning to leave again.

"They are in Heaven," I called after her. "But you will never see them."

Both she and Ira stopped and turned.

"What do you mean?" Ira growled.

"She is slated for the Pit," I told them.

"Wait. What?" Raven said. "You mean I'm going to Hell? What for? For stealing?"

"Oh, no, not for stealing," I said. "That would barely get you into Purgatory now. Christian doctrine has become pretty lax on that commandment, especially when it was justifiable in your case, being for survival and all…although stealing Iratus's book—"

"Enough," Ira said. "Where in Hell is she slated?"

"Poena's ring," I told him.

"But that ring is for murderers. She hasn't murdered anyone," Ira said. He turned suddenly to Raven. "Have you?"

Shocked by the question, she said, "No."

"According to Christian doctrine, you have," I told her.

"The time you were off Sheik Nimr's compound, where did Ahmad take you?"

"But that shouldn't count," Raven said.

"But it does," I said.

"What happened?" Ira said, stepping back into the room toward me.

Looking at the floor, Raven said, "The sheik didn't know I was pregnant. I begged Ahmad to sneak me out so I could get an abortion."

"Which, thanks to Christian doctrine, is perceived as Poena's realm now," I said. "So, no, young lady, you won't be reunited with your parents. But you *will* be able to see Ahmad again."

"What?" Raven cried.

"Yes, I'm afraid that the sheik found out about your little trip. Why do you think he sold you?"

"Because I was a pain in the ass."

"No. Because he wanted to recoup his losses on you. As for Ahmad, eliminating another potential son for the sheik… such betrayal—"

"The sheik killed him?" Raven squeaked.

"I'm afraid so. You and he can face Poena together."

"He went to Hell because of my abortion?"

"No. He went to Hell for killing people. He was the sheik's bodyguard. They weren't very nice people, the sheik's men. So now you and Ahmad will be able to spend eternity together and—"

"Enough," Ira roared, grabbing me and pulling me over the table by the sides of my cloak.

"There's nothing you can do, demon. Tying me to a tree won't change anything this time."

His grip tightened on me, but the girl interrupted him.

"Let's go, Ira," she said, her voice low, defeated. She walked out the door. Ira dropped me. He snatched the lantern from the table and followed her out of my home. Leaving me in darkness. But the light hadn't been for me.

8

After leaving the bar, Jacobs drove up along the coast, past Saint Sebastian's Church, past Molly Simmons's and Uncle Stewie's houses—both with For Sale signs on their front lawns. He stopped at the Half Moon Pond Campgrounds on the edge of Parson's Woods. After grilling the kid working in the office about recent campers, he wandered the grounds for an hour, searching for any sign of the girl, unsure what that sign might possibly be. A giant demon, maybe?

He walked to the edge of the campground, looking down the coast. About a mile away was a place the kid in the campground office told him was called Damon's Point, but which the locals called Demon's Point. "See any demons?" Jacobs had asked the kid. The kid had looked at him a moment, trying to decipher if he'd not been clear enough that Demon's Point was only a nickname, or if this FBI agent was pulling his leg. "No, sir. No. That's just what people call it."

"Yeah, I get that," Jacobs had said. "But you, personally, haven't seen any demons, right?"

The kid had squinted his eyes and shook his head and left it at that.

Jacobs saw a vehicle creeping along the road from the point. A black Denali. It looked like the type issued to government agencies.

Time was running short, and Jacobs decided he'd best take the guy from the bar's advice.

9

Raven and Ira plodded back down through the woods. It was dark. Time runs differently in the Realms (Heaven, Hell, etc.), and my "home" is no exception, which is why our short conversation took most of the day. It's not so much that time in the Realms runs faster or slower; it's more that it doesn't run in the linear fashion humans are used to.

"Well that sucked," Raven called to Ira, who was trudging ahead of her.

"Forget everything he said to you. He is using us in some way," Ira said, picking up pace.

"But I thought he knows everything," she called, trotting after him.

"Just because he knows everything doesn't mean he tells everything. He is a liar and a manipulator, and a snake."

(I was not taking any of this personally, mind you.)

"So I might not really be going to Hell?"

"I don't know. Regardless, you need to be absolved."

"Get thee to a nunnery, you're telling me?"

He stopped and turned to face her. "Perhaps. Either way, we need to part ways."

"But we're a team. I know you're dangerous, but we'll find your book."

"My book is my responsibility. You need to be away from me."

"I still owe you a life-debt. Like five life-debts by now."

"You must go," he said.

Raven almost tripped over a branch. "I know, but I still think we could fix this."

"You said it yourself. I am no longer who I was. I'm too dangerous."

"Ira, I've been thinking about that, and that's the dumbest thing I ever heard."

"I am not human. I am Wrath."

"But this whole thing makes no sense. If you really were Wrath, then you would have killed me when you found out I stole your book."

"That was then. I am truly Iratus now."

"You're still Ira to me," Raven said.

10

Jacobs walked along the edge of Parson's Woods. The sun had fallen, darkness coming on quicker than he'd expected. He tried to split the darkness of the woods with his flashlight, but the woods seemed to have a different kind of dark. It was somehow mucky. The guy from the bar had told him that fifty-two people had gone missing in these woods in the past 400 or so years. Jacobs didn't like the vibes of the place. Didn't like the movements the trees were making in the light. His hand went to his sidearm a half-dozen times. He was about to abandon the trek and head back to the campground when he spotted an emergency vehicle access point, the gate hanging slightly ajar.

He walked to the gate and shined his flashlight at a broken padlock on the ground, its shackle sheared at both ends. He thought about the bolts in the church's basement. Sheared, not cut. Jacobs raised the light and shined it into the woods. Something glinted in the light. Reflectors on the side of what looked like a U-Haul truck.

Jacobs entered the woods and was inspecting the vehicle when he heard rustling.

Spinning around, his hand going to his sidearm again, he

saw a figure duck behind a tree. Jacobs's hand loosened on his sidearm, and he said, "Diaz, you motherfucker."

No one emerged from behind the tree.

"I know you're there. Come on out."

Diaz came out from behind the tree.

Jacobs said, "This is how you were going to solve the case better than me? By hiding—poorly, I might add—behind trees?"

"It's how I *did* solve it better than you," Diaz said. "All I have to do is call my contact, and this place is swarming with spooks. I've been promised a cushy cabinet job if I can deliver your giant."

"By who? Agent Thayer?"

"Hill."

"Whatever. Guy's a fucking liar. You know, you could have at least surprised me by not being such a fucking weasely dick?"

Ty was now walking up along the path into the woods, pointing at Diaz. "I knew it was that motherfucker."

"What is this, a Marx Brothers' routine?" Jacobs said. "How many people are following me?"

Ty said to Diaz, "What did you do? Bug us? Listen in on our conversations?"

"I didn't listen in," Diaz said.

"But you did bug us," Ty said.

"Surveilled you," Diaz said.

Jacobs said, "I swear to God, Diaz, if—" He was cut short as Diaz drew his gun.

Jacobs drew his own sidearm, saying, "I don't want this, I—"

But then Diaz dropped his weapon and ran away.

"That was unexpected," Jacobs said, turning to Ty.

Ty's jaw hung slack and his bugged eyes were transfixed on something behind Jacobs.

Jacobs took a deep breath. He suspected what it was, and as he turned, he saw it illuminated in lamplight. It towered over him, that chiseled face and fiery eyes. Those eyes looked somehow as shocked as Jacobs's own. The thing stepped forward and Jacobs raised his gun. Jacobs only vaguely heard the girl screaming, "Ira," as he discharged his weapon. The thing grabbed him, Jacobs feeling his feet leaving the ground. Somehow, impossibly, he had a memory of being a toddler lifted over his father's head.

Then he heard Ty say, "Oh, shit. Help."

Jacobs thought, *Why's he calling for help? What help are we going to get out here? You're the help, Ty. Do something.*

Then Ty said, "She needs help." And it registered. The girl. She had jumped in front of the demon. Both Jacobs and the demon looked down at Raven. She was in a heap on the ground with Ty bending over her.

The demon dropped Jacobs. Jacobs felt his bones rattle as the impact stole his breath. He climbed to his feet as the demon crouched beside the girl.

"Raven?" the thing said.

She didn't answer. Her face was squashed in pain and was rapidly paling in the light of the lantern. Ty had his hands on her chest, blood spilling between his fingers.

"Shit," Jacobs said, taking a step toward the girl.

Raven coughed, a fine mist of blood rising from her lips.

The demon regarded the blood pumping between Ty's fingers. The speckles of blood from her cough dotted her face. The demon pushed Ty aside, placing its hand on her chest. "Don't worry," the demon said to her. "You are going to be all right."

A knowing look came into the girl's eyes, a recognition of comfort in the lie. More blood speckled her face as she coughed, gasping for breath.

The demon looked up at Jacobs.

Jacobs took a step back, but he did not raise his gun.

"You must get her to a hospital," the demon said. "There is one on this island."

Jacobs stared dumbly at the demon. But then he said, "My car is over a mile from here."

It looked at Ty.

"Mine, too," Ty said.

Ira nodded at the U-Haul. "Can you not drive this?"

"There isn't time." Ty said. "She's—"

"Drive it," the demon said.

Jacobs wanted to say, fuck, yeah, we'll drive her. I'll carry her if I have to. But he didn't say any of this. Nor did he move to help. Instead he said, "What did I do?"

The demon said, "You need to take her—" He stopped as Raven began clawing at his arm. He looked down at her as she struggled to speak. Her eyes focused on him with great earnestness as she tried forming the words, but they were squelched by a coughing fit and a large hiccup of blood that spilled down her chin.

"She's trying to say something," Ty said.

The demon watched her for a moment before saying, "She's trying to tell me that it was pretty dumb of her to take a bullet for someone who is bulletproof."

Raven stopped clawing at his arm and she stopped trying to speak, a smile spreading across her bloody lips as she stared up at the demon. The life left her eyes.

The demon stayed crouched a moment, looking down upon the girl.

"Oh my god," Jacobs said, he, too, staring down at the girl's lifeless body. He sensed the bulk of the demon rising from the ground. Rising above him. Jacobs did not bother looking at the thing. He was sensing, rather than seeing everything now. Realizing Ty was pulling his own firearm, but the demon flung Ty away. Sensing the thing's fiery gaze returning to him, Jacobs recalled his dream, that fist smashing onto his skull. Would it make that hollow slamming sound like a car door? Jacobs allowed the gun to fall from his hand and he took a shuffling step toward the girl. He then looked at the demon. Saw its fist raised above him for its hammer blow. Saw the wrath in the thing's eyes. But all Jacobs could say was, "This is all my fault."

The demon froze. Then it lowered its arm. To Jacobs's amazement, the thing took a deep breath and said, "You panicked and you didn't see her." It took another breath. "It's not your fault." The thing stooped and picked up Raven's body. It turned and began walking back into the woods.

Ty, climbing to his feet and again raising his gun, called, "Hey, hey, you can't…you can't take her body. Hey, stop."

The demon stopped and looked at Ty.

Jacobs said, "He's right, Ira."

The thing's gaze snapped back to Jacobs.

Jacobs said, "We can't let you take that girl's body. She must have a family. She needs to be with them."

The demon looked down at the girl in its arms, and Jacobs saw the answer in the thing's eyes. She *was* with her family.

The demon turned and walked off, carrying the girl, Ty's futile protests the only thing following him.

Revelation

Iratus climbed the steps of Saint Sebastian's Church and yanked the front door open, popping the lock off the wide wooden doors for the second time in the past week and a half. He strode down the aisle between the pews, cradling Raven's body in one arm, the lantern from my dwelling in his other hand. He headed diagonally across the transept, cutting in front of the apse and altar, to the door in the back corner. Cradling Raven tighter to him, he opened this door and squeezed down the narrow steps to the basement.

He strode to the metal door. He had determined that if I was telling the truth, her soul was in Hell, and he would do whatever it took to reunite her soul with her body and get her out of there. He knew, at that moment, she'd be bobbing down Styx toward Poena's Ring, and those who saw the horrors of Poena's face lose all sense of self. If Iratus didn't get her out of Hell before she reached the end of the river, she'd be truly gone forever.

(I was telling the truth, by the way. Her soul was there, but he wouldn't be able to save her. There was only one being with resurrecting talent, and he wasn't in Hell. Iratus didn't know this, and what's more, he didn't care. He would fight all of Hell if he had to. One way or another, Iratus had decided he'd be leaving with a living, breathing Raven.)

He stopped. There was something just inside the doorway. Something in the dark.

Iratus stepped back as an eagle's head the size of a barrel thrust from the darkness. The head, rising almost to the twelve-foot ceiling, was attached to a wide, muscular body. It had the hands of a man, the arms and shoulders of a lion, the legs of an ox, and gleaming brass hooves. Upon its torso it wore the brass armor of a Roman legionnaire, engraved with a hundred eyes. The creature spread three concentric sets of wings from its back.

Iratus, protectively cradling Raven's body, lifted the lantern. The light reflected in the creature's black, eagle eyes. It squared its body to block the demon's path.

"Out of my way," Iratus told the creature.

The creature let forth an eagle's shriek and knocked the lantern from Iratus's hand. The lantern smashed and its flame spread across the floor with a fire that did not consume. Shadows danced across the basement's walls.

Iratus's free hand tightened into a fist as he said, "I don't know why you're here, cherub, but I am going through that door. So get out of my way."

"I put him here," a booming voice called out. A man in silver armor stepped from the doorway, his white wings hanging down his back like a cloak. Black hair flowed from his scalp in exquisite waves and his face was the chiseled perfection of a Renaissance sculpture. He looked like a man on fire, the flames flickering in his silver armor and his silver eyes.

"Michael," Iratus growled.

"You finally recognize me, demon," Michael said, his voice projecting like a Shakespearean actor upon the stage. "Took you long enough to unriddle my identity. And do you not remember Uriel?" He gestured to the cherub.

Iratus glanced at the creature. "I remember."

"You should. They gave you his book, after all," Michael

said. "I've got to admit, I am amazed you stuck to that silly thing. Not a single non-sanctioned death."

Iratus started toward the door again. "You're wasting my time. I'm taking her to Hell."

Michael, holding his hands up in a calming manner, said, "Why go to Hell?"

"To find her soul." Iratus stepped forward again.

Michael, again with his hands up, "You cannot save her. You must realize that. So why not return to what we've started?"

"What you've started. Out of my way," Iratus said. He took another step.

Michael, stepping in front of him again, said, "But I would like you to finish it."

"How did you find me?"

"I was just by to see the Keeper. Right after you left. I asked where you were going, and he told me. I've been in touch with him quite often lately."

"He didn't tell you that you will destroy the universe if you proceed."

"How is that?"

"The Rapture will throw the universe off balance."

"Didn't you pay attention to his little spiel about the perceptions of these humans? We can get around that Rapture thing. We'll have Gabriel proclaim that there is no Rapture, and all Christians need to stay put. We'll be fine."

"They will expect their Rapture."

"Then I make them not expect it."

"I think you underestimate these humans' sense of entitlement," Iratus said. He took a deep breath, shifting Raven's body in his arm. "I don't know why we're wasting time talking about this."

"I thought it might be nice for you to know who you are dealing with. And then you shall do my bidding."

"I won't be doing your bidding," Iratus said. "Now get out of my way."

"You will be doing my bidding after I tell you what else The Keeper told me."

"That Hell froze over?"

"The Keeper not only told me who *you* really are, Wrath. He also told me what manifested concept *I* am."

"Loquaciousness?"

"Conquest." Michael spread his arms, giving the flames the best chance to reflect upon his silver armor. "I am Conquest."

(He's not actually Conquest, by the way. I may have bullshitted him on that one a little. However, he *is* the physical manifestation of a concept. I'll leave it to you to guess which one.)

"Sure, whatever, go conquest then. I'm going to Hell," Iratus said.

"Come on, Wrath, unleash your inner being and complete your destiny. Join the glory."

"Get out of my way. I won't tell you again."

"Demon, you should—"

Iratus punched Michael in the face. The archangel flew off, tumbling across the stone floor, his armor sounding like a garbage can being dragged down a street.

Iratus took a step toward the door again, but the bulk of the cherub was before him. "I have no quarrel with you, Uriel," Iratus said, "Allow me passage." He cradled Raven tighter. "She hasn't much time."

The eagle's black eyes, reflecting the flames, were expressionless, but the thing's head bobbed in that bird manner, as if grasping at air currents for comprehension.

"He will do no such thing," Michael said, climbing to his feet, his voice now as squashed as his face. His perfect chiseled features were reversed into a concave bowl. He shook his head, as if clearing his long hair from his face, and, with a pop, his face reverted back to its usual perfection. "It is unwise to provoke Conquest. Perhaps I shall kill you. Leave your body for the government officials to find.…" He paused, looking into the flames as if in thought, his right hand absentmindedly testing the alignment of his chin. "Actually, finding a dead demon would…I mean, I do enjoy your killing sprees and would love to see Wrath truly unleashed, but just handing your malignant mug over to the government to prove your existence shall help my cause more. Why did I not think of that in the first place? You are accurate, demon; I do not need you."

Michael turned to Uriel and nodded.

The cherub's eagle head turned, as though to look over its shoulder; the eagle head, seemingly folding into the back of the angel's neck, was replaced with that of an ox.

Iratus, looking up at the giant being, shifted Raven's body. "You don't need to do this," he said to the cherub.

The cherub lowered its horned crown and drove forward. Iratus had time to turn his body, protecting Raven's corpse, and he deflected the horns, taking the cherub's shoulder full on. The cherub drove Iratus into the basement's far wall, cratering the concrete and bringing flecks of plaster down from the ceiling.

Iratus dropped to one knee, catching his breath. The cherub, standing over him, snorted smoke from its snout. Iratus gently laid Raven's body to one side. "I'll be right back," he said to her, patting her shoulder, as if she could hear him. He stood, squared his body, and shrugged his shoulders. "All right, cherub, let's do this."

The cherub lowered its head and drove again. Iratus grabbed hold of the oxen horns, pulling the thing's head down and driving forward, pushing it back across the basement. The cherub's brass hooves spilled sparks from the concrete floor.

The cherub lowered its head further, putting Iratus off balance, then flung its head upward, launching him through the ceiling and into the church's main hall. Iratus landed on the nave's wooden floor, toppling several rows of pews like dominoes.

Below, in the basement, the cherub turned its head again, replacing it with that of a lion. It spread its six wings and, with a lion's roar, flew up through the hole in the ceiling, landing beside Iratus. From his place on the floor, Iratus could see the two testicles hanging from the bovine flanks beneath the cherub's legionnaire skirt. Iratus punched the angel right in its oxen balls. The cherub's lion head let out a high, soft mew as the engraved eyes on its armor crossed.

Iratus grimaced.

While the cherub bent to catch its breath, Iratus grappled with it, throwing it into the altar. The thing lay in a heap of splintered wood on the far end of the church. Iratus clapped the dust from his hands and called toward the crumpled cherub, "I told you, you can't stop me, I—"

Uriel climbed to its feet, shaking its mane and releasing a roar that shattered the church's stained glass windows.

"Here we go again," Iratus huffed.

The cherub leapt from the apse, grabbing Iratus by the front of his leather shirt and smashing him onto the floor, the impact toppling the remaining pews. Iratus gripped the angel's forearm with both hands, trying to break its grip, but the angel did not let go. It spread its six wings, rose to the vaulted ceiling of the church, and then dropped, smashing Iratus through the church's wooden floor and driving him into the basement's concrete floor below. Iratus left a crater in the concrete at Michael's feet. Uriel landed beside him.

"Egad," Michael said, "you must really have gotten under Uriel's skin. I haven't seen him this worked up since Sodom and Gomorrah." He turned to the cherub and said, "Finish him."

The lion face turned, replaced by that of a man, the steadfast cold expression of Michelangelo's David upon it. The cherub took a bladeless hilt from its belt. It held the hilt up, tightening its grip, and a blade of fire burst from the guard. Uriel raised the sword, about to smite the demon.

Iratus looked back toward Raven, then up at the cherub. "Let me get her out of there," he said. "Before she faces Poena."

The human face looking down at him was emotionless.

"You waste your final breath, demon," Michael called. "Nothing can stop the mighty Uriel."

The cherub's grip on the hilt tightened and the flaming blade began its downward swing.

A voice commanded, "Stop."

The cherub stopped, sword held over Iratus, the human face looking like a child caught stealing from a cookie jar.

The room filled with the bright, orange glow of sunrise. Above them, a man was looking down from the hole in the ceiling. He dropped to the concrete floor, his sandaled feet making no sound.

"Enough," the man said, his flowing golden hair seeming to dance in a nonexistent breeze, his intense blue eyes regarding the two angels from above a perfectly trimmed beard.

"Jesus," Michael said.

"How dare you go behind my back like this," Jesus said to the angel.

Michael looked at his feet, toeing an invisible stone. "I did it for you."

"Excuse me?" Jesus said. "What was that?"

Michael looked up at Jesus. "I did it for the glory of your kingdom."

Jesus sighed and walked to Iratus. He reached out his hand. Iratus regarded him for a moment and then took the hand. Jesus helped him to his feet and said, "You know, unlike the rest of you heavenly beings, I was once a man before I became an ideal. I can still remember the man I once was." He looked Michael in his silver eyes. "And that man railed against glory and kingdoms."

"But—" Michael said.

Jesus held up his finger, silencing the angel. He looked up through the hole in the ceiling, to the nave, seeing the figure on the crucifix staring down at them. "I lose a piece of that man each day as people fill my mouth with promises and condemnations I never made." He looked sternly at Michael again.

Michael said, "I never—"

Jesus silenced the angel with raised finger. He chuckled and then in a pondering tone, said, "I mean, if my old self were to walk the Earth today, apparently, I would have to condemn *me*." He shrugged. "I long for the day that I can be that man again, even if he doesn't recognize the face reflected back at him." He spread his arms. "Look at this; when did I even become a blond? I mean, what is this? I'm a Middle Eastern Jew. Blue eyes? The white robes? And this glow? It's like I'm radioactive or something. Father help me if I ever get invited to a surprise party. You try hiding in the dark glowing like this."

Iratus laughed.

The two angels did not.

"See what I did there?" Jesus said to Iratus. "Father help me?"

Iratus chuckled. "Yes, I got it."

Jesus winked. He then snapped his attention to the cherub and said, "You, back to Eden. Git."

The cherub's fire sword fizzled out and, with lowered shoulders, it skulked away.

"And you," Jesus said, turning to Michael, "it's your turn to hold up the throne."

Michael groaned. "It's Raphael's turn."

"Your turn now," Jesus said. "And I'll deal with you when I return."

Michael skulked off with Uriel, the two of them vanishing.

Jesus turned to Iratus, the smile returning to his face.

Iratus said, "How did you know to come here?"

"The Keeper told me."

(It's true. I did tell him.)

Iratus said, "I thought he wanted Michael to succeed."

Jesus shrugged with a sheepish grin. "I can be convincing."

(I have to admit, he can be convincing.)

Iratus went to Raven's body. He lifted her up and headed back toward the door to Hell.

Jesus raised his hand.

"I'm taking her to Hell," Iratus informed him. "You can't stop me."

"I got a better idea," Jesus said, placing his fingers and thumb on her temples. His glow flickered a moment, and Raven gasped a deep breath.

Her eyes opened. Her body jerked. Her eyes darted around the room in horror as she flailed and cried out. Her eyes fell on Ira, her screams intensifying, then fading as she registered what she was seeing. "Ira?" she whispered before passing out.

Jesus grinned and shrugged. "I suppose being a perceived ideal can be helpful at times." He brushed her hair from her forehead. "Let her rest for now. She's been through Hell." He snapped his fingers and said, "Oh, by the way, you lost this." He handed Ira his book.

Ira shifted Raven in his arms and took the book. "Thank you."

"What you hold has caused you a lot of trouble," Jesus said.

Ira held up the book. "I will be more careful with it."

"I meant her," Jesus said, nodding at Raven.

Ira nodded. Then he asked, "What do I do now?"

Jesus said. "You're part human, you decide."

"I'm not human."

Jesus shrugged and placed his hand gently on the demon's arm. "That's all up to perception."

"I don't understand," the demon said.

"And that's okay," Jesus said, and he turned and walked away, vanishing as the two angels had done.

Ira looked down at the girl in his arms, her breaths steady and measured. He looked at the doorway to Hell. He looked at the stairs leading out of the basement. The One True Son of God did giveth unto the Son of Moloch a choice. And it was good.